Why did he keep thinking of Miss Lockwood?

Why did her face flash disconcertingly across his vision as it had a habit of doing so often of late? Why did he find himself drawn to the library when he knew she would be working?

How could he let a woman affect him as this one did? He was quite bewildered by it. All he knew was that it was different from anything he had felt before. She was not for him, coming from the class she did, but he could not stop thinking about her.

There was something about Juliet Lockwood—a loveliness not just in her face but in her heart and soul. It shone from her like a beacon. In her naivety she was completely unaware of it, and that was what was so special about her.

Helen Dickson was born and lives in South Yorkshire with her retired farm manager husband. Having moved out of the busy farmhouse where she raised their two sons, she has more time to indulge in her favourite pastimes. She enjoys being outdoors, travelling, reading and music. An incurable romantic, she writes for pleasure. It was a love of history that drove her to writing historical fiction.

Previous novels by Helen Dickson:

THE DEFIANT DEBUTANTE
ROGUE'S WIDOW, GENTLEMAN'S WIFE
TRAITOR OR TEMPTRESS
WICKED PLEASURES
   (part of *Christmas By Candlelight*)
A SCOUNDREL OF CONSEQUENCE
FORBIDDEN LORD
SCANDALOUS SECRET, DEFIANT BRIDE
FROM GOVERNESS TO SOCIETY BRIDE
MISTRESS BELOW DECK
THE BRIDE WORE SCANDAL

SEDUCING
MISS LOCKWOOD

Helen Dickson

All the characters in this book have no existence outside the imagination of the author, and have no relation whatsoever to anyone bearing the same name or names. They are not even distantly inspired by any individual known or unknown to the author, and all the incidents are pure invention.

First published in Great Britain 2011
by Mills & Boon, an imprint of Harlequin (UK) Limited,
Eton House, 18-24 Paradise Road, Richmond, Surrey TW9 1SR

ISBN: 978 0 263 88806 5

Harlequin (UK) policy is to use papers that are natural, renewable and recyclable products and made from wood grown in sustainable forests. The logging and manufacturing process conform to the legal environmental regulations of the country of origin.

Printed and bound in Spain
by Blackprint CPI, Barcelona

SEDUCING
MISS LOCKWOOD

Chapter One

London—1817

The Fleet prison loomed towering and intimidating as Juliet approached the huge doors. Unconsciously drawing her cloak tighter around her, she shuddered as she was admitted. How she hated the place. The guard knew her from her weekly visits and conducted her through the lobby and past the warden's office and up to her brother's cell. The guard pocketed the necessary coin she gave him and turned the key to admit her.

Robby was stretched out on a narrow bed, seemingly fast asleep. Thoroughly frustrated by her brother's inactivity, she shook him roughly by the arm.

'Robby! Wake up.'

At twenty-eight Robby, her half-brother, was five years Juliet's senior, but prison had taken something away from him and she was for the moment the strong one, the support, her female instincts for her sibling flooding to comfort, to relieve his suffering, for despite his devil-may-care attitude on the outside, she knew as only a sister can the depth of his pain, his anger and frustration directed at himself for allowing himself to fall so low.

At last, to her relief, he showed signs of stirring. His eyelids flickered in his gaunt face and he stared lazily around him, as if surprised to find himself in prison at all. Then he caught sight of Juliet and his eyes lit up with pleasure.

'Juliet! I must have dozed off.' Throwing his legs over the side, he sat up, smoothing his long white fingers through his fair hair.

Robby was in the Fleet because, with an eye for the main chance, he had lived beyond his means. Every opportunity had been expended upon him by their father, and after finishing years of advanced learning he had declared an intense dislike for it and resigned his position as a teacher of history at a prestigious boys' school in Surrey. At twenty-one, coming into a small inheritance from his mother, he had taken off on the Grand Tour with some of his contemporaries. The money spent, he had returned home.

Living on his wits and boyish charm and possessed of arrogance, pride and a good deal of pigheadedness, he indulged in the usual pastimes open to a gentleman of urbane habits and wealth, spending his nights drinking and carousing and being over-generous to his friends. He was good looking—at least the ladies seemed to think so, for they hung around him like flies and he knew how to charm and coax. But his debts had finally caught up with him and he had ended up in this place.

'You really should be at some kind of employment, Robby,' Juliet said, wrinkling her nose with distaste at the dreadful odour that pervaded every corner of the prison, 'not kicking your heels in this place.'

'I admit I want to be out of here,' he murmured, straining at this restriction to his freedom, 'but what can I do?'

Juliet placed a wrapped bundle on the table. 'Here, I've brought you some food—bread and cheese—and some books to read to help pass the time.'

He grinned at her fondly. 'You and your books, Juliet. Where would you be without them?'

'I really don't know, Robby. Where would either of us be? It's because of my love of books and what I've learned from Father that I'm able to do the work I do. And you may mock, but it's my knowledge that enables me to pay the guards to provide you with special favours. It's better than taking in washing, and, if I am to get you out of this dreadful place, I must earn all I can.'

Robby was immediately contrite. 'Sorry, sis. I know how hard you work and the small luxuries I have are down to you. I am grateful. I'm proud of you. Father would be, too…were he still with us. You've proved yourself as resourceful as you are clever. How's Sir John?'

'That's what I've come to tell you. I'm leaving his

employ, Robby. My work is finished. I've found new employment—out of London.'

'And naturally you'll be too busy to come and see me.'

It was the undercurrent of disappointment in his voice that touched Juliet. 'Not too busy, Robby. Too far away. I'm to take up a position for the Duke of Hawksfield in Essex, so I won't be able to visit you for a while, but I will write often.'

Robby's look of surprise was quickly followed by one of displeasure. 'Dominic Lansdowne?'

'Yes—I believe that is his name.'

'Well—Dominic Lansdowne of all people!'

'You know him?'

'I know of him—a military man, fought in Spain.' He frowned, suddenly anxious for his sister. 'He's also a spectacularly handsome rake, Juliet, superior, arrogant, a despoiler of innocent girls and constantly gossiped about, but rarely seen. If all the stories are to be believed, the Duke of Hawksfield and his friends spend the majority of their time when in town perusing sexual conquests, and when he isn't in London prowling the gaming halls, he's roaming the countryside on his stallion searching for a complaisant wench to assuage his appetite.'

Juliet flushed at Robby's unsavoury description of the man she was to work for. 'Really, Robby, you paint an unflattering picture of my future employer.'

'With good cause. Have you met him?'

'No. He was willing to employ me on Sir John's

recommendation and my written application. He can't possibly be as dissolute as you have painted him.'

'I'm sorry, Juliet, but that's the way he is. You mean the world to me and I care about you—what happens to you. I know how independent you are, but when it comes to men like Dominic Lansdowne, then you are way out of your league. The ladies love him. Be wary. He'll not make you a duchess.'

'I don't want to be a duchess, Robby. I only want to earn enough money to make your life bearable while you are in this place. Another few months and you'll be out.'

She left, leaving her brother lost in his own depressed thoughts.

As Juliet left the town of Brentwood in Essex the wind had risen, bringing with it a cold, dense rain that whipped against her face. Her bonnet was soon soaked, as was her cloak and her dress beneath, and saturated strands of hair clung to her face. Mr Carter, whose trap she was in, handed her a rug.

'Sorry about the weather, miss, but don't worry. We'll soon be at Lansdowne House.'

'I do hope so, Mr Carter. I really do, otherwise I dread to think what I shall look like when I get there. I only hope we arrive before dark.'

Gratefully she took the proffered rug and draped it about her shoulders, hunching her back against the downpour. Disregarding the water trapped in the folds of her sodden collar, she did her best to ignore the discomforts of the weather, concentrating wholly upon the route they were following.

When at last she caught sight of some tall, wrought-iron gates ahead, she breathed a sigh of relief. Passing through them, they followed a curved drive. The house at the end of it looked enormous, very impressive and very grand, which was what one would expect a duke's house to be. It was three-storeyed, with leaded windows and a white marble portico in front.

Mr Carter halted at the entrance and climbed down, going to assist his passenger. The hem of Juliet's cloak became caught on a nail on the side of the trap. Pulling at it in exasperation, she uttered a cry of dismay when she heard it rip. Knowing there was nothing to be done, with a resigned sigh she followed Mr Carter to the door.

'Thank you, Mr Carter,' she said as he set her trunk down. 'You'd best be getting back. It will soon be dark and you still have a way to go before you reach your home. I'll be all right now.'

She watched him go before turning her attention to the door. She had been anticipating this moment for days, and now it was here she was strangely reluctant to enter. With butterflies in her stomach—a mixture of nerves and excitement—she lifted the highly polished brass knocker shaped in a lion's paw. Letting it fall loudly, she waited.

There was no sound from within, which she thought strange for a house as grand as this. After letting the knocker fall again and still getting no response, she turned the knob and pushed. It opened soundlessly. Sternly quelling a tremor of apprehension and stepping inside the house, she looked around. There wasn't a servant in sight.

It was a magnificent house, she thought as she moved into the centre of the spacious and elegant hall—a palace, that made her feel even smaller and more insignificant than she already felt, as she dripped water all over the floor. Straight ahead was a sweeping central staircase, the handrails highly polished and glinting in the diffused light of the chandelier. The walls were hung with paintings: men in military uniform, family portraits, scenes of days gone by. Seeing a door slightly ajar, with her heart pounding a nervous tattoo within her chest, she went towards it and opened it further, realising her mistake when it was too late.

All but one pair of eyes moved as one, as if in slow motion, to look at her. It was like a bizarre tableau. The man at the head of a table littered with nutshells and orange peel and glasses and bottles, the air thick with tobacco smoke, was the last to turn his head and look at her, his face a picture of irritated bewilderment. What he saw was the bedraggled figure of a woman in a sodden cloak with its torn hem trailing on the floor. Wet strands of hair clung to her face and a small feather in her bonnet drooped pathetically.

Dominic Lansdowne, the seventh Duke of Hawksfield, knew all the servants in his house, if not by name then by sight, and he didn't know the woman in the doorway. If she was looking for the domestic quarters, then she had lost her way.

'Oh—please excuse me. I'm sorry to intrude upon you like this. I really didn't mean to. I—appear to be lost.'

Her appearance caused a stir of lewd and bawdy comments from five young men at the table, who, because of a good day shooting birds on the Duke's estate, were already in their cups. Not so the man seated at the head of the table, who gave his guests a look of bored nonchalance and the supreme indifference of the true aristocrat.

His authority was obvious, a man used to giving orders and having them obeyed. Juliet felt a prickling of unease. It wasn't just his fine clothes and bearing that marked him out. Even from a distance she could feel the force of his personality and charisma.

Rising from his chair, he sauntered indolently towards her.

He was tall and lean of waist and hip and of powerful build, with broad shoulders, the body of a soldier, an adventurer rather than an aesthete. His hair was thick and shining black, curling vigorously in the nape of his neck. He was clean shaven and amber skinned, and dark clipped eyebrows sat above silver-grey eyes with pupils as black as coal.

He was an attractive man, his face strong, his mouth stubborn and his chin arrogant. But there was a hint of humour in the curl of his lips, which told Juliet he took pleasure from life. He had removed his jacket and his silk waistcoat was unbuttoned, his shirt thrown open at the neck. Towering over her, he said, 'And you are?'

'Miss Lockwood.' She was very pale and her expression seemed strained, but her candid dark eyes met the Duke's with almost innocent steadfastness. His eyes held hers entrapped, and hidden in them was amusement, watchful, penetrating and mocking, as though he held the world an amusing place to be. 'I—am sorry to arrive unannounced, but there was no one on the door to let me in.'

Dominic uttered a sound of annoyance and stepped briskly round her. Peering into the hall, he shouted for someone called Pearce.

'I was not expecting you until tomorrow, Miss Lockwood.'

'Yes, I know, but I arrived in Brentwood early and didn't think you would mind if I came here straight away,' she explained, the truth being that the accommodation in Brentwood was expensive and she had wanted to conserve her limited capital.

'And you have come directly from London—from Sir John Moore?'

'Yes, your Grace.' Juliet felt uncharacteristically daunted. She had been her own mistress for so long she was used to being in command, but there was something rather disconcerting about this man's self-assurance.

'And Sir John is well?'

'Yes, perfectly.'

When a loud guffaw rose from the table, irritated, Dominic looked at his friends. 'I must apologise, Miss Lockwood,' he said on a dry note. 'It's the shooting season, you see, and it's been a long day for all concerned.'

'And a damned enjoyable one, too,' one of the gentlemen piped up, taking a long swallow of his brandy.

Juliet couldn't see what being a long day had to do with anything, but didn't dare say so. Her gaze was drawn to the people seated at the table. Endowed from birth with financial provision made them the superior beings they so obviously thought themselves to be. They possessed also the glorious belief that they were unique in the world. They were all lounging lazily in their chairs with a bored languor, having become quiet and eyeing her rudely, as if sensing something about her which promised to be entertaining. Their neck linen had either been removed or unfastened, and their clothes and hair were in disarray.

She was disconcerted at being subjected for the first time in her life to a situation like this, to being visually harassed by such poor specimens of men as these, and she felt a surge of resentment that they were having fun at her expense. Certainly she was not used to people like this. She had been at the Academy with girls who had rich and influential parents, but that's where it ended.

One gentleman, Thomas Howard, drew deeply on his cigar, the smoke wreathing about his head, and another had an attractive-looking fair-haired young woman seated close beside him. Lifting his quizzing glass to his eye, he trained it upon Juliet and boldly inspected her.

'Good Lord! Who is this unkempt creature, Dominic? Lost her way, has she? Doesn't she know to use the back door?'

'Shut up, Sedgwick,' Dominic said. 'You're being outrageous, exceedingly rude and embarrassing Miss Lockwood.'

'But servants never enter a gentleman's house by the front door,' the woman commented, her voice sounding like a purr, 'unless, of course, she's new to service and doesn't know any better.'

Juliet's eyes narrowed and anger stirred inside her. 'I am Lord Lansdowne's employee, not his servant,' she was quick to retort.

The woman looked at Juliet with a malicious twist to her lips and an uninterested shrug of her shapely shoulders. 'What's the difference? If he pays your wages, you are the hired help.'

'Enough, Geraldine,' Dominic chided, his smile softening the reproach. 'Please remember your manners.'

Juliet was beginning to doubt that this Geraldine had any. The woman was sumptuously attired in a deep pink silk gown with an overskirt of pink net lace sewn liberally with tiny pink beads that twinkled in the light. The bodice was so low as to prove an almost inadequate restraint to the swelling ripeness of her breasts. Her hair was auburn and adorned with diamond pins. Around her throat she wore a gold necklace inset with blood-red rubies. The stone cast a rosy light upon her white flesh and Juliet felt a total inadequacy stir within her.

Sedgwick smiled, his smooth face easily accommodating the ingratiating expression. 'Then let your— employee come and join us? It could be fun.' His voice was low and laced with mockery. His fingers rhythmically stroked the stem of his glass and his knowing eyes bore into her.

The beautiful woman laughed softly, provocatively. 'Don't be lewd, my darling. Can't you see the poor girl is positively terrified? Better she should be directed to the kitchen.'

Dominic saw the horror and shock that flashed across Miss Lockwood's face. 'Pay no attention to Sedgwick. He's not normally rude, but his manners are somewhat lacking at present.'

He was amazed at his own concern, for what did he care about a woman he had never met? Perhaps it was because of her wretched appearance, or because she was to undertake a project that was important to him and he didn't want her bolting for the door before she had taken up her post. Whatever it was, it annoyed him slightly, since he didn't really have the patience to be fretting himself over a woman he did not know.

Sedgwick reached out and trailed his skilled fingers down the soft nape of Geraldine's neck. She sighed and arched with pleasure, like a cat, Juliet thought.

'Ah, Charles, you know what I like.'

He chuckled low and leaned over to trail his lips where his fingers had been before.

Juliet watched, unable to tear her eyes away. Never had she seen anything so blatant, so decadent, so— so disgraceful. She felt she was about to collapse, not because her sensibilities had been shocked, but from a swift rush of anger such as she had never before experienced in her life.

Now she was being possessed of another strange

emotion. She had never hated anything or anyone, but at this moment she became so afraid of the intensity of the feeling that was causing her heart to beat violently, that she dropped her gaze from the rude woman and down at her tightly clasped gloved hands that were gripping each other so that her knuckles stood out through the material.

She had ceased to see what was in front of her, for her gaze had turned inwards and she was seeing herself as she must look to this roomful of fashionable people—dull, soaked, her soiled boots and ripped cloak with its muddy hem giving her the appearance of a vagrant.

Witnessing the birth of a new creature, someone born out of frightening emotions, all she wanted to do was strike the mocking smile from the woman's lips, to rush towards her and topple her from her chair on to the floor. All eyes were watching her.

Thankfully at that moment the butler appeared. For once Pearce, usually the picture of dignified calm, looked somewhat flustered as he fumbled to do up the buttons on his waistcoat, which he had unfastened when he had gone to sit in a comfortable position with Mrs Reed, the cook of many years, in front of the kitchen stove, hoping for an hour or two's respite while the young gentlemen seemed intent on getting more inebriated than they already were, which was certainly nothing new when they had spent the day shooting at birds or galloping after the fox during the hunting season.

'There was no one on duty at the door, Pearce,' Dominic said sharply but without reproach. 'Miss Lockwood had to let herself in.'

Somewhat disconcerted, Pearce allowed his features to relapse momentarily into an expression of disbelief. Then, his lips pursed in a suitable disdain, he said, 'I apologise, your Grace.'

'I think your apology should be directed at Miss Lockwood, Pearce. Show her to her room and make sure she has everything she requires.'

'Yes, your Grace. Miss Lockwood's room is prepared.'

Dominic looked down at his new employee. 'Goodnight, Miss Lockwood. I hope you have a comfortable night. I'll see you in the library in the morning. Nine o'clock sharp.'

'Yes, of course.'

Pearce half-turned to Juliet. 'If you would come this way.'

'Thank you. If you gentlemen will excuse me.' Juliet's voice was low, cool and slightly contemptuous as her eyes passed over them, before she turned about and went out.

Pearce was already walking away. When the door closed behind her, for a moment there was silence, and then, as if on cue, that roomful of ugly people erupted in loud guffaws of laughter.

'Good Lord, Dominic,' Sedgwick cried, loud enough for her to hear, 'I doubt you will be tempted in that direction. Why, the girl's pathetic, as plain as a pike staff and—'

'I know, Sedgwick, and with no feminine appeal

what-so-ever and more unfashionable than Farmer Shepherd's scarecrow,' the Duke interrupted, laughter not far away.

Juliet seethed.

A scarecrow!

Upon her soul, she couldn't remember ever being so humiliated. Having no wish to hear more, she turned away and strode after Pearce, unable to force any coherent thought to the forefront of her mind. She was dazed, numb. All she could hear over and over again was the carelessly brutal opinion of her spoken in jest by the man she was to work for.

It wasn't until she found herself traversing the many corridors and staircases of Lansdowne House that the anger in her began to subside, and, like a mist clearing from her eyes, she looked at her situation. But as she did so a sickness assailed her, for she knew that no matter how she came to view her employer, there would remain in her an intense dislike of him while ever she remained beneath his roof. If she had any alternative, she would leave right now, but, she thought as she suddenly shivered and sneezed, she needed the work and a roof over her head and the money to help Robby, so for the present she would have to bite the bit and put up with it.

Pearce turned and gave her a baleful look. 'Oh dear, Miss Lockwood. I do hope you haven't caught a chill.'

'So do I,' Juliet murmured, fumbling for her handkerchief as she sneezed again and felt the beginnings of a stabbing headache.

Alone, she looked at the room that was to be her

home for the next few months. It was a well-appointed chamber, both handsome and comfortable with a large bed, overlooking the lawns to the south of the house. It was close to the servants' quarters, yet far enough away to make her different in their eyes. She sighed. As if she didn't have enough to contend with without resentment from the domestic staff.

Feeling her headache getting worse, she poured herself some water from the pitcher and drank thirstily. When a footman brought her valise she quickly unpacked and got ready for bed, relieved when she finally slipped between the cool sheets. She closed her eyes to stop the hazy waves in front of her eyes, feeling herself slipping into a swirling mass.

The next thing Juliet heard was a knocking on her bedroom door. Her bemused mind refused to function, preferring the anaesthesia of sleep. When the knocking continued, she struggled to open her eyes. Sunlight slanting through the windows almost blinded her and she quickly closed them again.

Realising she had slept through the night, she tried to remember where she was, and then she remembered and groaned. How could she be so unfortunate as to fall ill on her first day in her new position? Her eyes hurt so much, and her throat was so sore—in fact, everything was hurting, from the top of her head to the soles of her feet.

The knocking became persistent, accompanied by a voice. 'Please, Miss Lockwood, say something.'

Juliet groaned again. What did the woman want?

Why on earth was she being bothered when all she wanted to do was to go back to sleep?

'Please—come in,' she managed to croak—too late, for whoever it was had gone.

Dominic strode into the library at nine o'clock exactly, fully expecting to find Miss Lockwood to be waiting for him. Sunlight sifted through the windows, casting a golden glow across the highly polished round table in the centre of the room. He stopped and looked around. The room was empty. Miss Lockwood was not there.

And so he waited, pacing the carpet as he struggled with his mounting annoyance at being made to wait. He was not known for his patience. Where the hell was she? He had the most ridiculous notion that she had been so hurt and humiliated by his friends' loose banter last night that today she was demonstrating her rebellion against him by being late to begin her work.

Striding swiftly across the room, he jerked the bell rope. Almost immediately, Dolly, one of the chambermaids, answered his summons. When he enquired after Miss Lockwood, she paled and swallowed nervously.

'I—I've just been to her room, your Grace, but there was no answer. I—I think she must have overslept.'

Astounded, he stared at her, his anger and frustration mounting. 'Overslept? Oh, for God's sake!' he exploded, heading for the door. 'Which room has she been allocated? Show me.'

'Y-yes, your Grace.'

Dolly skittered off, the Duke stalking hard on her heels. Servants going about their duties stopped to stare, wondering what could possibly be amiss to raise his Grace to such a fury so early in the morning.

After rapping on Miss Lockwood's door, Dominic turned the knob and flung it open, seeing the young woman was indeed still abed and feeling himself about to explode. His brows snapped together as he stared down at her. She was lying on her stomach, her face, hidden by her mass of dark hair, turned away from him on the pillow.

'I'm sorry to wake you, Miss Lockwood. You've made your point,' he told her curtly. 'Now I'll make mine. I did not employ you so that you could idle your days away in bed. I said nine o'clock and I meant nine o'clock—not one minute later. Now, if you are not out of that bed and in the library in fifteen minutes, you can pack your bags and get out.'

Juliet became aware of a presence in the room as she floated in a swirling grey mist, drifting in and out of sleep, her mind registering mild confusion.

Reining in his temper with a supreme effort, Dominic said icily, 'If you have anything to say by way of explanation that will soften my attitude to you, then you'd be wise to speak out now.'

Juliet's tousled head raised itself off the pillow. She tried to bring the world back into focus. On seeing the figure at the bottom of the bed, hands on hips, glaring like some forbidding black thundercloud, slowly she sat up, pushed back her hair and then the covers and put her legs over the side of the bed. With a racking cough and her eyes streaming, she eased herself to her feet and took a few steps.

'I—I'm sorry,' she managed to whisper. 'I—I don't feel well…'

'Miss Lockwood?'

The voice was insistent, cold and commanding and vaguely familiar. He was speaking to her. She forced her eyes open and blinked, trying to focus, but her vision was blurry. The floor lurched and pitched beneath her and she swayed like Robby when he'd drunk a drop too much. A terrible dizziness assailed her and, putting her hand to her head, she crumpled to the carpet.

'Good God! You're ill.'

Juliet was disconcerted, but eternally grateful when strong arms lifted her, when a man's voice she had come to recognise called for someone to call Dr Nevis. When she was carried as though she weighed no more than a feather, which, to the man, she didn't, to the bed and returned her to her warm cocoon, knowing she was safe, she couldn't have said why, she let herself drift away, allowing the now gentle voice of the man to say what he pleased.

Juliet awoke to the sounds of someone moving about the room. Though her eyes were still closed, she was conscious of a shaft of light glowing red through her eyelids. She stretched and yawned, warm and rested and with a growing sense of well being, and with no sign of the dreadful headache that had plagued her when she had become ill.

For a while she lay listening to the rare sounds that broke the deep silence of the countryside. The dawn chorus of the birds and the sloughing of the wind as it sifted through the trees were more pleasant by far than the sounds of the vendors and the traffic of London streets.

Opening her eyes she turned her head, the movement attracting the attention of the maid bending over a tray. Suddenly everything became clear and she groaned. The maid, in a starched black dress, white apron and white cap, came and looked down at her, her round young face lit by a cheerful smile.

'Well, miss, feeling better, are you?' Dolly asked, her voice soft spoken. 'You gave us a rare fright, you did, especially the Duke.'

'Yes,' Juliet managed to say. 'I'm feeling much better...'

'Dolly, miss. My name is Dolly Fletcher.'

'Dolly, and I'm sorry to have been so much trouble.'

'Nay, don't say that. You've been no trouble, and it wasn't your fault you were poorly. 'Twas the soaking you got that did it. Wet through you were.'

'The—the doctor came. I seem to remember...'

'He did, miss, on the Duke's insistence—right worried he was too—the Duke, I mean. Doctor Nevis left some potions that brought your fever down and here you are, better in a flash.'

'How long have I been in bed?'

'Two days—so I expect you're ready for something to eat. I thought I saw you stir when I looked in on you earlier so I've brought you some tea.' Dolly poured her a cup and carried it to the bed as Juliet struggled to sit up. 'You can drink it while I fetch you some milk and eggs—and I'll just inform the Duke on the way to the kitchen.'

Taking the proffered cup, Juliet looked at her sharply. 'The Duke? Inform him about what?'

'He made me promise to tell him the minute you woke up. Right concerned he's been, asking after you all the time.'

'No doubt that's because he's impatient for me to start work,' Juliet murmured, taking a sip of the warm beverage, the memory of her unpleasant arrival at Lansdowne House returning in all its humiliating clarity.

Resilience came to the fore, for a young woman who tried never to allow things to get her down showed a champion's resolve to fight back. Though the anger still lingered and she felt a deep resentment towards those utterly spoilt young men and the woman called Geraldine, she was determined not to let it affect her work.

The following day Juliet could get out of bed and walk about, and later the same day, feeling the need for some fresh air, on Pearce's direction she found her way to a bench on a quiet terrace overlooking the extensive gardens. The sky, blue like a bolt of silk, was shot through with pale slashes of light and fluffy white clouds. The slopes of the grounds were shadowed by trees and the velvety lawns shimmered with early morning dew.

It was here that Dominic found her.

She stood up as he approached, uneasy about meeting her employer, hoping her illness had not roused his displeasure. She studied him intently as he came closer, her eyes alight with curiosity and caution. He was certainly as handsome as she remembered; in fact, many women would find him attractive, for he had incredible presence, exuding vitality and an aura of brute strength. She remembered the flush of attraction that had come over her on first seeing him and hated him for it. No other man had possessed the power to stir her emotions so intensely, and in such a way, on so short an acquaintance.

He appeared to be in his early thirties and there was a vigorous purposefulness in his long, quick strides that bespoke an athletic, active life, rather than the overindulgence that she could ascribe to the other gentlemen who had been present on the night she arrived.

'Ah, Miss Lockwood. I trust you are feeling better?'

'Yes, thank you, much better.'

'I'm glad to hear it. Please—sit down. I did not wish to disturb you.'

Juliet sat stiffly, her hands in her lap. 'I want to thank you for having the doctor sent for. It was thoughtful of you.'

'Nonsense. While I am paying your wages, it is in my own interests to hasten your recovery whenever you become ill.' An amused, enigmatic gleam lit his eyes as he met her gaze. 'Are you susceptible to illnesses, Miss Lockwood?'

'Apart from contracting a few minor ailments when I was a child, on the whole my health gives me no reason for complaint. Have—you any objections to my being out here, your Grace?'

'None whatsoever. Feel free to go anywhere you please within the house and grounds while you are here.'

'Thank you. That is most generous.'

He walked to the edge of the terrace and, with his back to her, gazed at the scene before him, a scene that was as familiar to him as his own hand. 'I often come out here to sit. This is a pleasant garden.'

'Very pleasant,' she agreed.

He looked back at her. 'I'm glad you find it so. You are being looked after, I trust?'

'I no longer need looking after. Dolly has been kindness itself. I apologise for the inconvenience I must have caused, but I should be ready to begin work in the morning. I'm looking forward to starting.'

An easy smile curved his pliant lips. 'Not before you're ready. We don't want a relapse. You gave us all quite a fright.'

'And I must have looked a sight.' She laughed. 'Although probably no worse than I normally look.'

'Now you are being ridiculous and do yourself a grave injustice,' Dominic remarked, marvelling at the courage she displayed under such duress. The bedraggled creature that had arrived three nights ago was gone and in her place was a pert, self-assured young miss. What he saw was a girl of medium height and slender and with curves in all the right places; and with an eye for beauty, especially when beauty was displayed in feminine form, Dominic looked at her now with surprise and more than a little appreciation.

She had a long white neck—like a swan, he found himself thinking. Her waist was miniscule, above which her breasts were high and rounded beneath her dress. Her voice was soft and yet her expression was open and direct, and she had indicated a genuine concern about her appearance, then calmly admitted that she did not look her best. This gave him the distinct impression that pretensions were completely foreign to her and that she was refreshingly unique in many ways—delightful ways, too.

That realisation stirred his conscience—and his pleasure at the thought was banished and made him step back. There was nothing right in what he was thinking about her. He was her employer and common decency dictated that he must not forget that—difficult as it might be. He must keep his distance, mentally and physically, and he must not think about her in any personal way.

With a slight inclination of his head that told her the conversation was over, he said, 'If you'll excuse me, I have some work to do.'

'Of course. Please—do not let me keep you.'

She stood up quickly. It was a mistake. He was too close and with the seat behind her she could not retreat. He looked straight into her eyes, overwhelming her with the sheer force of his personality. She felt as if she had been stripped naked by the unexpected intimacy of that brief contact. She struggled to appear calm, but her cheeks burned with embarrassment.

He smiled, reading her perfectly. 'I was about to say don't get up,' he murmured, his voice as smooth as silk. 'Stay and enjoy the garden. The fresh air will be beneficial to your health.'

She relaxed slightly and began to breathe normally again, reproaching herself for acting foolishly. Surely she was far too sensible to be overawed by an employer. It occurred to her to wonder how much truth there was in the gossip that surrounded him. Was his reputation really as bad as it had been painted?

'Yes, I will. Thank you.'

He glanced at her, and she felt her cooling cheeks begin to burn again. A glint of amusement flickered in his intelligent silvery eyes, almost as if he had guessed what she was thinking.

'No need to thank me. Fresh air is free, Miss Lockwood.'

Juliet waited until he had disappeared into the house before resuming her seat. What sort of person was he, she wondered, this employer of hers? Her stomach churned when she remembered the harsh coldness of his words when he had come to her room, not realising she was ill, and when he had his kindness and concern had been exemplary.

Her position was becoming far more complicated than she had ever anticipated. Not only did she have her work to contend with, she also had to find a way of dealing with her own irrational attraction to her employer. She couldn't believe he had aroused such a strong response within her—no one else had achieved that.

* * *

The following morning, throwing back the covers, Juliet swung her feet down to the carpet, feeling much stronger and eager to begin work,

Sitting at the dressing table, she brushed out her hair before twisting it into a tidy bun at her nape. She lingered a moment, examining her features with a critical eye, remembering the attractive woman she had seen on her arrival. For the first time in her life she wished she were beautiful. Beauty meant delicate features, clear blue eyes and soft blond hair. Her hair was an indeterminate shade of brown, her eyes too dark and her cheekbones too high, her mouth too full. The girls at the Academy had teased her about her looks and about her figure, too, for it wasn't proper for a young woman to have a tiny waist and a voluptuous bosom.

She had never been concerned about her looks. She had thought only about learning, reading, her father and her brother, so that it left little room for anything else. A change had taken place, and it had come on her arrival to Lansdowne House. With it had come something that must be instinctive with every woman and she didn't welcome it. The meeting with her employer had awakened something new, something she had sensed fleetingly in the past but never fully realising it until she had looked into a pair of silver-grey eyes.

A rueful smile curved her mouth. The Duke's friend Sedgwick had called her pathetic, and if she were honest she must have looked a sorry sight. But there could be no excuse for what the Duke had said—about her looking like Farmer Shepherd's scarecrow. It was an aspect to his character that told her a great deal about the man. If she could leave Lansdowne House, she would, but she would never find another position as well suited to her qualifications and the generous amount of money she was being paid.

But to be near the Duke of Hawksfield, knowing the disdain with which he regarded her, was an intolerable prospect.

Leaving her room, she stepped out into the passage. The rest of the household appeared to be sleeping. Everything was still. Downstairs, the hall was deserted, although she could hear the sound of voices and the distant clattering of pots in the kitchen, which she entered.

It was a splendid room where delicious smells assailed her, whose every surface was so highly scrubbed and polished it hurt the eye. A massive range with glowing coals occupied one wall, and there were two enormous tables, copper pans and bowls and chopping boards, and a huge dresser with what seemed to be hundreds of pieces of crockery and silver-covered dishes.

Maids scurried about their work under the watchful eye of Mrs Reed. They all turned to stare at the newcomer. She returned each and every look with a cordial smile. Seemingly unimpressed, they looked away. Like them she was employed by the Duke, but her elevated position set her apart.

Mrs Reed, stout and full bosomed and holding a long-handled spoon, looked up and studied the new arrival from head to foot. 'You must be Miss Lockwood.'

'Yes, that's right,' Juliet replied quickly, awkward at her intrusion.

'You're not from these parts?' she said, as though Juliet had professed herself to be an alien from a place beyond the reach of civilisation.

'No, I am not.'

'And you're feeling better now, are you?'

'Yes, much better, thank you.'

'Good.'

'You are Mrs Reed?'

'I am. I'm the cook for his Grace—have been for thirty years.'

'Then I'm pleased to meet you, Mrs Reed,' Juliet said, already realising that it would need a delicate touch to deal with the ticklish task of keeping on the right side of the cook. 'It is you I have to thank for the excellent food Dolly was so kind to bring to my room. I wonder if I could have some coffee—and perhaps some toast sent in to the library? I'm anxious to see where I'm to work.'

Mrs Reed looked none too pleased at having one of the maids taken off their work to wait on the new girl, which Dolly had been doing too much of late, but she nodded all the same. 'I'll prepare a tray and have Dolly bring it to you, but in future I'd appreciate it if you fetched it yourself. They've enough to do without running back and forth to the library.'

The tone was courteous, but the dismissal clear.

Juliet smiled sweetly. 'I'm sorry, Mrs Reed.' Mrs

Reed sniffed as though to say and so she should be. 'In future I will do that.' She had no choice but to withdraw.

Sir John's library was impressive, but it could not compare with what she saw when she entered the library at Lansdowne House. Instantly she felt the room's peace and tranquillity. It was a square high room and smelled of beeswax and old leather, a wonderful smell she savoured. A globe of the world stood in one corner, alongside a glass display case containing a selection of artefacts and curiosities, and four beautiful miniature water colours by an artist she did not recognise. There was a richly carved huge round table in the centre and comfortable leather chairs.

The room was awash with books on shelves from floor to ceiling, huge tomes, some behind glass for preservation, and journals and pamphlets. She ran her eyes along each shelf in turn, reading the names on the polished spines, letting her fingers trail over the leather bindings, pausing now and then when a particular volume caught her interest. Some were dog eared and in need of attention.

There was a collection of religious texts, a section devoted to English literature, and in the furthest corner of the library was an alcove dedicated to books on history. She stared in awe at the priceless artefacts and the glorious collection of paintings in ornate frames, and she was sure that was a Rubens over the fireplace.

Dolly brought the tray with her coffee, a small jug of frothy milk and a bowl of white sugar cubes. She placed it on the table. 'Shall I pour it, miss?'

'No, thank you, Dolly. I can manage.'

'Very good, miss—and don't mind Cook. Her bark's worse than her bite, as they say. She meant no harm—in fact, she's sent you some of her special biscuits to have with your coffee, as well as the toast.'

'I can see that,' Juliet said, somewhat heartened by the cook's unexpected kindness. 'They look delicious. Please thank her for me, will you, Dolly?'

'I will, miss. And don't be put off by Pearce either. He might look as though he's come out of the laundry over-starched, but he's an old softy at heart.'

Juliet laughed. 'Thank you, Dolly. I'll remember that. And—and his Grace?' she ventured tentatively.

Walking to the door, Dolly turned and looked at her with a grimace. 'His Grace is better for knowing, miss. You'll get the measure of him soon enough.'

Chapter Two

When Dolly had left, selecting a book at random Juliet took it to the table and opened the hard-back covers, releasing the scent of dust and old papers and antiquity. She lifted the lid on the pot of steaming coffee, releasing the delicious aroma, and settled down to begin her work.

Thirty minutes later Dominic paused in the doorway. Miss Lockwood hadn't heard him enter and he paused for a moment to look at her, pleasantly surprised. She was wearing a plain grey dress, its only relief a small white linen collar and cuffs.

Sensing she was not alone, Juliet reluctantly pulled herself away from what she was reading and drew herself upright. Turning, she met the Duke's hard, discerning stare. She noticed how he had a habit of staring right at a person with an unwavering gaze that seemed to blot out everything else. An inexplicable, lazy smile swept over his face as he surveyed her from head to toe, and Juliet had the staggering and impossible impression that he actually liked what he saw.

She started to lower her gaze, then forced herself to return his appraisal with a measuring look of her own. Lounging in the doorway in his snug, buff-coloured breeches and polished brown knee boots and tan jacket, a strong, ruthless figure who made the room seem much smaller, he looked incredibly striking.

'Good morning, your Grace,' she greeted brusquely.

'Good morning, Miss Lockwood. You may address me as Lord Lansdowne. I always consider your Grace as being too formal.'

'Very well. I hope you don't mind me coming to the library, but I wanted to see where I would be working.'

'Why should I mind?' he replied, sauntering towards her. 'It shows you are keen to get on with the project. I like that. It is unfortunate your first few days have been blighted by your illness,' he said lightly. 'I am also sorry that your first impressions cannot have been favourable, but no matter. You are here now.'

Juliet watched him, noting that the man who strode towards her bore little resemblance to the relaxed man she had seen on the night of her arrival and again on the terrace.

Leaning over, he scanned the notes she had made, his face impassive. 'I see you've started already,' he comented, noticing the quill in the inkwell and the ink staining her fingers.

'I've just been familiarising myself with where I am to work and making some notes.'

He nodded. Her reply made no apparent impression on him and he raised his eyes and levelled his penetrating gaze on her, swiftly changing the subject. 'I must apologise for my friends when you arrived. They were out of hand.'

'Please do not think you have to apologise for their behaviour to me. If your friends choose to behave like that, then that is their affair.'

'Indeed, but their manners were quite appalling.'

'I quite agree. I am sure they're all fine, honourable gentlemen—when they're not in their cups, but it is not gentlemanly behaviour to make fun of defenceless females.'

Dominic cocked a sleek black brow and smiled. 'Oh, I think you are more than capable of defending yourself, Miss Lockwood.'

She lifted her chin and gazed squarely at him. 'Lord Lansdowne.'

'Yes.'

'There is one thing I would like to say before I begin working for you.'

'Really! And what is that, Miss Lockwood?'

'I have not come here to provide some kind of entertainment for your friends. I am here to work.'

'I see you speak your mind.'

'That is my way. In doing so it is not my intention to give offence, but I think it is best if we know where we stand. Don't you agree?'

His lips twitched. 'Oh, absolutely, and I shall

endeavour to keep tight rein on my friends when you are around.'

'Thank you. I would appreciate that.' His grey eyes locked on to hers in such a penetrating way that she couldn't look away.

'You seem very sure of yourself, Miss Lockwood.'

'I am independent. I make my own living. I like it that way.'

Closer now, Dominic saw that her eyes were a curious colour, being large and limpid and a warm brown, but in them were flecks of gold, reminding him of a young doe. Her skin was white and as unblemished as bone china, and her mouth was rosy and full. He took a moment to note her severely drawn-back hair was thick and silken, shot through with tones of russet and copper and gleamed with the gloss of good health.

His expression said he was astonished and that he liked what he saw. It was in his eyes and the curling expression of his well-cut lips, in the slight drooping of his eyelashes in admiration.

Resentment at being stared at as if she were a mare that had drawn his fancy stirred in Juliet, but she did not show it. Still she was determined to be on her guard, mindful of Robby's warning. She could now see for herself that he was terribly handsome, and his wealth and title only added to his desirability.

She had also heard all about maids in many of the big houses having to leave in a hurry when they found themselves in a delicate condition, because they had caught the fancy of the master or one or more of his sons, who thought young domestic girls were there to be used for their personal convenience. It was a way of life with them. For all she knew the Duke of Hawksfield might be no different, in which case she would do her work and avoid him whenever possible.

'You aren't, by any chance, one of those women who are committed to women's rights—equality and all that.'

'Being a woman, naturally I support it, but I am not involved with any group. Men will continue to make the rules for a good many years, just as they have always done, but one day I do believe women will overcome adversity and have the same freedom as men.'

Dominic was curious. 'Where do you live? Where are your family?'

'I live where I work.'

'And do you have siblings, Miss Lockwood?'

'I—have a brother—a half-brother.'

'A half-brother?' he queried.

'His mother was my father's first wife. She died. As did my own mother, Father's second wife.'

'And your brother? Where is he?'

She looked down at the open book on the table. 'We don't see each other very often,' she answered truthfully, having decided when she had accepted the position that she would withhold her brother's temporary embarrassment from him.

Sensing some kind of evasion, Dominic looked at her, but did not pursue the issue. 'And I understand you were educated at Miss Millington's Academy in Bath.'

'Yes.'

He cocked a sleek, inquisitive brow. 'An expensive academy, Miss Lockwood.'

'My father was a scholar—a professor. He taught theology and history at Oxford University, where he himself studied. He was an extraordinary man, a very private one, and his interest in books was wide ranging. He believed everyone had a right to an education, and where I was concerned he put that before anything else, which was why he chose to send me to Miss Millington's Academy.'

She did not tell him that it was only at her father's funeral two years ago that she learned that all his money was gone. The Academy had been very expensive and he had never let her suspect his financial difficulties. He had continued to pay her tuition and to send money for her clothes. On her visits to his rooms in Oxford he had put on a front and she had never suspected anything was amiss.

The money was gone, and she would have been homeless had Miss Millington not offered her a position to teach at the Academy. Of course there was someone she could have appealed to—her maternal grandfather, but he had disowned her mother when she had eloped with her father, and Juliet had too much pride to go begging to an old man.

'And you were a teacher at the Academy?'

'Yes, until I went to work for Sir John Moore—doing very much what I shall be doing here—and I must thank you for considering me suitable for the position. But you already know the work I did for Sir John. I included it in my letter of application, along with my references from both Miss Millington and Sir John.'

'And glowing references they were, too, which was why I considered you suitable for the position without asking to see you first. You are apparently well read and uncommonly well educated. You speak fluent French and read and speak Latin and Greek, so why shouldn't I consider you a suitable person to catalogue my books?'

'Because I am a woman. There are many who think it unnecessary and impudent for females to be tutored beyond the basics of womanly duties.'

'That doesn't trouble me. Does it trouble you, Miss Lockwood?'

'No, not in the slightest, but many men are too prejudiced when it comes to women working for them.'

'It does not concern me. I am merely interested to know that you can do the job to my satisfaction.'

'And did you have many applicants to consider, Lord Lansdowne?' she dared to ask.

'Just the one. You, Miss Lockwood.'

'Then there really wasn't very much to consider, was there?'

'No.' He went to the desk and picked up a book she had been looking at. 'The library here is quite extensive and has been neglected for a good many years. There are many first editions and rare volumes, which I am certain you will find interesting—along with a good selection of novels. There is a great deal of work to do, and the pace will become quite stressful. You may find it tedious, but it is necessary if the books are to be preserved. Cataloguing was undertaken in my grandfather's time and the library needs updating. More books have been added and some of the volumes are in need of repair. There will be much to do.' He passed a keen eye over her face. 'Are you up to such an undertaking, Miss Lockwood?'

'I would not be here if I didn't think so. As you pointed out yourself, Lord Lansdowne, I am well qualified.'

Dominic glanced down at the title of the book and opened it, the gold signet ring on his left hand flashed as it caught the light. He smiled. 'You like Greek mythology?'

'Yes, very much.'

'Which you have read extensively?'

'Of course,' she admitted.

'And I was under the impression that reading the classics branded a female a blue stocking.'

'It usually does, in the circles in which you move, but in my case society is not important to me. I am interested in things beyond *petit point* and fashion. No doubt you consider this unfeminine.'

'Not at all—but there isn't a lady of my acquaintance who thinks of anything other than clothes and meaningless gossip, so it makes a refreshing change to meet a woman who does not.'

'Well, firstly, I am not a lady, and, secondly, I actually find it tedious.'

'Do you sing—and play a musical instrument?'

'No, I'm afraid not. I'm tone deaf.'

Her candid confession brought a smile to his lips. 'No one's perfect, Miss Lockwood,' he cheerfully and magnanimously declared. 'Besides, it makes a refreshing change. I've long desired to meet a female who reads Greek mythology, and I shall not be deterred from employing you merely because you can't sing or play the piano.'

Despite herself, Juliet found herself smiling. 'That's a relief. It will make my work a whole lot easier knowing I shall not be required to break into song.'

'That will not help my project to get the library sorted.'

'Does it not please you to listen to ladies entertain, Lord Lansdowne?'

'No, not particularly. Between you and me, Miss Lockwood, some of them would be as well to keep their mouths closed. Permanently.' He put the book down and perched his hips against the desk, feeling drawn to her and curiously reluctant to leave and to keep the conversation flowing. 'I am sure we have many points of interest and I see no reason why we should not become good friends.'

'I see many reasons,' Juliet stated primly.

'And what are they?'

'Your elevated position, for one thing. You are a duke, well descended, a person with breeding, bloodlines and ancestry. I am your employee, and I have no intention of breaching the social code. You have already seen by my behaviour when I arrived—when I so rudely barged into the room where you were entertaining your friends—that my knowledge of protocol is negligible.'

'It is easily acquired.'

'I have no doubt it is, by those in a position to do so,

but because of who I am, I do not expect noble etiquette to concern me. I am happy with the present arrangement.'

His eyes narrowed. 'You are a cool customer, Miss Lockwood.'

'Like I said, that is my way. To make a living I have to sell my services; you as my employer are buying them.'

'And with the mammoth task ahead of you, it could turn out to be a costly transaction. My secretary James Lewis, will assist you when necessary, but you will have to refer to me on several issues, so it is inevitable that you and I are going to be on closer terms. Have you not thought about that?'

'Not really. Our respective positions make any kind of acquaintance other than a working one impossible. It would be like a Royal Prince consorting with a commoner.' He looked slightly taken aback by her outspokenness, and she felt the victory was hers.

Shoving himself away from the desk, Dominic fixed her with a level stare. 'We shall see, Miss Lockwood. Your room is comfortable, I trust—and the servants have helped you settle in?'

'Yes, thank you—although I don't think the staff know quite what to make of me.'

'Oh? And why is that?'

'I belong neither upstairs nor downstairs.'

'Then where do you belong, Miss Lockwood?'

'Somewhere in between.'

'Then since my own elevated position sets us apart, and the servants are not in your league either, it would seem you are going to have your work cut out—and I am not talking about your work in the library.' His eyes on the window, suddenly he frowned.

Juliet followed his gaze and saw a carriage approaching the house. 'You have a visitor.'

'Mmm,' he murmured thoughtfully. 'My sister, Cordelia. No doubt she's come to nag me some more about taking a wife.'

There were footsteps across the hall outside. A moment later the door opened and an elegant woman breezed in.

Cordelia, a brisk, businesslike woman, was tall like her brother, in her late thirties, slender and with the upright carriage of a woman who sat a horse superbly. Her light brown hair had lost most of its colour, but her face was still young, her angular cheekbones and well-defined nose had kept their lines and her complexion had a bloom many a younger woman would envy.

'Good morning, Dominic,' she said coolly, crossing towards her brother and offering her cheek, which he kissed dutifully.'

'Cordelia.'

'You enjoyed the shooting yesterday?'

'As always, Cordelia,' he answered drily.

'And no doubt you spent the night with your friends drinking yourself into oblivion,' she chided dryly, pulling off her gloves. 'I called on Maria Howard on my way here. Her darling Thomas looked dreadful—haggard and hollow eyed—clearly under the weather. Geraldine was still in bed—I'd wager she made a total fool of herself and disgraced herself with young Sedgwick as usual. Thomas and Geraldine are both spoiled, promiscuous and irresponsible. They drink far too much—in fact, the pair of them are over-indulged. Neither of them know anything of self-discipline—and you shouldn't encourage them, Dominic,' she reproached harshly.

Dominic's brows shot up in offended surprise. 'Me?'

'Yes, you, since this is where they make for whenever they wish to misbehave. Why on earth Geraldine's father doesn't take a crop to her backside I'll never know. Although that said,' she said wryly, 'I strongly suspect he's hoping young Sedgwick will offer for her.'

Interest kindled in her eyes when she turned and saw Juliet standing patiently by the desk. 'Oh, forgive me. I had no idea you had company. And who is this young lady, pray?'

'Cordelia, allow me to present to you Miss Lockwood. Miss Lockwood, my sister, Lady Cordelia Pemberton. Cordelia, I told you I was to employ someone to sort out the library,' he said, somewhat vexed that she had clearly forgotten.

'You did? I don't recall you doing so. Still, it does need updating, I suppose—but I am surprised you of all people should employ a woman to do it—and isn't she a little young?'

'Miss Lockwood may be young, Cordelia, but she is highly qualified and comes with excellent recommendations.'

'Well, that's something I suppose. I am pleased to meet you, Miss Lockwood. I do hope the task of cataloguing these dusty old tomes won't be too daunting a task for you.'

'Not at all, Lady Pemberton. In fact, I'm looking forward to it.'

'You are? Well, I suppose it takes all sorts. You are like Dominic. The library is close to his heart, but I fear I could not bear to devote myself to such a tedious task. My late husband was an avid historian and often came here to peruse, so to speak.'

Juliet wondered how anyone could call such work tedious.

'Don't let my brother work you too hard,' Lady Pemberton remarked, eyeing her brother as though he already had.

'But I enjoy my work,' Juliet counted. 'This is where I like to be.'

'I suppose you do, otherwise you would not be doing it, but you must not hide yourself away. You must have some kind of recreation. It's important that you get into the fresh air—take some exercise. Do you ride, Miss Lockwood?'

'No, I'm afraid not.'

Lady Pemberton waved her hand in a dismissive manner. 'Oh well, I suppose you can always learn.'

Smiling, Juliet shook her head. 'Oh, I don't think so, Lady Pemberton. I prefer to leave horse riding to others.'

As if reading her mind, Dominic said, 'I must warn you that outside pursuits are close to my sister's heart, and if you are not careful she will take you under her wing and before you know it you will have become an accomplished rider trotting about all over the place.'

Juliet could not help laughing at that. Lord Lansdowne's sister had a forthright friendliness she liked.

'She is the same with everyone,' Dominic went on, 'although it causes some of her friends much vexation.'

'I can't see why,' Juliet countered. 'I would be happy for you to visit me here in the library at any time.'

Lady Pemberton beamed. 'Good. Be assured I shall do just that and we shall have tea together. Since my dear husband passed on I find I have far too much time on my hands. I shall often come to see how you are progressing with your work, but I must insist that you do not impose a discussion of literature upon me. I prefer to chat about more interesting matters.'

'You heard what Miss Lockwood said, Cordelia. She is here to work, not socialise,' her brother firmly stated. 'Besides, she has already told me she has no interest in frivolous matters.'

'Well, I'm sure we shall find something in common to talk about.'

'When she accepted the position she took on an obligation to me through to the completion of this project.'

'Really, Dominic, you cannot keep the poor girl cooped up here all the time. And might I suggest that in making her feel welcome you do not terrify her with your ducal intimidation. Make use of the charming aspects of your character. Do not drive her too hard. Remember that she is a woman first.'

Dominic scowled and, taking his sister's arm, marched her to the door. 'I will keep what you say in mind, Cordelia. Now let us leave Miss Lockwood to do what I am paying her a great deal of money to do and we will go elsewhere to discuss why you are here.'

'Oh, very well. Goodbye, Miss Lockwood. I shall visit you very soon. You know why I have come to see you, Dominic, so don't pretend you don't,' Lady Pemberton retorted as she was led away, unaware that the library door was ajar and that she was being overheard by Juliet as they crossed the hall to her brother's study. 'There is nothing that would delight me more than to know you have found someone to marry, a young woman who possesses the requirements of birth and breeding enough to make her worthy of marrying into the Lansdowne family and producing your heir.'

'I know, Cordelia, since you never tire of telling me at every opportunity.'

'You are the Duke of Hawksfield, so you must marry well for duty's sake. I know you would prefer not to marry at all, but you are not getting any younger and you must secure an heir. You cannot go on postponing the inevitable any longer. Besides, it's about time you made me an aunt.'

Eight years ago, despite the fact that Dominic was an only son and had not produced an heir to ensure the succession, his father had bought him a commission in the army. He had fought many battles in Spain against Napoleon's army, his daring and courage in the face of the enemy earning him the reputation as an invincible opponent. Two years ago, after fighting in the battle at Waterloo, which was quickly followed by his father's demise, he had resigned his commission and returned to Lansdowne House to resume the duties and responsibilities of a dukedom, and it was Cordelia's opinion that it entailed taking a wife and producing the necessary heir.

'Cordelia, as usual you are being far too dramatic. You have raised this particular issue many times and it is becoming tiresome. I am quite content as I am, and I want nothing to mar my present contentment—a wife would.'

'You cannot continue evading the issue as you do, Dominic,' his sister persisted. 'Of course, if you do marry, you will have to give up your current mistress. You do realise that, don't you?'

Frances was no secret, but it was not the done thing for a gentleman to discuss his mistress with his sister. On this occasion, however, Dominic wanted Cordelia to understand his intentions. 'My choice of bride is not your concern, Cordelia, and neither is my mistress. I am not giving Frances up.'

'Are you telling me you intend to keep her on after you are married?' his sister gasped in shocked tones.

Standing by the partly open door, Juliet heard Lord Lansdowne chuckle low in his throat.

'That's what gentlemen do all the time, Cordelia. The English nobility, as you will know, marry only for prestige and money, then look elsewhere for sexual fulfilment. When I marry, the lady I choose will be well bred, healthy and gracious. I shall not be expecting to be made happy by it—which is where Frances will come in.'

'Marriage may surprise you. You might even be made happy by it—as happy as I was with my darling Edward, happy enough that you will not need the companionship of such women as Frances Parker. I beg of you to at least try to find someone you could love.'

'You always were a romantic, Cordelia,' Juliet heard Lord Lansdowne reply with irony, their voices getting fainter as they entered his study. 'You and Edward were blessed to have loved each other so devotedly—'

'As you once did,' Cordelia said on a softer note. 'Amelia had everything—looks, breeding and style—and I know you were dazzled by her looks. It was a wicked tragedy what happened—to you more than anyone else—and then for her to die so suddenly, but it was over eight years ago and life goes on.'

'What I felt for Amelia only comes once in a lifetime, Cordelia. You should know that. Anything after that is only second best.'

Neither of them heard the click of the library door as Juliet closed it to shut out their conversation.

'You never did get over that, did you, Dominic?'

'Oh, I got over it, Cordelia. I also learned my lesson. Never trust a woman.'

'That's a bit harsh, isn't it? Not all women are like that.'

'You are the exception, Cordelia.'

It was not in Juliet's nature to eavesdrop on other people's conversations, which was why she had closed the door without listening to the rest of what they had to say, but what she had heard told her more about her employer than she cared for. He really was a libertine of the first degree if he insisted on keeping a mistress when he acquired a wife, and she pitied the woman he would eventually choose to marry, but she was also saddened by his loss, a loss that had plainly been so traumatic for him that it had made it difficult for him to marry any other woman.

Over the days that followed Juliet embarked on the task to familiarise herself with her new position and to absorb everything that was required of her with all the determination and intelligence she possessed. It was a demanding task and Lord Lansdowne was a demanding employer. His secretary, James Lewis, a mild-mannered, middle-aged man, was indeed helpful in showing her the ropes, and Lord Lansdowne himself frequently came to the library. He was critical and yet at the same time he gave praise where it was due and was interested in the progress she was making.

Their encounters were beginning to disturb her. She was overwhelmed by the sensations he aroused in her. She could not believe how her heart leapt when she caught unexpected sight of him, the delight when he smiled at her. At the same time she did not like the feeling of weakness, of powerlessness.

Often he would come upon her when she was so engrossed in her work that she was at her most vulnerable, her guard relaxed. Without warning he would appear beside her and look over her shoulder. She would feel his warm breath on her cheek and smell the subtle tang of his cologne, and felt betrayed by the way her body responded to him in stark opposition to her wishes. His great virility alarmed her at such close quarters.

It was her day off, a glorious day, with the sun shining out of a deep blue sky and not a cloud in sight. With a book to read, an apple in her pocket and wearing a green bonnet to shield her face from the sun, she intended finding a quiet spot in the extensive gardens where she would be uninterrupted.

Encountering Dolly in the passage leading from the kitchen to the yard at the back of the house struggling with a large basket covered with a snowy white cloth, she paused. 'What on earth have you got there, Dolly? I hope you don't have to carry it very far.'

'To the field beyond the stables, miss, where they're cutting the winter wheat.'

Juliet knew the home farm, run by the competent Farmer Shepherd, whose scarecrow his Grace had likened her to, had started the harvest. True to tradition, the Harvest Horn was sounded each morning at five o'clock, summoning the workers to the fields. 'Here, let me help you. You'll strain yourself, carrying the basket all that way.'

'Thank you, miss. I'd be ever so grateful. All the baskets of food have already been taken to the field, but this is full of some late pies just out of the oven. There's a large workforce to cater for. His Grace is giving them a hand, so Cook wants to create a good impression by making sure everyone's well fed and watered—so to

speak.' She gave the basket a look of disdain. 'There
are enough pies and pasties in there to feed an army.'

Juliet placed her book on a window sill, and between
them they took the handle and went outside. The air
was hot and sultry and heavy with the scent of flowers
blooming in beds along the path that led to the stables
and the fields beyond.

'You say the Duke is helping with the harvest,
Dolly?'

'Always does. Loves it, he does. He's always there
come hay time and harvest. Seems to like the physical work—suppose it's got something to do with him
being in the army. There's no keeping him away from
it.'

'But don't the workers find his presence intimidating?'

'No—not a bit. They're used to him and treat him
like one of them—which is the way he likes it when
he's in the field. He wouldn't have it any other way.'

Reaching the field, Juliet thought what a beautiful
sight it was. It was full of people, young and old, with
men bending low, grasping the corn in handfuls and
cutting it with the serrated edge of the sickle, the metal
shining in the sun as the heavy heads of wheat fell in a
graceful form before being hooked into sheaves. The
men cut and the women gathered the sheaves together
with their bare hands. Each sheaf was bound with a
straw bond, which had been made from the cut corn
and tied with a special knot. They worked until the
mid-day sun baked the cornfield, making the uncut

wheat crackle and the reapers' hunger and thirst for food and drink.

A cobalt-blue sky smiled over the green crest of hills in the distance, golden sunlight pouring down the slopes. High overhead a hawk hovered, while a couple of noisy magpies perched on a fence. Dogs with wagging tales and tongues lolling from panting mouths watched and waited in a shivering, excited alertness to catch the frightened rabbits that would come darting out from the corn, disturbed by the cutters.

Juliet's eyes drank in the intoxication of it all. She suddenly felt like a gilded bird freed from its cage for a few precious hours.

Juliet and Dolly carried the basket to the shade of the hedge, where others from the house, who gave them no more than a cursory glance, were already unpacking baskets. Placing the basket on the ground, Juliet took a moment to let her gaze wander to the surrounding fields where the corn had already been cut and stooked and stood like aisles of cathedrals in long rows on the golden stubble.

Kneeling on the ground, she began helping Dolly. Juliet liked the young maid, who was easy to talk to and always went out of her way to make her life easy at Lansdowne House. Dolly looked at her and smiled.

'This isn't the kind of work I expected to see you doing, miss. You don't have to.'

'I know, but I'd like to. Besides, it's my day off, and it's much better than being by myself. Who are all these people, Dolly? Where do they come from?'

'The village mostly and surrounding hamlets. Casual

workers are paid by the day, others by the week. It's backbreaking work, with not many breaks. Too much time resting in the heat of the day and the target of corn to be cut, tied and stooked will not be reached. If the heavy rains come and lay the corn, it's difficult to cut so they keep going.' She looked up at the sun. 'They'll soon be breaking off. There's the Duke over there.' She pointed him out. 'He's handsome, don't you think so?'

'Yes, he is.'

'He's a lady's man, too, when he goes to London,' Dolly said in a matter-of-fact way. 'Randy as a ram in town, but he never brings any of the ladies back here. He's never been known to interfere with the female staff, either. He's sober and fair minded and generous towards those who work for him, and admired by everyone in the district.'

'You certainly place him in an amiable light, Dolly. It is not consistent with his behaviour when he is in London.'

She shrugged. 'He can do what he likes in town, it's how he behaves when he's here that counts. Take people as you find is what I always say. His friends are a bit lively, though, and he has a habit of setting the whole house in uproar during the shooting and hunting season, when every gentleman here abouts invades the house. Always puts poor old Pearce in a flap and Mrs Reed never knows how many she has to cater for. That Sir Charles Sedgwick has to be watched. Have you met him?'

'Yes, on my arrival.'

'He's an ever-so-charming rogue with the ladies

if ever there was, so you watch out for him,' Dolly
warned, pausing in her work to give Juliet a stern look,
as if she were instructing a child when in fact she was
younger than Juliet. 'He can be very persuasive.'

'Well, he is very good looking.'

'They all are, miss. That's the danger of it. Let them
have their way and the next thing you know you're in
the family way. Miss Geraldine Howard's got her hooks
into him, but he's not averse to trying it on with any
pretty face that comes his way. Always causes quite a
stir among the housemaids when he comes a-calling.'

Juliet laughed lightly. 'Never fear, Dolly. I'll take
heed of what you say, although I like to think I have a
cool head in matters of the heart and always keep my
feet firmly on the ground.'

Juliet paused to watch the workers toiling in the
field, becoming thoughtful about what Dolly had said
about her employer. Had she been mistaken about his
character, and that except for his dissolute behaviour
when he went to town, his actions when he was at Lansdowne Hall put a different construction on his character? To be fair to him, from what she had observed of
him as he went about his work, he conducted himself
with dignity and was always civil and courteous, and
had Dolly not given him an almost flawless character?

In her plain dove-grey dress, a few seasons old but
flattering with a modest neckline and short ballooned
sleeves, some of the workers began to take notice of
Juliet. Unlike the other maids in their white aprons
and caps covering their hair, from beneath her bonnet
Juliet's hair hung loose about her shoulders, the sides

drawn back and secured with a narrow ribbon. Young men in the field became fascinated by her presence, exciting them and thrusting from their thoughts all the other young maids who were unpacking baskets of food.

When there was nothing to do but wait for mid-day, sitting a little away from the others beneath the shade of a willow tree, spreading her skirts about her, Juliet watched those hard at work. It was a cheerful group of maids who, happy to be relieved from household duties for a short while, eyed the youths in the field with encouraging flirtatious glances, tittering and giggling and hoping they would be singled out when they came to eat.

It wasn't difficult for Juliet to pick out her employer, who was arranging up the sheaves in stooks of eight. Never had she seen a figure of such masculine appeal. Against her better judgement she allowed her captivated senses to propel her deeper into her own thoughts, and as often happened, she was filled with such longings and yearnings as she had never thought to experience, and she felt that melting sensation in her secret parts.

Like many of the other male workers, he was naked to the waist. His legs were clad in buckskin trousers that fitted him like a second skin, tucked into high black boots and secured around the waist with a leather belt. The hairs on his chest glistened like strands of polished jet as every time he lifted a sheaf caused hard muscle to tense and ripple under his bronzed skin.

In no way did he resemble the refined gentleman

who inhabited Lansdowne House. He was more like a gypsy, too swarthy for a nobleman, yet as much at ease in a fancy drawing room dressed like a duke as stripped half-naked in the harvest field, working and sweating like a beast of burden with everyday folk.

At mid-day it was a cheerful yet weary group of workers that drifted to the shade of the hedge. They gathered around the baskets, mothers picking up their babies and unashamedly bearing their breasts to feed them. They sat quaffing ale and cider, the women and children cold tea, before tucking into bread and cheese, fat bacon and Mrs Reed's succulent pasties and pies.

The air was languid, the warm, sweet smell of the cornfield prevalent, and butterflies and insects fluttered about. For a while silence reigned, as everyone was content to munch away, unfazed by the presence of the Duke among them, content to work side by side with him, their only concern being to get the work done.

Juliet watched him throw himself down on the ground with his fellow workers, and when one of the men spoke to him a slow half-smile curved his sensuous lips, and she saw him give a careless shrug before lifting his a flagon of ale to his mouth. Tilting his head back, he drank deep, the curved arch of his throat strong and muscular. Passing the flagon on to the next man, he wiped his mouth on his arm and bit into a pasty.

It wasn't until he'd finished that he raised his fine dark eyebrows at some remark and finally looked in

Juliet's direction. He sat watching her in silent fascination, then he smiled as their eyes met and he excused himself and hoisted himself to his feet.

Chapter Three

There was a mild stir of interest as the Duke made his way towards Miss Lockwood, but then everyone went back to filling their bellies. Dropping down beside her Dominic stretched out on his side, looking up at her.

'So, Miss Lockwood, you have deserted your duties in the library to wait on the workers.'

'I hope you don't mind.'

'Not at all. It's your day off so you are at liberty to do what you like.'

Uneasy by his semi-nakedness, Juliet tried to keep her eyes averted, but it was virtually impossible when he was so close.

Sensing her unease and amusingly aware of the reason, Dominic got up again and went and dragged his white lawn shirt off the hedge where he'd discarded it earlier. Shrugging himself into it, he resumed his position on the ground beside her.

'I would not wish my state of undress to offend your

maidenly senses, Miss Lockwood,' he said by way of an apology, 'so I will spare your blushes.'

She merely smiled, relieved that she no longer had to gaze on that wide expanse of firm flesh. How handsome he is, she thought, with his black hair wildly tousled by his exertions. The dark liquid of her eyes deepened as she became caught up in the excitement of his presence.

She was sitting on the ground in a position that was neither dignified not ladylike. In her wildest imaginings she had never expected to find herself sitting in a wheat field with the Duke stretched out beside her. He took the piece of bread and the lump of cheese she offered. For a moment their hands touched. His hand was tanned, with strong, elegant fingers. She was instantly conscious of the warmth and potential power of that hand and felt an answering spark at his touch that no other man had aroused in her.

She hesitated, unable to look away from his face. His gaze was strangely compelling, though she still couldn't decipher the expression in his guarded silver-grey eyes. She was torn between a desire to get up and run away, and a fugitive wish to prolong the moment.

'I—intended finding a quiet place to read my book, until I saw Dolly struggling with the heavy basket.'

'And so you volunteered to help her. How very considerate of you, Miss Lockwood.'

There was something about the amused tilt of his eyebrows, the sudden mischievousness in his eyes, that made her laugh. 'I like to oblige when I can.'

He cocked a brow, his silvery eyes glinting with reflected sunlight. 'You do?'

She flushed softly, hoping he didn't mean what she thought he did. When his smile curled and his lips lifted slightly at one corner, his eyelids drooping seductively over his eyes, she knew that was exactly what he meant and didn't deign to reply.

Seeming to be content in her company, he allowed his eyes to remain on her, gauging her, watching for her every shade of thought and emotion, his gaze missing nothing. She looked lovely and arresting and very interesting. Her body was rounded and disturbing in its femininity. The swell of her hips and the firm shapeliness of her breasts as she leaned over the basket were outlined softly beneath her gown.

Hauling himself to a sitting position, he idly took hold of the short handle of a sickle that had been left lying on the ground and set it down by his side before turning his attention back to his charming employee, his leg brushing the naked blade.

'Have a care, Lord Lansdowne. If you do not treat the sickle with respect, it could do you untold damage should you happen to...' They stared at each other in silence for several moments, then Juliet grinned impudently.

Dominic glanced sideways at her. There was a gleam in his eyes, and she saw a smile form on his lips. He was clearly amused by her gauche remark. 'What? Sit on it? I sincerely hope not since I intend to father many children one day. But, my dear Miss Lockwood,' he uttered with mock horror, 'you should be flayed to within an inch of your life as a warning to others for your disrespectful boldness.'

She flushed hotly, wondering how she could have been so unsophisticated as to speak her thoughts aloud, but then, seeing the funny side when she realised what he thought she was referring to, laughter bubbled to her lips and it was a moment before she could speak.

'Or hung from a gibbet at a crossroads somewhere,' she suggested at last, tears of mirth gathered in her eyes that were gently teasing, 'as a warning to others not to be rude to a duke—or transportation to the colonies, even. Goodness, the punishments could be endless.'

He grinned, the sunlight emphasising the distinctive contours of his face, his strong white teeth gleaming as he returned her gaze. 'You're far too attractive for gallows meat, Miss Lockwood, and were you to be transported to the colonies, then who would I get as efficient as you to finish cataloguing my library?'

'Who indeed?' She laughed. 'But no one is indispensable, your Grace.'

'I wouldn't count on that if I were you, Miss Lockwood.'

Looking around and seeing that everyone had eaten their fill and were lolling around before they would start the afternoon work, Juliet began placing the uneaten food and drink carefully back into the basket, studying her employer surreptitiously. He was the most assured man she had ever met, yet she sensed that his self-confidence wasn't founded on empty arrogance, but on hard-won experience.

He looked so relaxed, sitting there with his arms

resting atop his drawn-up knees. And yet, she had the
strangest feeling that beneath that relaxed exterior there
was a forcefulness, carefully restrained for now, but
waiting. If she were to make a wrong move, a mistake
of any kind, she felt that he would unleash that force
on her. Recollecting herself, she gave herself a hard
shake. Now she really was being foolish and fanciful.

As she turned her head away, her attention was
caught by a young couple several yards apart eyeing
each other with a certain look. Without a word she saw
them get up and saunter towards a break in the hedge,
come together and disappear through the gap, and a
moment later from behind the hedge came a fit of giggling. Juliet glanced at her employer, who had also seen
the couple disappear. He was watching and waiting for
her reaction with quiet amusement.

'They are sweethearts, Miss Lockwood,' he said
quietly by way of explanation, smiling broadly at her
sudden confusion and the hot flush that sprang to her
cheeks.

'Oh—I see.'

'You do? Every dinner time, when food and drink
have been taken, Mandy Cooper always gives Simon
Archer a nod and a wink and he knows what it means.
Mandy wants him to take her to the shade and privacy
behind the hedge and—'

'Please don't go on,' Juliet gasped quickly, before he
could go into detail about what they got up to behind
the hedge. He didn't seem to mind that Simon Archer
was only too happy to oblige Mandy Cooper in the harvest field. She lowered her head, grateful for the wide

brim of her bonnet hiding her embarrassed confusion. It would never do to let him think he had her at a disadvantage.

Dominic chuckled softly. 'They are to be married at Christmas,' he told Juliet, as if this made everything all right.

'Please don't go on. It isn't something I consider funny, even if you do,' she informed him haughtily.

'Of course I find it amusing. I'm always entertained by the amorous antics of others.'

'I expect you would be,' she retorted sharply before she could stop herself.

Comprehending her meaning, his eyes narrowed. 'So, Miss Lockwood, my reputation has preceded me.'

'Yes. Do you deny that you have a certain—reputation, your Grace?'

'I would do so with alacrity, if I didn't think the answer would disappoint you,' he answered, a faint smile playing on his lips. Reaching out he brushed her hair with his fingers. She pulled back in surprise and he laughed, holding a piece of straw that had become entangled. She sighed and met his gaze. 'At heart I am a true romantic.'

'Are you suggesting I find anything—remotely interesting about the idea that you are a womaniser, Lord Lansdowne?' Juliet exclaimed, colouring hotly at the implication that she might find something attractive about the fact that he enjoyed the reputation of a libertine.

He chuckled softly. 'It's a talking point, if nothing

else. Although it might be difficult for a monumentally respectable young woman like yourself to understand.'

'I don't know of any other womanisers, your Grace, so, yes, I do find such behaviour difficult to understand. But I meant no disparagement of your character.'

'And I would wager that you would not have said that if I were not your employer, Miss Lockwood. I'm sure you would give me a severe dressing down, which some would say I deserve.'

'Perhaps you do. It's not for me to say.'

'How old are you, Miss Lockwood?'

Her eyes locked on his. 'You know perfectly well how old I am, Lord Lansdowne. It was on my reference when I applied for the position.'

'Twenty-three, I believe. Not on the shelf yet.'

He grinned and she flushed, uneasy about this inappropriate turn in the conversation.

'I—I can't make out the time,' she said quickly, busying herself with the basket, 'but I suppose everyone will soon have to begin work. I'll stay and help Dolly with the basket. We can go back to the house together.'

His gaze shifted from the hedge to her. 'Not until I've heard you laugh again. You should laugh often.'

Juliet shook her head and lowered her eyes, unsure how she felt about the way he was looking at her. She relaxed and managed to smile, finding it hard not to when he spoke to her in that silken voice.

'I confess I haven't laughed so much since I was at the Academy—when I was eleven years old.'

When he realised she wasn't going to elaborate,

with his lips twitching with amusement, Dominic said, 'Since you're obviously reluctant to share it with me, as a duke and your employer I insist that you do, Miss Lockwood.'

'Must I?' she said, laughter not far away. 'Have you no mercy, your Grace?'

'None whatsoever—and not when you address me as your Grace.'

'But it wasn't that interesting.'

'I don't care. Make it up. That's an order, Miss Lockwood. Pray continue.'

She sighed and sat back on her heels. 'If you insist.'

'I do.'

'Well,' she murmured, her voice softening as she looked back into her past, 'at the Academy we had a particularly strict teacher called Miss Murdoch. She was tall and willowy with a pointed face and a pair of extremely penetrating green eyes. Nothing ever escaped her and if any of the girls failed to come up with the correct marks in lessons, she was vicious with a ruler over one's knuckles.'

'And what subjects did this monster of a teacher teach?'

'English, history and music. As you know, my musical talents are sadly lacking, my singing offensive to the ears, but Miss Murdoch would insist that if I tried harder I would get better. She made me play the piano in front of the whole Academy once, which turned out to be a total disaster; instead of blaming herself for making me do it, she blamed me not doing enough practice and gave me such a rattling on my knuckles that I couldn't have played the piano for a week if I'd wanted to.'

Dominic felt an unexplainable surge of anger at the dreadful Miss Murdoch. 'What has that to do with laughter, Miss Lockwood? It sounds more like torture to me.'

'There is a humorous side to the story,' she said with a breezy smile and waving her hand dismissively, 'and it wasn't just me she had it in for. A few of the girls got together and decided to wreak their revenge. We sprinkled itching powder between her sheets one night. The poor woman came out in a dreadful rash and couldn't stop scratching herself for days,' she confessed with twinkling eyes.

'I assume the *poor woman* never found out the truth?'

'Oh, no. Never,' she replied merrily. 'We would all have been expelled for sure. But I shall never forget the look on her face when she came down to breakfast the next morning. She had the reddest face you ever did see and she had to leave the room because she couldn't sit still.'

'And you got your revenge?'

'Absolutely. But nothing changed. She was still the same sour Miss Murdoch, but we were cheered by it at the time.'

Dominic smiled, but his voice was quiet, seductive, thinking how lovely she was. The light breeze had whipped strands of hair around her face into a frame of soft, feathery curls. 'After what you have told me, now I know what sadistic cruelties you are capable of,

I must remember never to get on the wrong side of you, Miss Lockwood. Next time your revenge may take you beyond itching powder.'

'Things were different then. I am no longer eleven years old.'

'So you didn't make it up?'

'No. It may surprise you, but I didn't and at the time it was more hilarious than the telling over ten years later.'

Seeing everyone returning to work, the men picking up their sickles, Dominic hauled himself to his feet and looked down at her. As she tried to get up, her legs stiff because she'd been sitting on them, he reached down and took both of her hands in his, drawing her easily to her feet.

She looked up at him, very conscious of how close together they were standing, and the almost casual intimacy of their actions, which nevertheless was most inappropriate considering her position.

'When all the harvest has been gathered in,' he said, 'you must come to the harvest-home supper. It's a night not to be missed, when everyone from miles around comes together. It's held in Farmer Shepherd's barn.'

'I'd like that. Thank you.' While Dolly shoved the remaining leftover food into the basket she watched him turn and walk away to begin work.

One afternoon, when she was sorting through some manuscripts, someone walked in. Raising her head, she felt a sinking feeling in the pit of her stomach when she recognised the young man, Sir Charles Sedgwick, who she had seen on her arrival at Lansdowne House, the same man who had been insufferably rude.

She caught her breath as he sauntered towards her. The picture of him and the lovely Geraldine flashed in her mind. She saw him leaning over to caress her neck, and how Geraldine had almost purred like a cat with the pleasure it. It was like an erotic engraving come to life. She forced the unwelcome images out of her mind and tried to compose herself. His pale blond hair was thick and as shiny as silk. He was good look-ing all right, no question about it, but fortunately she knew him for what he was and was completely immune to Charles Sedgwick's kind of potent sexual allure.

When he reached the table she managed to give him a cool, indifferent glance. Shoving some books aside that she had stacked up to be rebound and perching his hip on the edge, he folded his arms across his chest, looking very pleased with himself.

'Well, well, Miss Lockwood, we meet again,' he drawled, quizzing her at close range with open male interest. His seductive, smoky blue eyes appraised her and a lazy smile curved his mouth, for the ravishing young beauty bore no resemblance to the pale, bedrag-gled little sparrow who had interrupted their dinner.

Juliet raised one eyebrow at him and regarded him coolly. 'I am surprised you can remember, since I wasn't looking my best.'

'I must have been well into my cups not to see how lovely you are—and I shall endeavour to see a good deal more of you while you are here.'

'Really? I think I am right to be wary of you. You look like a scoundrel to me.'

'And you would know what a scoundrel looks like, would you, Miss Lockwood?'

She raised her eyes to his. 'Oh, yes, Sir Charles. I have come across men like you before and always stay well clear. Now, will you please go away? I am trying to work.'

He grinned. 'I am a very persistent fellow, Miss Lockwood.' His voice was pleasant, almost playful, but there was nevertheless a steely edge to it. 'I am a good-natured, gregarious sort of chap, and you are a beautiful young woman, the employee of my best friend—if I can make your life a little more cheerful while you are here then why should I not endeavour to do so?'

'Why not indeed?' Juliet uttered drily. 'It is obvious to me that you have a way with women—with everybody come to that, even the Duke himself—but my instinct tells me that you will do me no good. Do you flirt with every woman you meet, Sir Charles?'

His eyes twinkled mischievously. 'Only the ones that take my fancy. I find you quite a challenge. Did anyone ever tell you you have wonderful eyes?'

His smile widened and it was such a wonderful, infectious smile. Juliet found herself smiling back. 'Not lately.'

At that moment Dominic came in, looking most displeased to find Sedgwick perched on the table gazing at Miss Lockwood's upturned face. Her expression was soft, her generous, full-lipped mouth that raised her beauty to the extraordinary curved in a smile that carried both promise and invitation. A sharp barb of jealously pricked Dominic deeply.

'I thought I heard your voice, Sedgwick,' he uttered brusquely. 'I didn't invite you to come in here.'

'I took it upon myself. Always was the impetuous sort.'

'I see you've met Miss Lockwood.'

Sedgwick turned to Dominic with a grin. 'I most certainly have; had I known she was such a beauty, I would have come to Lansdowne House hot foot. So this is the attraction that keeps you at home, Dominic. I have to say I detect a definite improvement in your taste. My dear Miss Lockwood,' he said, looking again at Juliet, 'my hat is off to you. Since your arrival my good friend has not been seen, and I feared he had become a recluse.' He sent Dominic a twinkling grin.

An embarrassed flush spread over Juliet's cheeks. 'Really? If that is so, I assure you it has nothing to do with me.'

'Miss Lockwood,' Dominic said, 'bearing in mind the proprieties, perhaps I should formally present Sir Charles Sedgwick, who purports to be my good friend,' he growled with some measure of sarcasm.

'And I'm sure he is,' Juliet murmured absently, having instantly sensed that Charles Sedgwick was a born womaniser, accustomed to stealing feminine attentions from any other man in the vicinity.

'I feel I must apologise for my behaviour when you arrived,' Sir Charles said. 'I am not in the habit of being rude to young ladies. Say I am forgiven and I will leave a happy man.'

Juliet laughed lightly, finding it hard not to when he asked so touchingly. 'Very well. You are forgiven.'

Sir Charles smiled wickedly at his glowering friend. 'There you are, you see, Dominic. Miss Lockwood is indeed generous—a woman after my own heart. I intend to see more of her, so I shall have to call on you more often.'

'Miss Lockwood is here to work, Charles, not for your entertainment—and with your reputation she would be well advised to steer clear of you.'

'Your reputation is not a great deal better than mine.'

Dominic shot him an ironic look. 'I was never in your league, Charles. You have flagrantly violated the rules of morality, decency and ethics, and personal responsibility.'

Charles shot him a sideways look and noted his deep preoccupation with Miss Lockwood and his darkening expression. 'Good Lord, Dominic! You look as if at this moment you are looking for an excuse to draw my blood.' He smiled at Juliet and gave her a playful wink. 'I express my admiration for your courage in having survived a full two weeks with my most esteemed friend. I can well imagine how difficult it must be.'

'As you see, Sir Charles, I have survived.'

'And she will continue to do so,' Dominic quipped. 'Now will you kindly leave Miss Lockwood to do what I am paying her to do and wait for me at the stables. I would like to speak to her in private.'

Taking his leave of Juliet in the most charming manner, Sir Charles strode to the door. Dominic followed him, and growled, 'Back off, Charles. I meant what I said. Miss Lockwood is here to work and not open to seduction.'

Charles laughed softly, amused and not in the least offended by his friend's irate look. 'Worry not, Dominic. It there is any seducing to be done, you can be relied upon to do that yourself.'

He was still smiling that irrepressible smile of pure mischief, which Dominic knew he must be wary of if he were not to reveal the true nature of his feelings for Miss Lockwood.

Charles sauntered off, leaving Dominic alone with his employee. 'A word of advice, Miss Lockwood,' he said, crossing towards her. 'Never smile at Charles like you were doing when I came in. If you do, he will see it as an invitation to seduction.'

Juliet stared at him, unable to believe this was the same man she had whiled away the time with in the harvest field. 'I appreciate your advice, Lord Lansdowne, but I have taken the measure of Sir Charles Sedgwick and I believe I can manage him without any assistance from you or anyone else.'

Dominic could hardly contain his jealousy. His eyebrows dipped alarmingly and his mouth thinned with what appeared to contain his anger. 'Did you have to be so accommodating?'

'Accommodating?' she answered haughtily. 'We were only talking.'

'Then I would be obliged if you would confine your talking to when you are not working. Such distractions will lead to mistakes, and that would never do,'

he retaliated, his face darkening ominously, in a way
those who worked for him would have recognised. He
felt a sharp needle of exasperation drive through him,
directed at her, or so it seemed, as though, like a witch,
she had cast a spell on him which was so totally absurd.
It was not her fault that he found he was unable to get
her out of his mind.

Juliet gasped. 'I beg your pardon!' she retorted, putting her hands on her hips, her dark eyes flashing dangerously, evidently as put out as he was. 'I have been
working exceedingly hard and you have no reason for
complaint. Why Sir Charles came in here I really have
no idea—'

'You don't? It's pretty obvious to me,' he interrupted
sharply.

'Nevertheless, I am not so discourteous as to tell
him to leave. It is not my place.' She looked closely at
his angry features, wondering why he was being like
this. 'Is there something wrong? Do you not find my
work satisfactory, Lord Lansdowne?'

'Don't be ridiculous. Your work is exemplary, and I
think you should get on with it.'

Dominic turned on his heel and stalked out. He had
made a fool of himself and tried to get some order into
his mind to discover why. Why did he keep thinking of
Miss Lockwood? Why did her face flash disconcertingly across his vision as it had a habit of doing so often
of late? Why did he find himself drawn to the library
when he knew she would be working?

The sight of her looking up at Charles and smiling as
though she had not a care in the world had sent a wave

of jealousy surging through him. Dear sweet Lord, what was wrong with him? How could he let a woman affect him as this one did? He was quite bewildered by it. All he knew was that he felt different, strange, from anything he had felt before. It was something that had just happened, not there one moment but there the next as if she'd always been there. She was not for him, coming from the class she did, but he could not stop thinking about her.

He knew Charles and that he would want her—and how could he blame him for that? There was something about Juliet Lockwood—a loveliness not just in her face but in her heart and soul. It shone from her like a beacon, and when men saw her they recognised it. In her naïvety she was completely unaware of it, and that was what was so special about her.

Seething, Juliet stood for a long time staring at the closed door, deeply affected by what had just transpired and unable to understand why he had been so angry. Lord Lansdowne was persistent and he was ruthless too. His attractive looks and charm couldn't conceal that. It was evident in the hard glint in his eyes, in the set of his jaw and in the curve of his mouth. He might be able to set dozens of women's hearts to flutter just by cocking his sleek black eyebrow and a flash of those even white teeth, but she had no doubt he could be utterly unscrupulous if the occasion demanded.

Juliet was upset and angry, also, at the effect he was having on her. How dare he invade her mind like this, her life? Had she not enough to worry about without any new threats? Just when she had found new employment, hoping to earn enough money to help Robby. She hadn't earned nearly enough working for Sir John, despite all her hard work. She needed at least another six months, and this handsome, arrogant lord with mocking silver-grey eyes and determined manner had forced his way into her heart, adding yet another worry.

Following Sir Charles Sedgwick's visit, it was inevitable that every residence of note in the district got to know about the Duke of Hawksfield's beautiful new employee. As the drizzle of gossip and innuendo grew stronger, several of the Duke's friends and neighbours made curious visits, hoping for a glimpse of her, only to be disappointed, for apart from that one lapse when she had gone to the harvest field with Dolly, Juliet insisted on her privacy in the confines of the library.

The ebullient Sir Charles was the exception. He seemed to visit Lansdowne House more than usual and always made a point of popping in to the library. There was always a charming smile on his lips and a wicked gleam in his eye, though he wasn't really wicked, just spoiled and unprincipled. He had too much money and was too good looking. In fact, he had too much of everything and thought the world should pay obeisance to him, and Juliet could only hope that one day he would change and grow up.

His visits always drew the Duke's deep displeasure, but short of barring him from the house, which would damage their friendship, there was nothing he could do.

* * *

When a letter for Juliet was delivered to Lansdowne House, she read it with a mixture of amazement, joy and a certain measure of trepidation. It was from Robby. He had been released from the Fleet prison and had come to Brentwood. He wanted her to meet him that very afternoon. But how did he get out of the Fleet?

In town to visit an acquaintance, Dominic was getting out of his carriage when his attention was caught by a young woman who was dashing along the street. It was her laughter rising on the warm air above the hubbub of the crowds that he recognised.

Startled, he stopped dead and looked and looked again. Good Lord, she was running. The prim and respectable Miss Lockwood was actually running. Her hair was unbound and her bonnet, secured by a ribbon around her neck, was bobbing against her back and a wide smile stretched her lips. She was running towards a tall, lean man who was striding quickly towards her, with eyes for no one else on the busy thoroughfare. He caught her up in his arms and swung her off her feet, and her arms went round his neck and she hugged him tightly.

A jolt of some kind of emotion he didn't recognise shot through the part of Dominic's body where he supposed his heart lay. His eyes became colder than an icy winter sky and there was a thin white line about his mouth. He wanted to go and tear them apart, to fling the man away from the lovely, laughing girl and punch him in the mouth. How dare he put his hands on what should be Dominic Lansdowne's?

Running trembling fingers through his hair, he recollected himself. Dear Lord, what was wrong with him? How could he let a woman affect him as this one did? And who was the man who was acting so familiar with her? God damn him! Turning away, he pulled open the carriage door and flung himself inside, ordering his driver to move on.

When Robby finally set Juliet on her feet, she laughed up into his face. 'Oh, Robby. I can't describe how I felt when I got your note. It's so wonderful that you're out of the Fleet. But how did it happen? You weren't to be let out for another six months.'

Robby laughed and tucked her hand into the crook of his arm. 'Come, let's walk and I'll tell you.'

They sat in the shade of a giant oak as the sun stretched its rays over the grass. Juliet looked at Robby with a feeling of pride. He looked the picture of an up-and-coming young gentleman in his fine new clothes, pleasing and handsome enough to catch the eye of any young lady. He was still very thin from the time he had spent in the Fleet prison, but his eyes glowed with health and joyous vitality and with the content of a man well pleased with the world and his place in it.

'Now tell me,' Juliet asked, happy to see her good-looking brother with his laughing blue eyes, hoping there was nothing underhand about his release and that he might have to go back. 'How did you get out?'

He grinned. 'Don't worry, Juliet, I didn't escape or

anything like that. I merely called in a few favours owed me by some of my friends. I was surprised they paid up, but I was relieved they did. After settling my debts, at least it got me out of that place.'

'But if they owed you, why did you wait so long to ask them to pay you back?'

'Because I didn't know where they were. It was when a friend of mine came to see me and told me two of those I went to Italy with—having lent them money to see their way since they were strapped at the time— were back in London that I wrote to them. They are good chaps, their families well off, and they gave me what I was owed. With my debts settled I find I have some money left, so you will by happy to know I am not as destitute as you thought.'

Juliet sighed and patted his hand. He would never know how desperately anxious she had been for him when she had been told he had been sent to the Fleet prison.

'Well, I wish they hadn't taken their time in coming back. What they owed would have kept you out of prison and saved me a lot of money.' She looked at him fondly. 'But I don't begrudge you a penny of it, Robby. I'm glad you're out, but I hope you've learned your lesson and that you will find yourself a good position—and start to put on weight. Look at you. You're so thin.'

'With good food I'll fatten up in no time. And you will be pleased to know I have found employment already.'

'You have?' She hugged him laughingly. 'Oh, Robby, where?'

His look became grave as he prepared to drop his bombshell, not knowing how she would take it. 'In America, Juliet, in New York,' he said quietly. 'Someone I know who lives in New York and runs a school for boys has offered me a position teaching history and English.'

Shock rendered Juliet dumb. She stared at him, feeling as if all the breath had been knocked from her, and then she felt tears prick her eyes. 'America? But—but that's so far away. Oh, Robby, I don't know what to say.'

'You could say that you're pleased for me. It's a good opportunity for me, Juliet. I'm hardly likely to get such a good position here with my prison record.'

Juliet quickly pulled herself together. 'Yes, you're right. I am happy for you, Robby, and very proud, but—I shall miss you. All I ask is that you do not to go back to your wild ways. It's the road to nowhere.'

His expression became serious. 'I know that, Juliet,' he said softly. 'And I won't. One stretch in the Fleet is enough for any man. I won't go back. It's hard to wash away the stink of that place. It's in my hair, my clothes. Does your employer know about me?'

'He knows I have a brother...'

'But you haven't told him I was in the Fleet.'

'No, I couldn't.'

'Then better not. I asked you to meet me here because I didn't want to embarrass you by going to the house. Are you enjoying your work?'

'Yes. Lord Lansdowne often comes to the library to

see how things are progressing, but apart from that I rarely come into contact with him.'

'I'm relieved to know that. Given his reputation, I confess I was apprehensive about you working for him.'

'Then you needn't be, Robby. Besides, I won't be at Lansdowne for much longer. The work is not nearly as extensive as I thought. It should be complete in the next couple of months.'

'And then what?'

'Oh, I'll find something else, I suppose.'

'Juliet, why don't you write to your grandfather?'

The words seemed to drop like lead into the warm air and the smile faded from her face. 'You know why. After the way he treated my mother, I couldn't.'

'Your mother hurt him deeply when she ran off with our father, and now he's probably a lonely old man who more than likely regrets the estrangement.'

Juliet tensed, her mind locked in furious combat against the idea of reconciling with her grandfather. Robby's words brought back that terrible day when her mother had died, and later, when her father, having notified the Earl of Fairfax of his daughter's death, had received a letter from the old gentleman's lawyer informing him that, as far as the Earl was concerned, his daughter had been dead to him from the day she had left his house.

'When Father wrote and told him that my mother had died, he was given short shrift by Grandfather's lawyer. He couldn't even be bothered to put pen to paper himself. I will not communicate with him, Robby.'

'His grudge was with our father. You are your grandfather's legitimate heir, Juliet. There is no entailment to the estate. Who else does he have to leave his money to?'

She shrugged. 'I don't care. I don't want his money. I've managed very well on my own so far. I don't want anything from him.' Forcing a smile to her lips, she took his hand. 'When do you leave for New York, Robby?'

'Soon. I've found accommodation for a couple of weeks to enable me to see as much of you as I can before I go—if you can get away.'

'I put a lot of hours in with my work, so I am able to have time off—perhaps the day after tomorrow.'

He squeezed her hand. 'Don't worry about me— you've done enough of that in the past—my courageous, steadfast little sister.'

As they strolled arm in arm back the way they had come, Thomas Howard pulled his horse up sharply when he saw them.

'Good Lord!' he exclaimed, causing his sister to draw rein beside him.

'What?'

'I do believe that is Robert Lockwood.'

'You know him?'

'No, not a bit. I've seen him and his cronies about London's gaming haunts, but I had nothing to do with him. Thought he was doing a spell in the Fleet—no idea he was related to the delectable Miss Lockwood.'

Sudden interest kindled in the depths of Geraldine's eyes. She cast a contemptuous look at the couple as they walked on by, unaware that they were being observed.

A thin smile curved her lips. So, Miss Lockwood's brother had been in prison. Was Dominic aware of that? she wondered.

The sheaves had been gathered from the harvest field, the wagons pulled by heavy cart horses going to and fro from the fields to Farmer Shepherd's rickyard. When the last load was hauled from the field it was the turn of the gleaners. Juliet went to see the blue and red, and yellow and red four-wheeled carriers of corn pass by, and what a sight it was to see the women with their children, little things, with hard red legs shining amongst the stubble, stooping to pick up an ear of corn, snipping off the long straw and putting the ears of corn into the bags that their mothers had tied on them, or raising their heads to scare away a crow.

Dolly told Juliet that these people from the village had no holdings of their own and that a family could glean and thresh enough wheat to keep them in bread for quite a while.

Then the whole village gathered together and women and children raised their voices in the shout of 'Harvest Home'. The smiling young girls wore straw bonnets decorated with wreaths of flowers. The huge cart horses were decked in the same way—each one led by one of the men browned with summer toil.

The Duke of Hawksfield, looking positively dazzling in black knee breeches and jacket and a white satin waistcoat and cravat, his stockings of fine white silk, stood at the gate of the home farm to welcome in another harvest.

In Farmer Shepherd's great thatched barn, where the barrels of ale and cider stood against the wall facing the huge double doors like sleeping black dogs, the harvest supper was prepared. Juliet had given in to Dolly's persuading and agreed to come, and soon became caught up in the excitement of the festivities.

Her eyes grew wide when she saw the long trestle tables groaning under the weight of food—all kinds of meat pies and fruit pies and tarts and steaming plum puddings. Juliet was astonished to see her employer with an apron around his waist, carving an enormous sirloin of beef while his servants were busy loading the villagers' plates and filling jugs of cider and ale from the barrels.

Women were dressed in their best frocks and the men in clean white smocks, their faces ruddy with toil and health. There was much joking and laughter and old stories were told and old songs sung. The local orchestra played on their drums and flutes and violins, and among the candles and rapidly emptying plates the Duke sat supreme at the top of the table with Farmer Shepherd and the local mayor on one side and his wife on the other.

And then the dancing began. Dolly was lively and unreserved and danced every dance, dragging a protesting yet laughing Juliet with her. She was never in want of a partner, and all the while as she was spun around in first one country dance and then another, she was aware of the Duke on the sidelines, speaking to people he knew. Often when she caught his eyes, she would find him watching her thoughtfully.

* * *

It was towards the end of the evening and the harvest home was almost over when Dominic found his way to Juliet's side.

'May I have this dance, Miss Lockwood?'

Juliet didn't resist. 'You may,' she said.

All eyes were on the couple as they stepped on to the floor of Farmer Shepherd's barn. It was a rare sight to see the Duke dance with anyone, but they all agreed that his Grace and Miss Lockwood in her deep rose-coloured dress made a handsome couple. They danced the waltz, which was more in keeping with the mood of the late hour than a robust country dance. The musicians excelled themselves. The music was sublime, rising and swelling, filling the barn with a beauty as touching and as tangible as the flowers that decked the walls.

Dominic looked into Juliet's eyes and smiled. 'You're trembling, Miss Lockwood. Nervous?'

'Terrified,' she confessed. 'Everyone is looking at us. I'll probably stumble and fall flat on my face and then every-one will laugh at me and say it serves me right for being presumptuous.'

'Presumptuous? And why would they accuse you of that?'

'For agreeing to dance with the Duke.'

'I asked you to dance, and the reason why I asked you is entirely my own affair. Let them read into it what they like. It matters not one jot to me.'

'Even though I might stumble and fall?'

'No, you won't. Not when I am here to hold you up.'

'You have made me look conspicuous by singling me out from the others. Dolly told me it is virtually unknown for you to dance at harvest home.'

'It strikes me that Dolly says far too much. You must take what she says with a pinch of salt.'

'I like Dolly. She does tend to have a lot to say, but she means well and talks a lot of sense. She has gone out of her way to befriend me.'

'And you need befriending, do you, Miss Lockwood?'

'Of course not, but, apart from Pearce, Dolly is the only member of staff who feels comfortable around me. Because of my slightly elevated position in your house, most of the servants stand a little in awe of me, which I regret, but there doesn't seem to be anything I can do about it. I've managed to win over Mrs Reed, who always greets me amiably whenever I find it necessary to go to the kitchen—so you see why I value Dolly's friendship.'

'Her heart's in the right place, I grant you. Are you enjoying yourself?'

'Very much. I nearly didn't come, but I'm glad I did. Dolly insisted.'

'Then I thank God for Dolly,' he uttered blandly. 'You look charming by the way. Little wonder everyone is looking at you.'

Others began drifting on to the floor—although after quaffing large amounts of liquor throughout the evening, their dancing resembled more of a stumble and a shuffle and it was difficult to work out which of the partners was holding the other up. Mandy Cooper and

Simon Archer, both terribly flushed and their eyes half-closed, could hardly keep their hands off each other, and Mandy seemed to be immensely proud of the bulge beneath her dress, for she made no attempt to conceal it. Remembering the day in the harvest field when they had disappeared behind a hedge to make love, Juliet found it impossible to keep the smile from her lips.

Dominic read her mind and laughed low in his throat. 'It would appear those two have spent a great deal of their time behind hedges, Miss Lockwood. As you see, they are to have a child come February.'

She looked at him directly, unabashed at his implicit allusion to what the young couple had been doing that day. 'Then it's a good thing they're getting married at Christmas. Will they live in the village?'

He nodded. 'I've promised them a cottage.' When Juliet raised a questioning brow, he said, 'It's the way of things. They work on the estate. They're entitled to accommodation.' Glancing at the couple in question, who chose that moment to collapse on to a bench, his smile broadened. 'By the look of them, I would say the sooner the dancing is over and they find their beds, or bed, whichever the case may be, the better.'

'The evening has certainly been a success—a wonderful end to the harvest's toil. Everyone must be relieved to have managed it before the rains come.'

'That's how they see it—when all is safely gathered in.'

'And is it? I'm sure I saw a field of oats left uncut.'

'How observant of you, Miss Lockwood, and you are quite right. All is gathered in—apart from a field of oats left until the last in case there is some moisture in the sheaves or green ears.'

'Having no concept of farming procedures, I haven't the slightest idea what you're talking about.'

'Then I shall explain. I am most particular that the threshed oats are not mouldy or heated when my groom feeds them to my hunters. So we observe the old maxim that oats should hear the bells ring in the village church before they are ricked.'

'Oh, I see.'

'You do?'

'No, not really. But I will take your word for it. What would happen to your hunters if the oats were heated?'

'Like as not they would get a belly ache, Miss Lockwood.'

'And you would be concerned.'

'Of course. My hunters are valuable horses.' He looked at her sharply as a thought occurred to him. 'Have you ever seen a foal being born?'

'I've never had anything to do with horses, so the answer is, no, I have not.'

'Would you like to? It's a remarkable sight.'

'Yes––I think I would, but I doubt I ever will.'

'It's not impossible. I have a mare that is about to foal here in Farmer Shepherd's stable tonight. If you're not too tired after all the gadding about, I shall take you to see it when we've finished the waltz.'

'Thank you. I'd like that.'

Throughout the dance Dominic maintained eye contact with Juliet. He was a marvellous dancer, executing each step with graceful perfection. The barn seemed to swirl, the people a blur as Juliet tilted her head and gave herself entirely to the magic of the moment and the man who held her in his arms. She felt strangely light headed and gay—perhaps she had drunk a little too much cider herself.

A familiar slow smile played on Dominic's lips and the challenging gleam in the silvery eyes was very evident now, and as he gently but firmly spun her round, there was no mistaking the provocative way in which his gaze lingered on her eyes and soft lips.

She gazed back at him, her dark eyes wide and questioning, her lips parted slightly in surprise. She had tried to convince herself that she had misinterpreted their open and easy conversation in the harvest field, a conversation too casual, revealing and inappropriate between a duke and someone of her lowly station, but the fiery spark of intimacy she had sensed between them that day was even stronger now.

Despite her attempt to remain cool and detached, Juliet's heart beat with an uncontrollable rhythm of excitement, for she fully believed the Duke was flirting with her. He had not said one word to suggest he was, but his eyes were far too eloquent, far too bold, and she could feel the virile power in him as he held her in his arms. It half-frightened her, but a tiny flame of giddy joy burned within her as she danced.

Chapter Four

Entering the warm, orange glow of the lantern-lit stable, they were met by the pleasantly fecund smells of fresh straw and grain, warm animals and manure. It was filled with shadows, all hazy and dreamlike. The lithe shadow of the stable cat slunk away. Several hens nestled in a pile of hay stacked by the door, fluffed into brown and white balls of yellow-eyed resentment at being disturbed at this late hour. They muttered among themselves when Juliet and Dominic entered, but were too embedded in their nests to do more than shuffle and cluck.

The huge chestnut mare about to give birth was lying on the straw, her breathing laboured as she turned her head, giving the newcomers no more that a cursory glance. A groom, his shirt sleeves rolled up and sticking to his back with perspiration, was on his knees beside her.

'Hello, Ben,' Dominic said, shrugging out of his jacket and throwing it over the stall door. 'How goes it?'

Ben raised his head and nodded a greeting before fixing his attention once more on the labouring horse. 'Nearly there, your Grace, nearly there,' he muttered, social position forgotten in the wonder of the shared moment.

Her eyes having adjusted to the dim light, Juliet rested her arms on the top of the stall door and gazed in wonder at the enchanted scene, excited by the whole event. The Duke dropped down on one knee beside Ben. He looked at the hunter then grinned up at Juliet.

'It would appear we are just in time, Miss Lockwood. Another five minutes and it will all be over.'

No longer looking at the horse but at its master, Juliet saw the lantern light turn his hair to polished ebony, softening the hard planes of his face and turn his eyes to liquid silver. As he assisted in the delivery of the foal he murmured soft, gentle words of encouragement to the mother and stroked her quivering flanks.

And then the foal began to emerge. Juliet watched in a state of wonder as first of all a watery bag appeared, followed by a pair of front feet, the hooves soft like jelly. They were followed by a nose and then a head appeared and finally its ribcage and its legs. Holding her breath, her eyes enormous and shining in her flushed face, she watched as the foal—a stallion that delighted the two men and had them slapping each other on the back—slithered free of its mother.

Almost immediately the proud mother, despotic in

her protection, was up and licking the foal off, toss-
ing her head challengingly at the entranced group of
humans looking on, until it was dry. By this time the
foal was trying to get up. His stick-like legs were everywhere, his shy, liquid eyes looking anxiously at his
surroundings. Drunkenly he staggered about until she
found his balance, and soon found his way to his mother's teats. His tiny rump and sloping shoulders were
echoes of his mother's muscular perfection. He had the
same large, kind eyes, fringed with long brown lashes,
but instead of the sleek hide of rippling chestnut, he
was a dark reddish-brown and fuzzy as a rabbit, with
an absurd little tail.

Juliet laughed with delight. 'What a beautiful sight,'
she enthused. 'Never have I seen anything as beautiful
as this. And how brave his mother has been. And would
you look at that? He's beginning to suckle already. Oh,
what a darling little thing he is.'

After standing for a moment, his eyes narrowed in
admiring contemplation of the mare and her foal, Dominic came to stand at the door with Juliet. He was as
enchanted by the look on her face as he was with the
birth of the foal.

'It's a wonderful thing, the birth of any animal. It
never ceases to amaze me no matter how many times
I witness the event. Every time is like the first.'

'Thank you for letting me see. He is so little—and
just look at those long legs and knob-like knees—and
the glorious colour of him. Why, he's the colour of the
bracken that covers the hills in autumn.'

'So he is—and it is my opinion that to name him

Bracken would suit him well. What do you think, Miss Lockwood?'

Juliet felt something stir in her breast, making it difficult for her to breathe, the feeling moving down to the pit of her stomach where it lay, warm and comfortable. She looked up into his face and for a long moment could not look away again, unable to believe he was allowing her the honour to name this beautiful creature.

'Do you mean I am allowed to name him?'

He shrugged. 'Why not? He has to have a name.'

'Oh, then Bracken it is.'

'Good, then that's settled.'

She sighed, reluctant to leave the barn when she saw the foal peer cheekily out at her from beneath his mother's legs. 'It's so peaceful in here.'

'Stables on the whole *are* peaceful, horses and the people who look after them being generally kindly sorts.'

'But it's so warm and the light so mellow—and quiet, I can almost feel a heartbeat,' she murmured softly.

'That's mine—and you are right, it is all those things,' he said, turning to her. 'And beautiful as well.' He wasn't looking at the mare and her foal, but rather at Juliet, a faint smile on his face.

'Yes,' she said, feeling a small, obscure twinge of unease. 'Yes, they are very beautiful.'

Juliet took a step to the side, under the pretext of looking at the horses again. The foal was nuzzling at the mare's swollen udder, scraggy tail waggling with enthusiasm. 'I must be going. Dolly will be wondering where I am. I told her I wouldn't be long and she'll be wanting to get to bed.'

Dominic followed in her wake as she left the barn, appreciatively watching her hips as they swayed with a natural, graceful provocativeness. The air outside was fresh, and smelled of straw and barbecue smoke.

Juliet turned to him, unable to move for a second, stunned by sheer disbelief at the expression that showed quite clearly on Dominic Lansdowne's face. 'Why are you looking at me like that?' she asked blankly. Surely she was wrong, she thought.

She wasn't.

'I wasn't talking about the horses in there,' he said softly, and moved closer. She was bathed in moonlight and surrounded by shadow. The gentle night breeze stirred her hair and stroked the bare flesh at her throat. 'You are beautiful—and much more, Miss Lockwood. You are delightful and a pleasure to be with.'

Juliet was so shocked and alarmed that she didn't move for a moment, then she took several steps back and drew herself up straight. 'And I think you have had far too much of that cider—it has turned your mind, Lord Lansdowne. I am terribly sorry if you have some-how misunderstood the situation, but you are quite wrong if—if you thought...'

One quizzical black brow rose. 'Wrong? Was I?'

His low chuckle and the way he was looking at her, in that deliberate roguish manner that half-mocked, half-devoured her, brought a rush of flaming red to Juliet's cheeks. 'Yes, you were—quite wrong, and now if you will excuse me, I will go and find Dolly.' She turned and sped away before he had time to react.

Juliet glanced about her to see if they had been observed. She didn't know whether anyone had seen her going into the stable with the Duke—she could only hope no one had seen her hasty exit.

Tired, replete yet still merry, it was a happy band of revellers that began to wend their way home, some worse for drink but harmless. Juliet found Dolly and together, in the moonlight, they walked back to Lansdowne House behind a weary stream of housemaids, footmen and others who worked at the big house.

Juliet knew tonight would remain with her for a long time. It had been a pleasant interlude in many ways— although what his Grace had on his mind when they emerged from the stable did not bear thinking about.

There were times when Juliet took Lady Pemberton's advice and went outside to take the air and to exercise. She took pleasure in walking and there were so many delightful places to see at Lansdowne House, the principal residence of the Lansdowne family. The grandeur of the house and grounds, both much admired, was the result of restoration carried out by the present Duke's father and grandfather.

The gardens were exquisite and Juliet found one in particular that was shut in by a tall, well-trimmed beech hedge containing a lawn with a small fountain and seats painted white.

It was a favourite spot of hers. This particular afternoon she went to sit with a book. She had her back to the gate, which had been set up in the hedge, when she heard the latch click. Instinctively she knew who it was.

'So this is where you escape to when you are not working, Miss Lockwood.'

'I come here often. I find it a most restful place.'

'Have you any objection if I sit with you a while?'

She had her book open on her lap. It was the first time she had seen her employer since the harvest supper. She still flushed when she remembered how he had looked at her when they had left the stable—and she had still not forgotten their heated altercation in the library before that.

'You are a complex man in many ways, Lord Lansdowne—if you don't mind me saying so.'

'Of course not. I always like people to speak their mind.'

'So do I. The night at the harvest home, your behaviour towards me was—inappropriate—and I have still not forgiven you your unjustifiable comments in the library when Sir Charles came to call. So if you are going to be cross again then you can go away,' she dared to say with spirit. 'However, if you are prepared to be nice, then you may stay.'

His lips quirked with quiet amusement. 'Thank you. I shall endeavour to be as charming as my nature will allow.'

Juliet looked to where he was standing. 'It's your garden, Lord Lansdowne. Please—sit if you wish, and if you think I should be working then understand that after working all morning this is my rest period.'

'I apologise if my—inappropriate behaviour offended you at the harvest supper. Like you said at the time—' he laughed, his eyes dancing with humour '—I must have drunk too much cider. It must have been stronger than I realised. I also apologise for my harsh words in the library. I'm sorry if they upset you.'

'They were unwarranted, and I cannot for the life of me understand why you were so angry.'

He levelled his eyes on hers. 'No,' he uttered quietly, 'you wouldn't. I know how hard you work, Miss Lockwood. I'm not a slave driver and I'm happy for you to take time off when you feel you need to.' He was hoping she would disclose something of what she had been doing in town when he had seen her greet that fellow she seemed so fond of, but he was disappointed for she was not forthcoming.

'Thank you. I'll bear that in mind. How did you know where to find me?'

'What, that you'd be here?'

'Yes.' She did not look at him and continued to look straight ahead.

His smile deepened appreciatively. 'That was easy.' He sat on the bench with his back to the corner, one ankle resting on his knee, facing her. He could not believe she was the same young woman he had seen in town, behaving with complete abandon as she had literally thrown herself into the arms of the unknown man. Nor could he believe she was the same young woman who had danced the night away at the harvest home and been so enraptured at seeing the birth of the foal. She had unpinned her hat and placed it on the seat beside her. Her hair shone bright as she sat, as ever, demure and perfectly straight, her boots peeking out from the bottom of her grey skirt.

He had been riding with Charles. He wore black riding boots and his shirt beneath his tan jacket was open at the neck, which showed off his strong brown throat and the fuzz of chest hair in the vee of his neck. 'I followed you. I saw you leave the house with your book.'

'Why did you follow me? What is it you want to say to me?' She pushed a rogue strand of hair from her face and gazed at a blackbird perched on the rim of the fountain taking a drink.

Dominic watched her, as he had watched her during the time she had been at Lansdowne House, bemused by the loveliness of her, and he wanted her. More importantly, he knew, since he was a man of the world, that she was attracted to him.

'I have been instructed by my sister to invite you to a soirée at her house tomorrow afternoon. She has accused me of working you too hard. She also said I had to tell you that she will be mortally offended if you refuse.'

Juliet sighed deeply and turned for the first time to look him in the face. 'A soirée? But I cannot possibly. Has Lady Pemberton forgotten that I am the hired help and socialising with one's employers is not the done thing?'

'No, she hasn't, but she happens to like you—and don't forget what I told you about her taking you under her wing.'

'I am not a lame duck, Lord Lansdowne. I don't need saving.'

'The invitation is well meant.'

'I don't doubt that, and your sister is indeed generous. Will you be there?'

He nodded. 'I will escort you.'

She looked away. 'I don't think that would be appropriate.'

A scowl of displeasure furrowed his brow. 'You know, your pride really is a nuisance, Miss Lockwood.'

'My pride, along with my reputation, would be in shreds were I to do as you ask.'

'And that matters to you?'

'Of course it does. It may surprise you to learn, Lord Lansdowne, but even the reputations of hired help need protecting. When I leave your employment, I shall be looking for another position. Who would consider me suitable if it were known I was in the habit of being escorted to soirées by my employer?'

A wicked gleam shone from his narrowed eyes. 'You never know. Out of sheer curiosity, it might enhance your cause. I will give you a glowing reference.'

'I would advise you to wait until my work is complete before agreeing to do that. It may not be to your satisfaction.'

'I am well satisfied so far, Miss Lockwood,' he murmured, his voice low and soft, adding a double meaning to his words.

Averting her eyes, Juliet felt something stir in her breast, the feeling moving down to the pit of her stomach, where it lay, warm and uncomfortable. She felt herself blush at the way his eyes seemed to strip her bare, feeling her skin grow hot. She also felt a *frisson* of attraction, then fear. Both were pleasurable. Both alarmed her.

Dominic's eyes narrowed as if he could read her mind, his head nodding slightly, and the faintest hint of a triumphant smile curving his mouth. 'What are you reading?'

She forced herself to look at him and for a long moment could not look away. Somehow she found herself unprepared for the sheer force of feelings that swept through her and she knew, with a kind of panic, that she was in grave danger, not from him but from herself, and she was aware that she absolutely must not let him come any closer. Lord Lansdowne was her employer and an arch-seducer, and she must never forget that.

'A book about the French Revolution and Napoleon Bonaparte's rise to power. I am looking forward to reading books about his demise.'

'Indeed?' He glanced at the brown volume and read the gilded title stamped on its front. 'It was a cruel, brutal time for France, when the citizens were united as equal partners against the ruling class.'

'But an interesting one.'

'If you really wish to make a study of that time, there is a much better account somewhere in the library.'

'If there is, I'm sure I'll come across it in time.'

'You enjoy reading history?'

'Very much. I get that from my father.'

'Did he live his entire life in Oxford?'

'Mostly,' she answered carefully.

'And he had no family—siblings?'

She glanced at him, her face as unreadable as the Lockwood statues that adorned his gardens. 'My father was an orphan.'

She bent her head, returning her attention to the book in her lap, and he studied her profile, wondering for the hundredth time what went on behind that calm exterior. He wanted to know what she was thinking, what she was feeling, for she was an enigma, a mystery he wanted to solve.

'And your mother?'

Juliet closed the book and looked into the distance. She did not want to discuss her parents, especially her mother's family, or the shame of being unacknowledged and unwanted by her grandfather, the man who had disowned her mother when she had eloped with her father.

'My mother never talked about her family.'

'But she must have, at some time.'

Pressed, Juliet lifted her head high with an imperiousness that said her mother might have worn a crown, and admitted, 'I know that she came from Scotland—and that my grandfather disowned her when she eloped with my father. She was the most loving, caring mother anyone could wish for, and when she died I missed her terribly.'

'And is your grandfather still alive?'

'Yes.'

'Does he know about you?'

'Yes, he does.'

'And you are his only grandchild?'

'I am.'

'And has he not tried to make contact with you?'

'No. My father wrote and told him of my mother's demise, but, apart from a curt letter from his solicitor in reply, there has been no further communication.'

'Do you not think he might want to get in touch with you now your father is dead?'

Juliet sighed and looked down at her hands. 'In truth, I don't know.'

'Of course it's possible he might think you wouldn't welcome the contact. After the rift caused by your mother's elopement, he might think your father has prejudiced you against him.'

'Father would never do that. The rift between my mother and her father saddened him deeply and he always blamed himself.'

'In cases such as this, it's not uncommon for an assumption to be made—sometimes rightly so—that any approach would be rejected. Once contact is severed, it can be hard to repair the damage. The way I see it, whether or not the breach between you and your grandfather can be mended is up to you. Personally I would give him the benefit of the doubt and go and see him.'

'No.'

'He is your family.'

'My half-brother is my family. I acknowledge no other.'

'But you are his only grandchild.'

'That's his problem, not mine.'

'And when he dies? How will you feel then, not having at least attempted to heal the breach?'

'I don't know. I'm not in the business of forgiveness.'

Dominic fell silent. After a moment, he said, 'When I asked about your parents it was not my intention to pry into your affairs. I apologise if I have upset you by stirring the ashes of your past, only it upsets me to see a young lady unprotected and forced to work for a living.'

Juliet smiled. 'Please don't be upset on my account. I'm perfectly capable of looking after myself, and I am happy doing what I'm doing. How is the foal, by the way?'

'Thriving. Already he is running rings around the paddock. He'll make a fine hunter one day. You must go and see him.'

'Yes, I will.'

'And you will attend Cordelia's soirée? I am willing to escort you, but I don't intend staying.'

'Won't your sister mind?'

He laughed lightly, shaking his head. 'Definitely not. It is not my habit to attend tedious soirées, listening to ladies gossiping about mundane matters.'

No, Juliet mused. She couldn't imagine him doing anything so mundane.

The following day Juliet had a long, hard look in the cheval mirror, tilting it to obtain a full view and twisting first to the left, then the right, to see her reflection better. She was wearing her best dress, green silk with a scooped neck that fell in shimmering folds like water touched by sunlight. She smiled, pleased with what she saw. The dress was neither too plain nor too extravagant. It flattered her colouring and her figure. She had wound a thick handful of her tumbling curls around her hand and twisted them up on to the top of her head, holding them in place with pins and two tortoiseshell combs inlaid with mother of pearl.

When she was ready, she went down to the hall where Lord Lansdowne was waiting. Had she been a lady of the upper class, it would not be acceptable for him to escort her without a chaperon, but since he was her employer and she very much his social inferior, that kind of protocol didn't apply.

She could feel his gaze on her as she descended the stairs. He was darkly handsome today, Juliet thought, her throat catching. When she stood before him, his gaze swept over her, from her shining head to her daintily slippered feet, lingering for a moment on the swell of her breasts, before his eyes moved on and looked deep into hers. An unspoken tension took hold of her, and she had to look away to stop the trembling in her limbs. She wondered how she could bear it if he were truly as wicked as Robby had said.

Of late he had invaded her dreams, but she was sensible enough to know her dreams would not become reality, and she was wise enough to understand and accept that this casual friendship she shared with her employer was all there was ever going to be.

'Well, well, you look quite stunning—far too lovely to be anyone's employee, Miss Lockwood.'

'I am surprised,' she murmured, a secretive, mischievous little smile playing on her soft lips.

'Why should you be surprised when a gentleman pays you a compliment?'

'Because on my arrival at Lansdowne House I recall you saying I had no feminine appeal whatsoever and that I was more unfashionable than Farmer Shepherd's scarecrow.'

Juliet saw a flicker of something in his expression, and she went on, 'I was standing outside the door when you and your friends went on to talk about me. I also recall Sir Charles saying that I was pathetic and as plain as a pike staff.' She glanced at him obliquely. 'The comments were most uncomplimentary. Do you recall the conversation, your Grace?'

Comprehension dawned in his face. 'You are right. I did say something about Farmer Shepherd's scarecrow,' he murmured. 'I had forgotten. It meant nothing at the time.'

'Not to you, perhaps, but a great deal to me.'

'And you were angry—and rightly so. I am grieved that you overheard me say anything so thoughtless and insulting and I beg your forgiveness. As I recall, the weather that night was appalling and you were drenched and not looking your best. Please believe that I have nothing but regret for what I said. Wounding your feelings was never my intent.'

'My pride took a battering, but as you can see I have recovered from the experience. Now, have you changed your opinion of me and do I no longer look like Farmer Shepherd's scarecrow?'

Suddenly he grinned and a wicked gleam shone from his eyes. 'My opinion of you changed as soon as I saw you after your illness. Now when I look at you, I do not see Farmer Shepherd's scarecrow. I see a very beautiful young lady I shall be proud to escort to my sister's soirée.' He offered her his arm. 'Shall we?'

Placing her shaking fingers on his arm, he escorted her out to the waiting carriage. When they were settled, seated across from each other, Juliet, finding herself in such close proximity to her employer, could not help but admire his physique. While his head was turned away from her, she let her gaze travel over the sweeping breadth of his strong shoulders and his long legs crossed over each other. She found herself wanting to reach out and touch him.

Scandalised by the impulse, she raised her furtive study from his powerful body to his strong features. The mellow sunlight illumined his bold profile, that aquiline nose that gave him a stamp of nobility and stark, brooding intensity. He was an attractive man, sleek and fierce as a bird of prey, with his black hair and silver-grey eyes.

Lady Pemberton lived just a short drive away. When they arrived at the gracious old house surrounded by well-tended gardens and fields beyond, a large crowd of elegant people were already milling about. Despite the smile on her lips, there were butterflies in the pit of Juliet's stomach.

'It's quite a gathering,' she murmured to her escort.

'Don't be nervous. Cordelia and I will look after you.'

'But you are leaving.'

'I'm tempted to stay a while.' He looked down at her, his eyes appraising. 'The company is to my liking. Come,' he murmured, giving her a wink of encouragement, 'my sister can't be far away.'

Juliet entered the elegant salon where Lady Pemberton was surrounded by her guests and where maids flitted about offering tea and cakes. She tried to take an interest in her surrounds, profoundly conscious of Lord Lansdowne by her side and that they were attracting much attention. Except for her treacherous heartbeat, which insisted on acceleration as she moved further into the room, she managed a polite, fixed smile at those who stared with open curiosity.

A woman approached them. It was Geraldine Howard, the mean-spirited sister of Thomas Howard. In sky blue silk she was every bit as beautiful as Juliet remembered, also just as arrogant and haughty, she thought, as the coldest blue eyes she had ever seen appraised her in grudging acknowledgement. Juliet smiled and bent her head in polite greeting, whereas Miss Howard gave Juliet no more than the coolest nod, for she knew a nobody when she saw one; besides, one did not greet a servant except to issue an order.

'So, we meet again, Miss Lockwood,' she uttered, making an exception on this occasion, with an air of hostility and self-importance, 'and I see you are certainly better attired than when you arrived at Lansdowne House.'

'I would have to be, since I had travelled some considerable distance that night in the rain,' Juliet said tremulously, at the same time annoyed with herself for the shake in her voice.

Geraldine shifted her gaze to Dominic and smiled prettily. 'Hello, Dominic. Your employee has captivated Charles, you know. In fact ever since he visited you and met Miss Lockwood, he has not stopped singing her praises.'

'As a man who has always had a weakness for beauty, Geraldine, I cannot begrudge him for that.'

'Actually, it's beginning to wear a bit thin—and you are also taken with her, if gossip is to be believed. Why else would you be seen out with the hired help? It's highly irregular. There will be talk.'

Whatever the snide remark was meant to convey, it had the opposite effect on Dominic Lansdowne. Usually he would have responded to such an insulting remark with a cutting set-down, but instead Juliet felt his gaze linger on her face and he smiled a slow smile.

'What's new in that? I'm used to people gossiping about what I do. You know that, Geraldine.'

'Miss Howard,' Juliet said, unable to hold her tongue in the face of such rudeness. 'Where I am concerned, I assure you his Grace has observed all the proprieties.'

'And you are defending him like the loyal servant that you are, Miss Lockwood,' she sneered, her voice reeking with malice as she reminded her of her place. 'What extraordinary arrogant impertinence.'

'Plain speaking cannot be construed as arrogance, Miss Howard,' Juliet retorted sharply.

Affronted, Geraldine stiffened. 'And I will not be

spoken to like this by you. You should apologise for
your rudeness.'

'I most certainly will not. The rudeness is all on your
part, Miss Howard. I am merely reminding you of his
Grace's good name.'

'I need no reminding from you Miss Lockwood.
Excuse me.' With her nose set at a lofty angle, Geraldine walked away. She did not approve of the way
Miss Lockwood had been thrust to the fore by Charles
and even her lovestruck brother, Thomas, and Dominic
himself to a degree by bringing her to mingle with her
betters, and the upstart giving herself airs and behaving as though she had every right. She even carried herself like his duchess, not his employee, and Geraldine
liked it not one bit. Perhaps it was time to disclose to
Dominic the criminal tendencies of Miss Lockwood's
brother, and yet, on second thoughts, she might find it
advantageous to withhold it for the time being.

'Oh dear! I don't think Miss Howard likes me very
much,' Juliet murmured when they were out of earshot.
'Although I doubt I shall lose any sleep over it. Since
she first set eyes on me she took against me. I do not
trust her. Her manner is certainly not what I would
expect of a young lady of breeding.'

Dominic did not say anything in response, but raised
his eyebrows in such a manner as to confirm he shared
Juliet's misgivings. 'Geraldine is quite besotted with
Charles Sedgwick—has been since they were children—and she has high hopes that he is finally going
make her the offer she and her parents have long been
waiting for. It is only natural that she will not take

kindly to hearing him sing another woman's praises, and I don't suppose you can blame her if she is not accommodating towards you.'

Juliet was only too well aware of that. Geraldine Howard had made it plain right from the start that she was not ready to make her life an easy one. If she could cause trouble, she would.

Cordelia Pemberton greeted Juliet warmly, although she was surprised that Dominic had decided to remain and favour them with his presence when normally he avoided her soirées like the plague. Soirées were not his forte so was it possible that the lovely Juliet Lockwood had something to do with his presence here today?

Cordelia had quietly witnessed their encounter with Geraldine Howard and sensed Geraldine's resentment. It was with some surprise that she saw Miss Lockwood was a rapturous beauty, something that had quite escaped her when she had first seen her. No male could be immune to her charms. Her serene, secretive smile and smooth, graceful bearing had everyone quite fascinated—Dominic especially seemed to be unable to leave her side. In fact, he looked more relaxed and easy going than she had seen him for some time. But he was late and she had been beginning to wonder if he would turn up.

She gave him a reproving look. 'I'm pleased you've deigned to arrive with Miss Lockwood at last, Dominic.'

Dominic's bland, amused expression settled on his sister. 'For what am I to be called to task, Cordelia?'

he asked, a lazy, white smile sweeping across his features.

'For being late, you naughty boy!' she said, but all traces of animosity were vanishing from her voice as he aimed that lethally attractive smile directly at her. 'For making me think Miss Lockwood had changed her mind about attending my soirée—and for being far too handsome for your own good! Now,' she finished, forgiving him entirely, 'go and have a word with Dr Goodwin, will you? He's keen to introduce you to his son, who has just got back from a tour or Europe. You may find something of interest to talk about while I chat to Miss Lockwood.'

Reluctant to leave Juliet's side, Dominic wasn't at all sure he wanted to speak to anyone else, but, meeting his sister's implacable gaze, he relented and went to do her bidding.

'Miss Lockwood, I'm so pleased you are here. You have settled in at Lansdowne House?'

'Indeed I have. It is such a lovely house,' she ventured, allowing Lady Pemberton to draw her to one side.

'And you went to the harvest home, I hear. I was so pleased.' When Juliet glanced at her in surprise, she smiled. 'Don't worry. When anything of an unusual nature occurs, it is gossiped about and discussed at length by everyone for miles around.'

'Unusual? It was an evening for everyone. What could possibly be so unusual about me going to the harvest home along with everyone else?'

Registering the heightened colour on the younger woman's cheeks, Lady Pemberton laughed softly, her look one of understanding. 'It was brought to my attention that my dear brother broke his own rule and danced. He never takes to the floor at the harvest home—if he dances with one woman, he feels obliged to dance with them all, you see, so from the very beginning he decided against it. It would appear he made an exception in your case and I could kiss you on both cheeks for giving him the incentive to dance. You—enjoyed yourself, I hope?'

'Yes, it was an extremely enjoyable evening. I—I didn't realise—that dancing with his Grace would give rise to gossip. I certainly gave him no reason to single me out for particular attention; had I realised it would create such interest, then I would have declined.'

Lady Pemberton arched her brows in mock horror. 'What? Refuse to dance with Dominic? At your peril, my dear Miss Lockwood. At your peril. But I am glad you went. If you are to be at Lansdowne for several weeks, then it is good that you get to know the people hereabouts and to get to know the area.'

'Apart from that one night, as yet I've had little chance to see beyond the house and the immediate grounds. I have been so busy with my work.' Her precious meetings with Robby in Brentwood she kept to herself. 'I must admit to finding the air quite wonderful in the country after what I was forced to breathe in London.'

'Of course. I recall Dominic saying that you worked there for a time, for Sir John Moore. Have you always been in some kind of employment, Miss Lockwood?'

'Yes. I taught for a time at the Academy in Bath where I was educated, before I went to work for Sir John.'

'And what do you do for pleasure and excitement?'

Juliet smiled and shook her head. 'I'm afraid I have neither the time nor the money to partake of the kind of excitement I think you mean, Lady Pemberton. My friends are in Bath and I don't see them very often.'

'Dear me! Your life must be exceedingly dull.'

'It may seem like that to you, but there are many things I enjoy doing—mainly reading, and walking when I have the time. And living at Lansdowne Hall is a luxury I never imagined I would experience.'

'And marriage? You must have given some consideration to that.'

'Not really. I have little opportunity to make new acquaintances, so it is unlikely that I will find a husband.'

Cordelia stared at her in complete astonishment. 'But how can you know that? You are young and exceedingly lovely, with your whole life before you. Surely you don't intend sorting out other people's dusty old libraries for the rest of your days.'

'I am twenty-three and many would consider me to be already on the shelf. Besides, if I did marry, it would only be for a deep and abiding love, so you see, Lady Pemberton, the odds are stacked heavily against me.'

Cordelia did not reply, but Juliet could feel her gaze on her as she contemplated what she had said. Lord Lansdowne reappeared at her side and his sister smiled up at him.

'What horse are you riding for the steeplechase tomorrow, Dominic? Have you decided?'

'Most certainly, Cordelia. Eclipse—the horse I rode last year.'

'What, that huge chestnut? And I suppose you'll beat every other rider into the ground like you did last year.'

'I intend to try, but there are some good horses racing, so I shall have my work cut out.'

'You will be going, won't you, my dear?' Lady Pemberton turned to Juliet. 'It's always an enjoyable and exciting day for all concerned.'

'Oh—I—I don't think—'

'Of course she'll be going,' Dominic interrupted firmly. 'The annual steeplechase draws people from every village and hamlet for miles. It's a feast day, a holiday. You cannot miss it.'

'But I'd rather not. I won't know a soul.'

'Yes, you will, dear,' Lady Pemberton was quick to say. 'You will be with me. I shall collect you and we shall watch the races together—and perhaps you might like to toss a few hoops or have your fortune told by the gypsy woman who sets a booth up every year.'

In the face of so much determination, Juliet relented and smiled. 'Very well, Lady Pemberton. I would love to go.'

Lady Pemberton was clearly delighted. 'Good, then that's settled.'

Juliet's gaze ventured to the long French windows opening on to a sun-filled terrace that gave way to splendid gardens. The temptation to explore was overwhelming. 'Would you mind if I take a stroll in your lovely gardens, Lady Pemberton?'

'Of course not, my dear,' she replied absently, curiously preoccupied with this young woman's situation.

'What a good idea. I'll come with you,' Dominic offered.

'But you needn't,' Juliet said quickly.

'I insist. Cordelia has some rather fine delphiniums, which I think you might find pleasing.'

Cordelia looked at him in wide-eyed amazement. 'Delphiniums, Dominic? Since when did you become interested in delphiniums—or any other flower come to that? I didn't even realise you knew what they looked like.'

He grinned wolfishly. 'Since Miss Lockwood expressed a desire to see the garden.' He held out his arm to Juliet. 'Shall we?'

His voice sent a shiver down her spine. She hesitated for only a moment. Then, as if in slow motion, she saw herself reaching out her gloved hand and resting it upon his grey sleeve.

Cordelia watched Dominic escort Miss Lockwood out on to the terrace, where others were milling about, enjoying the rather fine weather. After years of waiting for her dear, handsome brother to find a suitable bride, she could be forgiven for hoping it wouldn't be long before he put his mind to it.

Cordelia would have been shocked had she been made privy to her brother's thoughts as he sauntered with Miss Lockwood along the garden paths like a doting swain, attentive but not inappropriately so. It was seduction that was uppermost in his thoughts, marriage a million miles away. The conversation between them continued along predictable lines—the beautiful garden, the weather, those present at the soirée, the splendour of the surrounding countryside.

They followed the sand-coloured path winding between trees and bushes, sweeping lawns and well-tended flower beds filled with exotic blooms. They reached the far side of the gardens, quite isolated and out of sight of the house. It was peaceful. They were surrounded by a tall box hedge, the dark green leaves fragrant and sharp. The only sounds were the birds, the occasional crack of a twig underfoot, and the murmur of voices drifting across from the house.

They were so close as to be almost touching. Juliet could feel the heat of him beside her, as if the entire left side of her body was facing an open fire. She felt quite unlike herself, but nevertheless realised the danger, that in the intensity of the moment she might say and do things she would subsequently wish she had not.

Suddenly she felt awkward and turned her head away. 'I think we should turn back. Our departure will have been noted.'

Dominic turned the full force of his silver-grey eyes on her. 'And?'

She looked at him directly. 'Commented upon. I— didn't realise we had come so far.'

'In which case we will walk back, but first there is something I have been wanting to do for some time.'

'Oh?' He fixed her with a look and, for a fleeting

instant, Juliet felt they were bound together, as if she was being inexorably drawn towards him, hooked and reeled in like a fish on a line.

A wisp of hair fell forwards and rested against her cheek. He reached out, tucking it back, feeling the velvety softness of her ear. She froze to stillness as he ran the tip of his finger along the line of her jaw and down the column of her throat. Juliet caught her breath as a shot of heat surged through her. Slowly he moved closer, then curled his hand around the back of her neck.

'Please don't,' she whispered, hardly trusting herself to speak, her heart beginning to pound in her chest. 'You forget that you are my employer.'

'I do not think of you as my employee, Juliet.'

There was something in his eyes, something intense and passionate. They were clear, and nothing had prepared her for the thrill of excitement that gripped her now, beginning in the middle of her chest where her heart lay, and trailing delicately through the whole of her body. She was aware that this was an important moment in her life and a great revelation, but could not yet comprehend it. She clung to her self-control as if it were some kind of lifeline, to prevent her being sucked down, but it was already too late, for she experienced a longing for something she had never known before that only this man could give her.

She could feel herself shaking inside. His nearness was powerful and potent, and undermining everything honourable she had ever thought about herself. She stepped away from him; with a movement she had not anticipated, he closed the gap and, placing his hands on her upper arms, drew her into his embrace. Though her heart soared joyfully, she struggled nevertheless.

It was useless, for his mouth came down on hers with a fierceness that paralysed her so that she became still in his arms. Never having been kissed before she had nothing to compare it with, but it was pleasant, warm, enjoyable, and she felt the instant unfolding of what she knew to be desire. She wanted him, but she also feared him—and herself.

As his lips began to move insistently against hers, she couldn't have anticipated the stormy rush of sensation that made her gasp and cling tighter to him, nor the compulsion to yield her mouth to his searching tongue that invaded her mouth, nor the frantic beating of her heart, his arms tightening about her while her body seemed to want to meet and forge into his.

When Dominic finally lifted his head and stared down at her flushed face, he was stunned by his unprecedented reaction to one virginal kiss from an inexperienced young woman who hadn't seemed to have the slightest idea of how to kiss him back. So much for the man into whose arms she had thrown herself; given his own experience with women, it was evident that Miss Lockwood hadn't had much practice at kissing. He watched her lids flutter open and gazed into her slumberous dark eyes.

He smiled, his voice like a purr of pleasure. 'Well, Miss Lockwood, you have hidden talents I knew nothing about,' he murmured, his desire making her sensitive to his mood, drawing her gently against him though his body wanted to throw her to the ground and take her.

The slow reaction to what had happened began to seep into Juliet's brain. He had been very sure that she would want him, she thought, the hot colour rushing to her face. And so she had. She had wanted him so much that, without thinking what she did, she had kissed her employer.

Placing the flat of her hands against his chest, she pushed him away. 'Let me go, please. This isn't right. I—I can't think straight when you are so close.'

'You don't have to think straight. I'll do that for you.'

'I like to think for myself.' Taking hold of her hands, he attempted to kiss her again, but she backed away. 'Please—don't. I don't know what it is you want from me, but I will be no man's plaything. Excuse me. I would like to return to the house.'

Dominic didn't try to stop her. He let her walk a little way on her own before he followed, a satisfied smile curving his lips. The seduction of Miss Lockwood would be easy. In truth, almost too easy. She was like a green girl, inclined to shyness with blushing cheeks and widening eyes and a serene beauty that delighted him, but she was inexperienced.

She was impressionable and young, ripe for the taking. His male body had demanded to go on, to satisfy itself as it had always done, and he could have enticed her, taken her there and then, had he so wished, but that did not suit his purpose. It was infinitely more satisfying to play with her emotions, to lure her into his bed and make her fall in love with him.

And she would fall in love with him, of that he was certain. It was plain that she was not in love with the man he had seen her with in town—a man, because of Miss Lockwood's reaction to his kiss, he did not see as a threat. When that happened, she would replace Frances as his mistress—Frances, with her acclaimed face and figure, pleasing to him and ready to satisfy any need he might have. However, of late she had become more like a demanding, nagging wife than the woman he had set up as his mistress. For twelve months they had enjoyed a remarkably open and highly pleasurable affair, which was about to come to an end.

Miss Lockwood's freshness and naïvety were something his jaded spirits badly needed and her innocence awakened a protective feeling in him he had never known before. All things considered, she would make him the perfect mistress.

Chapter Five

W alking back to the house, Juliet was all but oblivious to the people sauntering past her. The consequences of her dalliance with her employer were only now hitting her. She was deeply bewildered by what had happened and more unsure of herself than she had ever been. Dominic Lansdowne had challenged her preconceptions on several levels, and she had to think how she was going to deal with the growing complication of her situation.

She was well aware of his reputation, that he was a rake, eligible and sought after by a string of young ladies and with perhaps more than one mistress he kept in the lap of luxury, in which case it was not likely that an impoverished nobody he had employed to catalogue his books would become anything other than that.

When she stepped on to the terrace he caught up with her, halting her by capturing her arm. For a brief moment he was close, close enough for her to hear the whispered words when he spoke to her.

'You are very lovely, Juliet,' he said, using her given name for the first time. 'I mean to have you. Take my word on it.'

Juliet's gaze flicked to his hand gripping her arm, then up to his eyes. She was still trembling at the effect he could have on her senses and her emotions and her self-confidence. When she met his eyes she could read their meaning as if it were written in the stars.

'Your word? And just what is your word worth, Lord Lansdowne? Tell me that if you can.'

He released her arm. 'The word of a man who will have you.'

'No, you will not. I do not think that would be appropriate. I will not let that happen. Do you want me to carry on working for you, your Grace?' she asked quietly.

'I do. Of course I do.'

'And do employers take such advantage as this?'

Her words were more effective at stopping him than a kick on the shin. He stepped back and studied her features in the dappled sunlight that filtered between the leaves of a climbing rose trailing over the trellising. Miss Lockwood was a virgin, and he had no personal experience with virgins. At sixteen years of age when he had experienced his first sexual encounter, the woman had been experienced. There had followed a series of female companions and he had occasionally enjoyed the pleasure of demi-reps when in London, and until recently Frances had satisfied his needs perfectly, but not one of them had been a virgin.

He could feel Miss Lockwood's apprehension as well as her desire, and desire had nothing to do with experience. But she was right. He was her employer, and at this moment she seemed very vulnerable. For the first time in years he felt the pain of uncertainty, and honour dictated his decision not press her just now.

'This is all wrong,' she whispered. With invisible threads, he was drawing his net around her and she was afraid, afraid of herself. 'Please leave me alone. I need to think and I can't do that when I'm with you. You are too distracting by far. I want to leave now—alone.'

He nodded, not unduly perturbed by her reaction to what had happened. 'As you wish. I will order the carriage to return you to Lansdowne House, but this is not going to go away,' he said, having no intention of giving up on her.

'I know.' Without another word Juliet turned and walked into the house, hoping and praying no one would see the change in her—her flushed cheeks and the excessive brightness in her eyes. She had allowed the Duke of Hawksfield to kiss her, and by doing so he would see this as an open invitation to seduce her whenever the opportunity arose. And with his expertise, she had no doubt that he would soon make the opportunity.

How could she possibly do her work properly after this, obliged to see him day after day, his presence always there, powerful and potent and undermining everything honourable she had ever thought about herself?

Back at Lansdowne House she took some little time to recover from the strong emotions her interlude with her employer had aroused in her. Little by little, self-consciousness and embarrassment at having revealed herself so openly, and so unexpectedly, began to give way to regret. How could she have forgotten so soon her determination not to allow him to come too close?

Seated across from Lady Pemberton in her open carriage, not having been to a fair since she had been a child, when her parents and Robby had all gone together, Juliet felt excitement course through her and her spirits lift as they left Lansdowne House. They followed a shallow, fast-flowing stream in the direction of the village, where a steepled church was surrounded by charming cottages.

Lord Lansdowne had already left to join the other riders who were to take part in the race. From the window of her room Juliet had watched him leave. Wearing gleaming tan riding boots and buckskin breeches, which fit him to perfection, he was riding a big powerful horse the colour of a fox in winter, with a flaxen mane and tail, picked from his large stable because its resilience and stamina, its speed and endurance, could be relied on.

The fair, where farmers and peasants mixed with the local gentry, had been set up in a vacant field close to the village. Juliet could hear the music long before they got there. The carriage jolted over the rough ground, Lady Pemberton, cutting a distinguished figure in purple silk and matching hat with an array of curling feathers, acknowledging those she knew with a slight nod of her head. As they entered the field, the music was louder now, almost drowned out by the din of the boisterous voices of young men who were riding in the steeplechase, discussing the thrills and hazards they would encounter in the race.

There was the sound of someone blowing a long blast on a trumpet, and the crowd turned in unison to where some of the mounted riders had gathered. Lady Pemberton chuckled as some of them set off for the neighbouring village to get ready for the first race, which would end after a two-mile ride over rough terrain and many obstacles. There were to be five races in all, which would take up most of the afternoon.

'Ever since men began riding horses they have no doubt argued over whose was fastest. Things will never change.'

Juliet gazed at the colourful scene spread out before her. It was a fully fledged country fair, with tents and stalls selling all kinds of bric-a-brac and food. Wagons and curricles were everywhere, and fashionably dressed ladies holding brightly coloured parasols strolled on the grass. Excited, happy children were flying paper kites, and there were acrobats and jugglers and even a dancing bear. The shaggy creature looked so mournful as its owner put it through its paces that Juliet's soft heart went out to it. A wrestling match was already underway, with men and country boys, some hefty, some not so, queuing up to take on the current champion. With the resilience and optimism of youth, they were in good spirits.

They attracted considerable attention when they left the carriage and strolled among the crowd. Juliet's eyes picked out Lord Lansdowne, who talked and joked with a merry group, Sir Charles Sedgwick and Thomas Howard among them. He looked so at ease atop his huge, powerful horse, pulling repeatedly on the reins to keep it steady while conversing with the men with such boyish good humour that she could hardly believe he was the same predatory seducer who had walked with her along the garden paths at his sister's house yesterday, who had held her in his arms while his hungry mouth devoured hers.

'Come, let's sit a while,' Lady Pemberton suggested. 'The racing will begin soon, I expect.' She ordered her groom to bring them two glasses of pink lemonade and proceeded to some tables and chairs that had been set up in a quiet corner. The sun was hot so they chose to sit in the shade of the trees to watch the crowds and sip their lemonade and munch on sausage rolls and oranges.

Letting her gaze roam over the crowd, Juliet's heart plummeted when she recognised a young woman strolling with her parents, a bored expression on her pretty face.

Seeing where Miss Lockwood's attention was directed, Lady Pemberton's brow creased with disapproval. 'That young woman attracts attention wherever she goes, and little wonder with her wild ways.'

Continuing to observe Geraldine Howard, Juliet noted the way she tossed her imperious head, the defiant stare that did not really see the low-born beings about her. There was insolence written in every line of her body.

'Geraldine is the daughter of two very good friends

of mine. They are well regarded, two of the wealthiest people hereabouts, but Geraldine is defiant of fetters that might attempt to bind her to a life which is tedious. Her parents have let her do as she pleases for too long and are unable to control her. She is arrogant in her complete belief in herself and her place in life, which is privileged and secure—and she is hellbent on securing young Sedgwick.'

'And will he—be secured, I mean?'

Lady Pemberton nodded slowly. 'Perhaps. It certainly looks as though the wind is blowing in that direction, although he seems to be in no hurry to settle down. They grew up together—her brother and Charles went to school together, so they know each other well enough.'

Juliet looked again at Geraldine Howard, who was scanning the crowd. Her eyes came briefly to rest upon Juliet. A look of contempt flitted across Miss Howard's face, before she moved on.

Lady Pemberton took a dainty bite of another sausage roll, savouring the taste and dabbing pastry crumbs off her chin. 'If nothing else, I like to come for the sausage rolls,' she declared, Geraldine Howard forgotten for the present. 'Somehow they never taste as good when my cook makes them. These are so spicy—don't you agree, my dear?'

'They are rather good,' Juliet agreed. 'Though I rarely eat them.'

Lady Pemberton lifted her eyebrows. 'You are a very interesting and accomplished young woman, Juliet—I hope you don't mind if I call you Juliet? I don't wonder Dominic considered you qualified to sort out his books.'

'I don't mind—and I was well taught,' Juliet replied, and found herself talking to this friendly, engaging older woman as she had never talked before. Before half an hour had passed she had told her about her life at the Academy, about her father and the difficult times they had lived through. There was something about her that inspired trust and put one completely at ease, but she was careful not to impart too many confidences, especially about Robby and her mother's background, since that could complicate matters.

After a while they fell silent, content to watch the riders of the first three races pass the finishing line and to watch the crowd milling about, quieter now, more languid as the afternoon wore on. Hunger and thirst satisfied, in the thick, late afternoon heat, some of the men stretched out on the soft grass or leaned back against the trunk of a tree and dozed, their bellies full of ale.

Juliet glanced in Lord Lansdowne's direction, she couldn't help herself. As if he sensed her scrutiny, he turned and looked directly at her, and she watched him excuse himself to his friends and come towards her, clearing a path, until he towered over her atop his magnificent, restless horse.

For an instant the sight of him drove everything from her mind. All was forgotten. She felt shy almost, captivated by his seemingly obvious pleasure and delight to see her, and she was under the illusion that the Duke of Hawksfield had singled her out from everyone else, until he swung himself out of the saddle, turned to his sister and dutifully and affectionately kissed her cheek.

'Cordelia. You're looking remarkably fit today.'

'Not as fit as you, I hope. I've got a lot of money riding on you, dear boy. I trust I will see some return.'

'Rest assured I shall do my best, Cordelia. When are you leaving for town?'

'Tomorrow. I'm looking forward to Lord Fitzherbert's ball—and I'm looking to you to escort me.'

'As always, Cordelia, it will be my pleasure. I shall be travelling down myself in a couple of days—as will the Howards and Charles Sedgwick.' His gaze shifted to Juliet, looking lovely in her blue-and-white striped dress and blue bonnet. At one and the same time she managed to be an alluringly beautiful young woman and yet bewitchingly innocent. She was a study of intriguing and beguiling contrasts. 'And you, Miss Lockwood. Are you enjoying yourself?'

'Very much. I haven't been to a fair in a long time.'

'And have you a fancy for the next race?'

'You know perfectly well I know nothing about horses and even less about racing and placing wagers. I am not that adventurous—besides, I cannot afford to lose my money. It is too hard earned for me to fritter it away on a horse.'

'Place your wager on me and you will not lose.'

Her eyes locked on his and she enquired with a radiant smile, 'And you can guarantee that, can you, Lord Lansdowne?'

He grinned roguishly, his gaze lingering on her

gently flushed face. 'Nothing is guaranteed, Miss Lockwood, but I aim to win.'

'Nevertheless, I intend to reserve my bets.'

'Which is your prerogative. But you will regret it.'

'Then I shall have to live with it and still retain my money. So in the long run I shall not be worse off.'

'But you could be better off.'

She smiled sweetly. 'But as you said, your Grace, you cannot guarantee that. Can you?'

He laughed down into her upturned face, thinking that in the course of her entering his household, she had treated him with cool disdain, tempestuous rebellion, and now with a jaunty impertinence and breezy impudence that he found utterly enchanting and intoxicating.

'*Touché*, Miss Lockwood. *Touché*.'

'But I really do hope you win.'

'So do I, and don't complain that I didn't warn you if I do.'

'I never complain.'

'No, Miss Lockwood, I do not believe you do. And I do admire your ability to hold on to what you have without squandering it on betting, which has been the downfall of many a good man.'

'I am delighted that you are at least willing to give me credit for my good sense.'

Dominic chuckled. 'If you had the slightest notion of how much credit I *do* give you, Miss Lockwood, it would astound you.'

Before Juliet of Lady Pemberton could consider that

staggering pronouncement, he had hoisted himself back on to his horse and galloped off to join his friends.

Cordelia sat in thoughtful silence. She had listened to their light banter with some surprise, and saw something in her brother's eyes she had not seen in a long time. He had looked at Miss Lockwood with a mixture of pride and ownership. The connection between them was strong and, she suspected, intimate. She was encouraged by it.

On the edge of the field as they prepared to leave to begin the next race, Thomas Howard reined in his horse to wait for Dominic to join them and raised his quizzing glass, inspecting Miss Lockwood from head to toe. 'Perfect, Charles. Just perfect. Pity we didn't see it when she arrived. Hmm, she's divine.'

'A beauty and no mistake,' Sir Charles Sedgwick agreed. 'If it weren't for Lansdowne standing guard over her, I'd court her myself—except for the fact that she's as poor as a church mouse, which makes her totally unsuitable to dear Mama.'

Thomas shot him a disapproving look. 'You seem to forget my sister, Charles. She's long been expecting an offer from you and you damn well know it.'

'And I will, Thomas. Never fear. I will not disappoint the lovely Geraldine. She will receive my offer when I feel like settling down to married bliss, but there's no harm in having a little fun in the meantime.'

'Not with Miss Lockwood, Charles,' Dominic said, hearing the object of their discussion and shooting his friend a disapproving look. 'I've already warned you to keep well clear of that particular young lady. Dis-

tractions of the kind you have in mind would disrupt
her work, and I will not have it. Now, are you ready?
We have a race to run and I aim to beat the both of you.
So, if you will follow me, I shall be happy to show you
how it's done.'

All three of them gave shouts of laughter as the
horses bolted and they shot off to begin the next race,
the Lansdowne stakes, which was to be the main race
of the afternoon.

From where she sat Juliet observed their merry
antics with a warm glow of admiration in her eyes as
she watched Lord Lansdowne's horse lunge forwards
ahead of the rest and vault effortlessly over a low Lockwood wall before disappearing from sight.

'I have not seen my brother so relaxed in a long time.'
Lady Pemberton's smile turned wistful. 'Based on what
I have just witnessed…' for she could not believe that
Dominic was immune to his young employee's attrac-
tion '…he seems much taken with you—and you seem
to like him very well, too.'

Juliet spun her head round to look at Lady Pemberton, startled by her comment. Juliet's head spun round.
'I'm sorry?'

'Don't be. Of course, he isn't getting any younger
and it's high time he married and produced an heir.
Each time he takes himself off to London I pray he'll
return and tell me he's found someone who will make
a suitable duchess and make him happy. Unfortunately,
the news I await is a long time in coming.'

'Clearly the right woman hasn't come along.'

'I suppose you think when she does it should be a love match?'

'It is important in a marriage. If two people have to spend the whole of their lives together, then they would be considerably more miserable without it. Don't you agree, Lady Pemberton?'

She nodded. 'Was your parents' marriage a love match?'

'Yes, very much so. They had a depth of devotion and companionship few can boast. One only had to see them together, to look at them, to know how much in love they were.'

'And you believe love is important in marriage?'

Juliet looked at Lady Pemberton, surprised that she should ask such a question when the answer seemed so obvious to her, but then, perhaps her marriage had not been a happy one. 'Of course, I do realise that there are some people who are of the opinion that love and marriage need not have anything to do with each other. My own opinion is that there is no other reason to marry.'

'That is a cynical opinion, Juliet, but I consider children an excellent reason for two people to marry.'

Juliet's lips twitched into a smile and a mischievous light danced in her eyes. 'Really? I did not realise it was necessary for people to marry for children to arrive.'

Lady Pemberton laughed low and playfully tapped Juliet's arm with her fan. 'What a wicked thing for you to say, Juliet. Were you to utter such a comment in society, it would make people think you quite outrageous.'

'I dare say they would, and I would condemn them for being shocked only because I dared to say such a thing, and not for the content. In my opinion, children need the stability of a family environment and loving parents, but I am not so naïve or ignorant as to know that sadly this is not always the case.'

Lady Pemberton's expression became almost melancholy as she studied her young companion. 'What a wise head you carry on your young shoulders, Juliet, but, you know, love can also bring its own measure of pain.'

'If love is only one-sided and one is not loved in return, then I suppose it can.'

Lady Pemberton sighed and stared absently into the distance. 'There was someone Dominic loved once—Amelia, her name was. He loved her very much—too much. What he felt for her almost destroyed him—for she…' She stopped herself, as if she didn't want to disclose too much. 'When she died, he vowed that he would never allow his emotions to become engaged by a woman again. It was pitiful to see what Amelia's death had done to him, which is why our father decided that a commission in the army would be good for him.'

'Lady Pemberton, why are you telling me this? I am Lord Lansdowne's employee. His private life is his own and nothing to do with me.'

'I am telling you this because you, my dear, are different. I've seen the way he looks at you, watches you. He hasn't looked at anyone like that in a long time.'

Juliet stared at her, lost for words. Mercifully she was let off having to reply, for at that moment the crowd suddenly roared. They looked towards the finishing line, and in the last leg of the race Juliet saw Lord Lansdowne was ahead of the rest, his mount covering the ground in long, devouring strides, seeming to slip along the track with the ease of an arrow. The crowd was shouting and urging him on. Caught up in the excitement, Juliet sprang to her feet and cheered and clapped as loudly and jubilantly as the rest when he shot past the finishing line a good three lengths ahead of the rest.

Victorious, he leaned forwards and gave his horse a hearty pat, laughing broadly, his black hair falling over his handsome face and his white teeth shining from between his parted lips, clearly well pleased with himself and his mount. Vaulting from the saddle, he accepted the congratulations in good spirit, the spectators who had placed wagers on the outcome of the race converging on him.

As Cordelia studied Juliet, noting the soft flush that mantled her cheeks and the gentle smile that curved her lips, a thought occurred to her, a thought so incredible that she could not set it aside. The two of them looked so handsome together, so right, somehow. How delightful it would be if Dominic were to fall for Juliet Lockwood in a big way—if he were to fall in love with her, flout convention and marry her. Of course, she was totally unsuitable material for a duke to marry, and there would be many who would challenge a match between them, but it could be made possible.

Juliet was intelligent and with good sense. She was a woman who knew her own mind, a woman who was not afraid to say what she thought. She was also warm and loving and would make the man she married a good wife. Why not Dominic? In addition to them coming together, there was also the benefit of prevailing over Francis Parker, the most notorious courtesan in London, for Juliet Lockwood was not the type of woman who would tolerate her husband keeping a mistress.

Juliet didn't see her employer again that day or the day after. He and several of his well-heeled friends had gone to stay overnight with friends to do a spot of hunting. It was around mid-morning when one of the servants came to the library and handed her a letter, which had just been delivered. At first she thought it was from one of her friends at the Academy, but when she looked down at the handwriting she found it was unfamiliar to her, and she saw that the letter had come from Scotland.

Taking the paper knife, she slit it open and unfolded the letter. Staring down at what was written, she felt her throat go dry. It was from her grandfather, the last person in the world she had expected to receive a letter from. Scanning it quickly, she then folded it and shoved it into her pocket, too confused and not knowing what to make of it just then.

She was both surprised and relieved when Robby came to the house that same afternoon to inform her he was leaving for London a couple of days early and wanted to say goodbye. She received him in the library, glad to see him, but apprehensive about what the servants would think about her entertaining a gentleman in the Duke's house.

'I won't stay, Juliet, but I wanted to see you before I

left, to tell you where I can be contacted if you should need me. A friend of mine has very kindly offered me a room in his house in Cheapside until I leave for New York.'

'I'm glad things are sorting themselves out for you, Robby.'

With his hands behind his back Robby sauntered about the room, looking around with admiration written all over his face. 'Well, Juliet, his Grace the Duke of Hawksfield lives in grand style. This is truly a magnificent place. You won't want to leave when your work is finished.'

'It is a lovely house. I've become quite attached to it.' She wondered what Robby would say if he knew how attached she had become to its owner, how enamoured she was of him. He would be both shocked and disappointed, so better he didn't know her true feelings else he would more than likely insist she left with him for London.

Remembering the letter from her grandfather, she took it from her pocket and handed it to him, as if she could still not believe the contents of it. 'Read it, Robby. It came today from my grandfather. I don't know what to make of it, whether to simply ignore it and tear it up or—or to reply. I really can't imagine why he is writing to me,' she said as Robby read it. 'After all these years when there has been no contact between us, he sends an invitation for me to go to his house in London. He says he is to return to Scotland shortly and would like to see me before he leaves.'

'Perhaps he wishes to make amends for his lack of familial duty. It is possible.'

'There is nothing in the letter to suggest that is the intention behind the invitation.'

'It's hardly the manner of thing one would commit to paper.'

Juliet folded her arms belligerently. 'Well, it's quite absurd of him to imagine that I should accept an invitation to visit a man who is a complete stranger to me.'

'He is your grandfather, Juliet—your family, despite what went on all those years back. What will you do?'

'Decline the invitation, of course. I can't possibly accept it, Robby.'

Robby smiled. 'Come now. Don't be too hasty to dismiss it. He's down from Scotland and staying in London, close enough for you to visit. It sounds just the thing. You could go when you have finished here—between jobs, if you like.' Taking her hand, he enclosed it between both his own. 'You know, Juliet, it wouldn't hurt to mend a few bridges with your grandfather—end this estrangement that was none of your doing. It was all a long time ago. Perhaps things are different now.'

'You think I should, Robby?'

He nodded. 'It think you should give it serious consideration. Besides, I shall feel a lot better knowing you are being taken care of when I go to America.'

'But Grandfather might be thoroughly disagreeable. And how would I occupy my time? There will be nothing for me to do.'

He grinned. The serious moment had passed. 'You? Nothing to do? I dare say there will be an enormous library at his town house that is just waiting to be sorted out,' he joked. 'Will you promise me you will write to him—to please me?'

'Very well,' she capitulated reluctantly. 'If it will make you happy, then I shall write. Look, I was just about to pour myself some tea,' she said, indicating the tea tray she had just fetched from the kitchen. 'I insist you stay and join me. Write down your friend's address where you will be staying and wait here. I'll go and fetch another cup.'

Returning several minutes later with an extra cup and saucer, she opened the door and looked across the room into the face of Geraldine Howard. She was smiling amiably at Robby.

'Ah, Miss Lockwood,' she greeted, sweeping towards her. 'I have just been acquainting myself with your brother.' She looked from one to the other. 'Although I would not have thought it. There is no resemblance between you whatsoever.'

'Juliet is my half-sister,' Robby explained, being his usual charming self, completely unfazed by Miss Howard. 'We share the same father.'

'Nevertheless, one would expect some likeness.' She looked at Juliet, her manner haughty. 'I am here with my brother. He borrowed one of Lord Lansdowne's horses the other day and is returning it. I thought I'd just come and see where you work while he's gossiping to the grooms.'

Juliet arched her brows and gritted her teeth. 'Really? I am surprised you would want to, Miss Howard.'

Robby sensed the tension between them. 'Juliet, I

won't stay for tea. I must be away if I'm to catch the Post for London.'

Disappointment clouded Juliet's eyes. 'But—must you go so soon?'

'Yes, sorry, love.' After giving her a bear-like hug he turned to Miss Howard with a polite inclination of his head. 'Goodbye, Miss Howard. It's been a pleasure meeting you.'

Juliet accompanied him into the hall and said her farewells, assuring him she would make a point of seeing him in London before he left for New York, before returning to her visitor, who had her back to her and appeared to be showing some interest in the display cabinets across the room.

'Might I offer you some refreshment, Miss Howard? Some tea, perhaps?'

Clutching her reticule to her waist, Geraldine turned and looked her up and down as if she were some beggar who had the temerity to accost her in the street. She smiled, showing her perfect teeth.

'I think not. I am not in the habit of drinking tea with servants. How long do you expect to be working for Lord Lansdowne, Miss Lockwood?'

'As long as it takes. But then, that is my business, Miss Howard, and Lord Lansdowne's, of course.'

'Of course it is, and you will be hoping to see it through to completion, I suppose.'

'I intend to. When I start a project, I finish it.'

'Naturally.' Geraldine smoothed down the lustrous velvet of her riding habit, taking pleasure in the feel of the rich and expensive material, her smile of self-satisfaction very evident, the diamonds in her ears as she threw back her head sparkling as they caught the light. She would never forgive this woman from the under-classes for drawing Charles's interest, the man she had earmarked for herself, and though she had high hopes of him offering for her, she intended to make matters as unpleasant for this woman as she could.

She crossed to the door. 'I really must go. My brother will be wondering where I've got to.' She spun round as if in surprise. 'Oh, I quite forgot. It must have been a great relief to you when your brother was released from prison—the Fleet, I believe. A dreadful place.'

Juliet stiffened and stared at her in horror. 'Did Robby tell you that?'

'No, of course he didn't. Spending time in prison and being branded a criminal is not something to be proud of and certainly not something one would want bandied about now, is it?'

'Then how…?'

'My brother told me. He spends a great deal of time in London and has seen your brother from time to time on the social scene and knew of his imprisonment. He recognised him when he saw you together in town one day. Of course he was pleased to know he had been let out, but it will be hard for your brother to put prison behind him and I can imagine how difficult it will be for someone in his position to find respectable employment. Like I said, whether or not you continue working for Lord Lansdowne is entirely up to you. If you choose to do so, then the consequences to you and your brother could be most unpleasant.'

With a brilliant smile she opened the door and went out, leaving Juliet as though turned to stone in the middle of the library. Her face had not a vestige of colour and her eyes had a haunted, almost desperate expression.

Juliet piled the long list of books she had been working on neatly on the table and pushed back her chair and stood up. To make up the time she had lost with Robby's and Miss Howard's visits, she had worked later than she normally would, and also because concentrating on her task stopped her from dwelling on the true purpose of Miss Howard's visit—that if Juliet didn't leave Lansdowne House of her own volition, she would make things extremely difficult and embarrassing for her by exposing Robby as a criminal.

The fire in the grate had burned down, and despite the summer night the room had become quite cold. She flexed her fingers, wincing at the ache in them from all the writing she had done. She yawned, knowing it was quite late. Suddenly her bed seemed very appealing.

She went out into the hall just as the house steward let someone in. It was the Duke, back from his hunting trip. Handing the steward his hat and gloves and giving orders to have the cook prepare a fresh meal for him and have water drawn for a hot bath, he walked towards her with that particular long-legged stride, that lounging arrogant grace that she would always associate with him. She straightened her back and lifted her head, unaware that she was holding herself stiffly, her shoulders slightly hunched as though to defend something vulnerable inside her.

'You're working unusually late, Miss Lockwood.'

'Yes. I had much to do. Please excuse me. I am just going to bed.'

'It's too early for that,' he retorted brusquely. 'Have you eaten?'

'I—I—no, I wasn't very hungry,' she answered hesitantly, truthfully. Ever since Geraldine Howard had left, food had been the last thing on her mind.

'Then after a glass of wine you might feel like something to eat. I would like you to dine with me. It's been an exhausting couple of days and I really would be glad of the company.'

Juliet hesitated, thinking she must be going quite mad, because she honestly sensed that he wanted her to stay. A cosy dinner with a duke was definitely not on her list of acceptable pastimes for a woman of her position, but even so, she was reluctant to refuse. But refuse she did, for the thought of Lord Lansdowne deliberately trying to charm and entice her was more than she could bear to contemplate, and the intimate implications of being alone with him made her face burn.

'I—I do not think that would be appropriate...'

His smile held a hint of mockery. 'There you go again, Miss Lockwood, allowing your pride to get the better of you.' He cocked a brow. 'What's the matter? Afraid you'll fall under my spell?'

'Of course not,' she lied primly.

'Then there is no harm in dining with me, is there?' he said, his eyes challenging.

Juliet relented. 'No, I suppose not. I would love to. Thank you. If you don't mind, I would like to go to my room and freshen up. It's been a long day for me, too, and I feel rather like one of the dusty old books I've been dealing with all day.'

'Then I shall see you in the dining room in an hour.'

Dominic watched her go. After what had happened between them at Cordelia's soirée, he knew she was deeply affected by the brief intimacy between them and, being the person she was, she would not treat it lightly. He had intentionally kept out of her way in the hope that his absence would deepen what she felt for him, and now, as he watched her retreating figure, the idea of making her his mistress seemed not only an ideal solution, but an achievable one.

Now that he had made it a specific goal, he saw no reason not to pursue it with the same single-minded efficiency and determination that he used to achieve any other desirable asset he wished to possess and of which, when he grew tired of it, he would dispose of.

The only remaining difficulty was to enlist her co-operation—a delicate problem, yes, but in his arrogance he was supremely confident that with a little gentle persuasion he would succeed.

When Juliet had washed and changed into a sensible sage-green muslin dress, she went to the dining room as instructed. The room was very grand, but the white marble pillars and gold-patterned ceiling high above her head, the long dining table and chairs of midnight-blue velvet, beautiful paintings and gilt-edged mirrors did not induce a relaxed and comfortable atmosphere.

His Grace was lounging in a large leather chair, a large brandy beside him. Having bathed and changed his clothes, his dark hair still damp, he looked terribly handsome. He rose when she entered, and crossed towards her, his shoes making no sound on the thick Turkish carpet. He had never seen her in the evening and he was pleased she had got rid of that unattractive bun and gathered her hair at the nape and secured it with a narrow green ribbon. It hung down her back, thick and gleaming a rich deep brown in the candlelight.

Juliet paused, waiting for him to come to her, her hands clasped together in front of her. When he stood before her she lifted her face to look up at him. The moment she did, he forgot everything. She had beautiful eyes, he thought, dark and warm and surrounded by thick black lashes. She was extremely attractive, and bathed in candlelight, with loose tendrils of hair around her face, she seemed softer than she ever had before.

'Lord Lansdowne?'

Her voice brought his attention back to the reason she was here. His prediction that dining together might bring them closer seemed likely to come true. 'A drink, Miss Lockwood—some wine, perhaps?'

'Yes, thank you.'

He handed her a glass of red wine. 'I do realise that by entertaining an unchaperoned female at my home means that I am committing an unforgivable breach of decency which could put your morality in serious question.'

Juliet suppressed a smile. 'Not to mention your judgement for doing so, your Grace. But since I am your employee, I don't count.'

'You don't?'

'No.'

As they drank their wine the food was brought in. Dominic insisted she sat facing him at the long table, explaining that he wanted to converse quietly with her, not shout down the length of the table. His manner was amiable, all consideration and regard, and his attention assiduous, but Juliet was not unaware of his intentions, for had he not told her what they were at his sister's soirée? She studied his hard, sculpted features. Even with the softening effect of the candles on his face, he looked supremely invulnerable.

Dominic watched her throughout the excellent meal. Whenever she looked up she found him watching her, with a strange sort of intensity she could not define.

'Why do you look at me like that?' she asked, spooning the last of the delicious dessert into her mouth.

Picking up his glass of wine, Dominic leaned back in his chair, his eyes narrowed as his gaze swept over her face with the leisure of a well-fed wolf. 'Like what?'

'As though I am some kind of mystery you cannot fathom.'

'Perhaps that's because you are a mystery to me, Miss Lockwood, an enigma. You spend every minute of every day in my house, I employ you, but I do not know you.'

'I assure you I am no great mystery. My life is quite uninteresting. I have no home of my own. You know what I do, where I was educated and that I worked for Sir John before coming here. What else is there?'

'What else, indeed?' he murmured. Even now she told him nothing about the man she had met in town. He was curious, but he would not ask outright. 'I cannot draw any conclusions from that.'

'You are my employer, your Grace. It is not necessary.'

'And I beg to differ, Miss Lockwood. You see, I want to know about you—all there is. I am curious. You intrigue me.' Shoving back his chair, he stood up and walked round the table to where she sat. Taking her hand, he drew her to her feet, and he tipped her chin up, wanting to see her eyes. 'Tell me,' he said before he could stop himself, 'how does a woman who would have me believe she has lived the life of a recluse, manage to look as lovely as you do?' He ran the tips of his fingers across her lower lip and let then slide gently over the curve of her cheek. 'You have wonderful eyes—did you know that? And your skin is as soft as velvet.'

Juliet opened her mouth and drew a deep, quivering breath, letting it out against the palm of his hand, doing her best to avoid his penetrating eyes. 'I—I've never thought about it.'

'Have you not?' His voice was low and seductive, his fingers curling round her nape and drawing her head closer. Suddenly there was a different quality to the atmosphere between them.

'No—not ever.' His lips were perilously close.

Her calmness in the face of danger was admirable. Only a slight tremble in her jaw told him she was affected by what he was doing.

'Are you trying to seduce me, your Grace?' she ventured to ask nervously.

'Contrary to certain reports, I am not as colourful as I have been painted, Miss Lockwood.' The corners of his eyes crinkled, though he did not smile. 'But I confess I am trying to seduce you.'

'Yes, I know.'

'And is it working?'

'What? This blatant attempt to trick me into your bed with charm and other tactics?'

'Ah, but you are far too clever to be fooled by trickery and charm. It is a different weapon I choose.'

'I know.' At last she met his gaze directly. 'I think it is called persuasion.'

'No. It is called temptation.'

'To tempt, you must have something to tempt with. What have you got, Lord Lansdowne? How would you know what would tempt me?'

'Passion would, Miss Lockwood. Passion would.'

A rush of intense warmth came over Juliet and she turned away before he could see that she was actually blushing. 'And that is something I need instruction for?'

'I think so.'

'Please don't toy with me.'

'I'm not. This is not a game, Miss Lockwood.'

Something in those words made her shiver with excitement. 'I'm relieved to hear it,' she replied primly.

He smiled. 'What I find interesting about you is that, while being prim and proper, you are capable of being both captivating and alluring.'

'Really? The kind of passion you speak of is unbeknown to me.'

Taking her arms, he drew her against him, and, kissing her ear, he murmured, 'It needn't be. I'll show you if you will be accommodating for this one night,' he cajoled. 'Is it too hard to imagine that we are lovers?' he asked, breathing against her throat.

His warm breath stirred shivers along Juliet's flesh, and a curious excitement tingled in her breast. His voice was low and husky in her ears, and she had to dip deeply into her reservoir of will to dispel the slow numbing of her senses. The wine had certainly had its effect on her, for her senses reeled in intoxicating pleasure. His arm came around her shoulders, and she had to fight to keep her world upright as his mouth, moist and parted, warmly tasted hers. Although she struggled not to, she found herself kissing him back, her arms snaking around his waist, and was shocked by it. What was the matter with her? She was not a woman of easy virtue. For goodness' sake, she was a virgin!

His mouth was insistent, demanding, relentless, snatching her breath as well as her poise. She was caught up in the heat of a battle she could not hope to win. Her weapons were useless. She should have found his kiss repulsive, but in truth it was wildly exciting. She was aware of the feel of his body, the hard, muscular chest pressed against her breasts, and the heavy beat of her heart as it throbbed a new frantic rhythm.

With trembling effort Juliet collected herself and pulled back, and as he stared at her, she drew a deep, ragged breath, her eyes searching the flames smouldering in the depths of his silver-grey eyes. 'This—has to stop,' she whispered in an unsteady voice.

'No, Juliet.' Dominic smiled leisurely. 'That isn't what either of us wants now, is it?'

Taking her hand, he walked to the door, drawing her after him, and before she knew what was happening he was leading her up the stairs. When they came to a break in the landing, she drew back. He turned and looked at her, his eyes questioning.

'Not—not your rooms, your Grace. I—I couldn't.'

He smiled. 'No? Then I have no objection to sharing yours. Lead the way, Miss Lockwood.'

Chapter Six

Juliet wanted him, she realised unhappily. Despite her own inhibitions and everything she had heard about his Grace, the Duke of Hawksfield—that he was a libertine and an arrogant, spoiled aristocrat—in the silence of her heart she knew she was no different from any other woman who came under his spell.

When he closed the door to her room, so they were totally enclosed in their own unique and enchanted world, she was made to realise that there was no going back, no escaping what was to happen and at last she accepted.

She did not object to the slow, languorous unwrapping and removal of her clothes by Dominic Lansdowne, who dropped them carelessly to the carpet, stopping now and then to gaze in wonder at the amber-tinted flesh and the smooth, gracefully arched back, the sweet curve of waist, hip and thigh, before he swung her up into his arms and laid her down on the bed, soft and ready for them, and she watched as he stripped himself of his own obstructive garments to reveal his beautiful male body, hard and eager.

Dominic stared down at her, his gaze running down the length of her and back up her body to the full curve of her breasts and on the rosy glow on her face. She was a woman, a lovely, vibrant woman, and as alluring and desirable as any he had ever known. Her brown eyes were deep and warm and glowing and the weight of her hair rippled down her back and about her shoulders like a dark, silken cloud.

She was as ardent as he was, as feverish for his embraces as he was for hers. When he lowered his mouth to hers, in his eyes she saw the flame that was lit, a bright, consuming flame of passion that spread and licked about their naked bodies. Her soft flesh began to glow and tingle, and the tingle spread throughout her, in her blood, in her bones. It was a wonderful kind of torture that continued to grow until she could feel a warm fountain within, soon to run over, soon to drown her in a flood of pleasure. Nothing mattered but each other.

Pushing his hand into her soft hair, with the last thread of rationality Dominic possessed, he lifted his mouth from hers and gave her one last chance to call a halt. 'Are you sure about this?'

Looking up at him, her eyes soft, warm and dazed and unfocused with that loveliness that comes when a woman is deep in the pleasures of the flesh, she nodded. She was going to let him love her and she felt a wild surge of excitement and anticipation. 'Yes,' she whispered, linking her fingers behind his neck and drawing his lips down to hers.

He took what she was offering, took what he had wanted the morning he had set eyes on her in the library. He took it mindlessly, driven by a violent compulsion to have her, took her with an urgency and hunger that stunned and aroused him, and he used all his sexual experience to knock down the defences of an inexperienced young woman who hadn't any idea how to withstand it.

The moment he entered her, he looked down at her face, surprised and a little ashamed to see her cheeks were damp with tears. 'I'm sorry,' he whispered, kissing her tears. 'Did I hurt you?'

Her choked, whispered words reinforced the need in her eyes as her hands splayed about his taut shoulders. She could feel the strength of him, the force of his arms and firm thighs, the soft hair on his chest brushing against her.

'No. Please—hold me—kiss me…'

Driven on by desire, by need, Dominic complied, letting the mindless pleasure overwhelm him. He was the first man Juliet had known and he knew it too, and his triumphant laugh echoed about the room, telling her she was his now.

They did not love casually, but what they shared was given complete consideration. Juliet was light against him, folding herself into his body, her head tucked beneath his chin while his hand smoothed and caressed the soft flesh of her body, moving to cup her breasts shivering with delight at his touch. He bruised her mouth with his and she moaned deep in her throat, returning his kiss and stretching to accommodate his hard, lean body, not stopping him as they moved slowly and surely towards the fire and ecstasy that embraced them both, and when it came they faced it together, the sound of their joy heard by no one but each other.

Whatever the reasons that had driven Dominic to Juliet's bed, they were forgotten as he wrapped his arms around her back and pulled her with him on to his side. She was exquisitely soft. In the flickering light of the candles, they lay together, not speaking, Juliet's face buried in his neck and shoulder, his against her tangled hair, then he sighed, replete for the moment, reluctant to leave, to end this moment, this marvel he had discovered, the heady, primitive sensuality of her.

With a hypnotic, heavy warmth seeping through her limbs, filling her up, devouring her senses, Juliet tipped her head back and, reaching up, trailed her fingers lightly over the outline of his jaw. 'I never thought the act of making love could be so pleasurable. Thank you. It was the most wonderful thing that has ever happened to me. I will not turn it into something of which I shall be ashamed. I do not feel guilty or ruined. I knew what I wanted and I took it—and so did you.'

Hearing the truth of her words in her voice, Dominic turned his head and placed a kiss in the palm of her hand. 'Lord, you're the loveliest, the sweetest—'

She silenced him by placing her finger on his lips. 'Hush…and kiss me.'

Dominic was only too happy to oblige. Afterwards

he held her close, feeling strangely protective of this woman who had come so suddenly into his life. He had made love to many women, but not one of them had given him what Juliet just had. Her responses had been real and uncontrolled. In fact, it had been the most satisfying encounter of his life. The ecstasy he had experienced was a wonder to him, for he thought he knew it all, but he had been wrong.

He was a virile and very masculine male who was accustomed to the women in his arms allowing him whatever he asked of them, a man well used to the lusty pleasures that were always available to him. He had not, until now, held a woman in his arms who was innocent, untouched and pure. A woman who had never known the hands of a man on her.

Gradually they drifted into sleep. The candles spluttered and died. Dominic and Juliet did not notice. They were not aware of the march of the silver moon across the sky, nor the purple light of dawn creeping over the horizon. They knew nothing but each other as they slept.

When Juliet woke, Dominic was gone. She reached out her hand to the empty space he had occupied beside her. The sheet was cold, but there was still the impression of where his head had been on the pillow, and the sharp tangy smell of his cologne.

The curtains were closed and it was still quite dark in the room. She looked at the time. Six o'clock. She assumed he didn't want the servants to see him and had gone to his own room. For a time she lay burrowed in the covers, thinking about Dominic and what they had done, thinking of how it had felt to have him beside her, within her, the emotions he had roused in her. With a sigh she knew she was completely in the Duke of Hawksfield's thrall, and it was only a matter of time before she must pay the price of her folly, but for now she was content to think no further than the night past.

Turning back the covers, from the corner of her eye she noticed the spots of blood on the sheets—her blood—and realised then that she had felt no pain, as she had expected she would. No, she had felt only pleasure, delirium.

Later that morning, Dominic strode into the library. He was wearing a brown jacket, buff-coloured breeches, and impeccably blacked, high riding boots. Not a hair on his head was out of place, and his cravat expertly tied. His square jaw was set with cool purpose, and there was a confident strength emanating from every inch of his broad-shouldered frame. Closing the double doors behind him, he crossed the room.

Juliet watched him approach the table where she sat, wondering a little desperately how he could look so utterly casual after the things they had done. But then, he probably went around making love to every girl he had a fancy for, so in all probability it had meant nothing to him at all. He smiled and she wished he didn't look quite so nonchalant, so calm, not when she was struggling to appear normal in the aftermath of their night together. Her fear and confusion promptly escalated to panic.

All morning she had secretly counted on her own ability to remain in control and not to read too much into what had happened between them during the dark hours, but the man whose brows were drawn together now looked about as malleable as a rock.

'Good morning, Miss Lockwood,' he said brusquely. 'I trust you are feeling well today?'

'Yes—I am quite well, thank you,' she replied, putting down her pen and folding her hands in her lap. In place of the seduction that had marked his mood last night, his tone today was impeccably polite, impersonal and businesslike—and he hadn't called her Juliet.

Perching his hips on the edge of the table, he crossed his arms over his chest and studied her impassively, his long leg swinging lazily to and fro. It seemed an eternity before he finally spoke. When he did his voice was calm and authoritative.

'I am to leave for London in a couple of days, but before I do there are certain things that have to be clarified between us.'

'There are?'

'I have an offer to put to you.' Dominic saw her eyes kindle with joy at the word *offer*, and could not believe that she truly believed he was stupid enough to actually offer marriage.

'What kind of offer?'

'A business proposition.'

'Different to what I am doing now?'

'Very much so. Once you've had time to consider

it—which you will, since I expect to be away for some considerable time—I think you'll find it sensible.'

'For me, or for you, your Grace?'

'Both of us—and I do wish you would stop calling me your Grace,' he said irritably. 'It is hardly appropriate after what happened between us last night. Certainly you'll find my proposition preferable to doing what you do now.'

Uneasiness settled in. 'But I enjoy my work. How can you say I'll find anything else preferable?'

'Financially it will be beneficial.'

Something in his manner made Juliet go cold and something began to die within her. 'Please, go on. What is it you want from me?'

'That you become my mistress. After what happened between us last night, it is obvious to me that we are compatible.'

Juliet couldn't believe what she was hearing. How could he describe what they had done with such clinical calm? He was standing with the still vigour that characterised him, simultaneously relaxed yet alert. There was an intelligent, amused understanding in his silvery eyes, which was very disconcerting.

Juliet hesitated, thinking over her choice of words before she said them. She knew she was on shaky ground. Her own nature would not allow her to play the part of a nervous female given to vapours. Pushing her chair back, slowly she got to her feet and looked at him directly, an angry light blazing in her eyes.

'I'm not sure I like your proposal, your Grace,' she

said, deriving pleasure from using the form of address
he disliked from her.

'I can't see why you should be against it. You
will share my bed. In return you will have a house
in London, servants, a carriage, the freedom to do as
you please, so long as no other man is given the use of
what I am paying for, and gowns and jewels to make
you the envy of every woman in town.'

'I have no interest in fancy gowns and jewels and
having servants do what I am capable of doing for
myself,' Juliet uttered tightly.

His lips curved in a smile. 'Then you will prove to
be an inexpensive mistress. Also you must never mis-
understand the nature of our relationship.'

'And what is that supposed to mean?'

'That you must not want more than I am prepared
to give.'

Juliet's chin came up. At least he didn't utter words
of love he didn't feel. Neither, however, had he proposed that she become his mistress with any show of
sentimental affection, so she acted in the same unemotional way it had been offered.

'Might I ask what would happen to me if you
decided to take a wife?'

'Matrimony is not on the agenda, but, if I did marry,
your status as my mistress would not alter.'

'I see. Then you would dishonour your wife as well
as me. Have you never thought of marrying, your
Grace?' she enquired coolly.

A bolt of pain and something Juliet could not define
flashed through his silver-grey eyes like lightening.

'Once—a long time ago,' he confessed. 'Her name was Amelia. At the time I could see no wrong in her. She was so full of life and very lovely, and I firmly believed she was a chaste and virtuous young woman.'

Unlike me, Juliet thought, somehow holding her taut features in control. Bending her head, she gazed at her clasped hands. Roiling shame churned inside her. She had to commend his devotion for his dead love, but didn't he see the insult he was giving her? But perhaps the insult didn't matter, since she was only good enough to be his mistress.

'And what happened to this paragon?' she asked quietly, knowing from her conversation with Lady Pemberton that the lady was deceased, but wanting to hear it from him.

His look was direct, his eyes shuttered. 'Amelia was no paragon. She died.'

'I am very sorry for your loss,' she murmured, confused by his remark that he had believed she was chaste and virtuous. Did that mean that he had found out differently? Whatever it was, Amelia must have meant a great deal to him. Disappointment nearly stole her breath, and she was careful to hide the twist of hurt inside her behind a thin smile. 'It must have been painful for you.'

His lips curled into a cynical smile. 'Painful is putting it mildly. Perhaps if I give you a brief account of what happened, you will understand me a little better. Amelia betrayed me. It was a bitter experience, one I never wish to repeat. I never forgave her, and now every woman who tries to get close I have no time for. After what happened I vowed that my emotions would never again become engaged by a woman. I want none of their treacherous deceit. But you are different. I sensed it the first time I set eyes on you.'

Juliet raised her head and looked at him levelly. 'Really? Forgive me if I do not feel flattered. Neither am I ready to give my heart,' she said, wondering what Amelia had done that was so terrible he locked love out of his heart. 'So now you go around collecting mistresses, do you, your Grace?'

He flinched at her defiance to continue addressing him as your Grace, but chose to overlook it for now, sensing the tension behind her controlled façade.

'Something like that. My sister is constantly nagging me to wed, and I shall, eventually, but as I said, it is not on my agenda at this time. While I am gone you will have plenty of time to think about my proposition. You are ambitious and clever. I am sure you will see the logic of it.'

Juliet gazed at the cool, dispassionate man standing before her. He looked powerful, aloof and completely self-assured. 'You think so, do you? How can you speak of me as being your mistress as if you're discussing a common business arrangement—without any feeling or emotion?'

He reached out and with the backs of his fingers caressed the soft, heated curve of her cheek. 'Because that's the way I am, and that's the way it is. There's no reason why we can't enjoy ourselves. I am not prepared to pledge eternal vows, but I do find you an adorable, enchanting creature and I happen to be extremely fond of you. You're delectable and engaging, and I want you quite madly. I don't offer you solemn love or soulful devotion. I offer you my protection, affection and fun. Come. Be sensible. There's no need for all this melodrama over a perfectly straightforward proposition.'

'Straightforward to you, maybe,' Juliet said passionately, 'but not to me.'

'It's the chance of a lifetime for you. You must see that.'

'Must I?'

'Think about it. You and I. We could have a very delightful arrangement. What we each enjoyed last night could become a regular occurrence. It could be good for both of us.'

His voice was like pure silk and his eyes became warm and appreciative and Juliet knew immediately, of course, what he was demanding of her and she felt fury explode in her, not just with him and the effrontery of what he wanted, but at the sudden excitement that stirred in her at the very idea.

Never had she been so humiliated in her life, she told herself, whipping up her temper until her cheeks were scarlet with outrage. 'Since I have not the slightest intention of repeating what happened between us last night, I intend to put it behind me.'

A humorous gleam appeared in his eyes and a tantalising smile played on his lips. 'That sounds remarkably like a challenge to me.'

'Forget it,' she hissed.

'Come now, Juliet, don't play the innocent with me. I know you better than any man, I would say. You are not so naïve as not to know what I am saying, so I don't think I have to spell it out. Not only do you know, but the thought excites you. You're a woman, Juliet, and though I've had my share before, not since...' he hesitated and Juliet knew he had almost said Amelia '...there's none to touch you when it comes to pleasing a man, and to take pleasure from it yourself. And don't pretend you don't know what I'm talking about. I can see it in your eyes. They are far too eloquent. So, what do you say?'

With all the time in the world and the unconcern to go with it, he reached for the decanter and poured himself a drink. Sitting in a chair, he drank it slowly, and waited.

Flinching from his words, Juliet glared at his hard, handsome face with feverish wrath. Swallowing convulsively, she shook her head, the calm she had maintained so carefully moments before having completely disintegrated.

'I will say this, your Grace,' she said, her voice shaking with anger. 'I simply work for you. You are not my lord and master. We spent the night together—a pleasurable night. It meant nothing more to me than that. You have an over-inflated opinion of yourself if you thought it did. Clearly it meant more to you, for I did not expect this.'

'Then pray tell me, what did you expect?'

'In truth, I did not expect anything from you. I will not be your mistress. You are asking me to dishonour myself more than I already have. Both the proposition and the terms you lay down are unacceptable to me.'

He took another drink of his fine brandy, his long legs stretched out indolently in front of him. 'Just as you please, Juliet,' he said, as though it was nothing to him one way or another.

Juliet moved to stand over him, glaring down into his handsome, haughty face. 'My father was a good man. He taught me right from wrong. The next time I give myself to a man it will be within the bounds of marriage—not some tainted liaison. I am worth more than that. After this I cannot possibly remain in your employ. While you are away I shall complete my work and I will be gone when you return.'

Apart from a narrowing of his eyes Dominic's face remained expressionless. 'I see. Where will you go?' he demanded, shoving himself out of the chair and putting his glass down, towering over her, purposely intimidating her as if he could frighten her into submission. 'What will you do?'

'What I have always done. Honest work. Decent work. Nothing tawdry or shameful, which is what it would be were I to become your plaything—your whore.'

The word hung in the air between them. Dominic looked at the young termagant hard before shrugging nonchalantly and turning away and sauntering across the room. They were not the most romantic circumstances under which to propose that she become his mistress and he had probably insulted and wounded her by suggesting it in such a blunt fashion. And he supposed it was rather arrogant of him to assume she would accept him—but for God's sake, he was a duke.

It was not as if he were of lowly occupation. Only royalty ranked higher than he, and it was not conceited of him to take her acceptance of his offer as a matter of course.

He knew that at this moment it would do him no good to argue with her. Let her get used to the idea, to the knowledge that he would take care of her and that she had nothing to fear.

'Is that so?' he said, his tone sharp. 'A true whore's life is earning coppers in back alleys from the kind of low life that inhabits such places. I am offering you something far superior to that. As I said, I shall be gone for some time. Don't do anything in haste. Think about it.' Glancing casually down at one of the display cabinets, he frowned. 'Where are the miniatures?'

Startled by the abrupt change in topic and the question itself, Juliet replied blankly, 'Miniatures? What miniatures?'

Dominic lifted the glass and peered inside. 'There were four, now there are two. They were painted by Mother, who was an accomplished artist. They are of no great value, only to her family, and wherever they are—whoever has taken them—I want them returned.'

Juliet went and looked at the empty spaces where the beautiful miniatures had been, clearly puzzled by their disappearance. 'They were there yesterday. I recall seeing them.'

'They cannot have vanished into thin air.'

At that moment the door opened and a servant announced Sir Thomas and Miss Howard. Juliet raised her head to look at them. Miss Howard was dressed in a coral silk gown and matching hat, which seemed rather overstated for that time of the day, but, considering Miss Howard's greed for attention, one could hardly suspect a less flamboyant arrival. She gave Juliet a derisive glance as she swept in and, without otherwise acknowledging her presence, focused her attention on Dominic.

'We were passing on our way home from visiting friends nearby and couldn't resist calling on you,' Thomas said. 'Hope you don't mind.'

'Be my guests,' Dominic replied, somewhat exasperated and annoyed that they had chosen this particular time to pay an unexpected social call.

Thomas, a willowy, dark-haired effeminate-looking youth, sank into a deep leather chair, stretching his long legs negligently out in front of him. 'Has Charles called on you recently, by any chance?' he asked absently perusing his fingernails with interest.

'He has. Twice this week.'

Geraldine's eyes hardened as they settled on Juliet. 'Has he indeed!'

'Why?' Dominic queried. 'Are you looking for him?'

'Not me—though Geraldine's getting a bit hot under the collar. I have to say he does seem to be avoiding us of late.' Thomas glanced at Dominic and smiled wickedly at Juliet. 'Methinks he's either lost his head over a brown-haired moppet, or he's suddenly developed an avid interest in books.'

Dominic cast him a look, his features carefully showing only mild amusement at Thomas's assessment of Charles's suddenly frequent visits to Lansdowne

House. Unfortunately Thomas was right in his assertions—one of them, at least—that Charles did seem to have developed a *tendre* for his employee, and Thomas would have been astounded to know that as Dominic languidly listened to him, he was seething inside.

Juliet didn't like what Thomas Howard was suggesting and her cheeks flushed crimson, partly from embarrassment and partly from a surge of anger. 'If the brown-haired moppet you are referring to is myself, sir, I assure you Sir Charles gets no encouragement from me.' In fact there were times when she looked on Sir Charles's visits as a nuisance since his presence distracted her from her work.

'The attraction will soon wear off,' Geraldine retorted peevishly. 'It does, you know, and quickly.' Raising her head haughtily, she turned her attention to Dominic. 'I'm so delighted to see you are still here, Dominic. We were afraid you might have left for London. We are to leave ourselves very soon.'

'As you see I am still here, Geraldine. I intend leaving for my house in Mayfair two days hence, although the way things are going I might be here for some time yet.'

'I see.' She looked into the open display case. 'Oh, what on earth has happened to those charming miniatures, Dominic?'

'They have mysteriously disappeared. How or when it's hard to say.'

'Are you saying they have been stolen?'

'It's beginning to look like it.'

'Then it must be one of the servants.'

Dominic looked at her sharply. 'That is a very serious accusation to make, Geraldine. We have never had a thief in this house.'

'It is a serious matter when things go missing.'

'But I was here all the time,' Juliet intervened. 'I would have seen if anyone had opened the display case.'

Geraldine glanced at her. 'You are certain you were in here *all* the time, are you, Miss Lockwood—every minute of the day?'

Juliet bit her lower lip uncertainly. 'No, only during working hours.'

Dominic walked to the bell pull in the corner of the room. 'I intend to get to the bottom of it. I will speak to Pearce.' He was about to grasp the bell pull, when Geraldine said in an over-loud voice,

'What about the gentleman who visited you yesterday, Miss Lockwood?'

Juliet glanced at her sharply. 'Robby?'

Dominic's eyes narrowed on her suspiciously. 'And who, may I ask, is Robby?'

'My brother.'

'And he came here, to the house, yesterday?'

Juliet stared at him, chills beginning to slither up her spine. 'Yes. It—had quite slipped my mind.'

'Clearly,' he ground out coldly. 'And is your brother in the habit of coming here?'

'No of course not. It was the first time.'

'And you did not think to consult me?'

'You were not here. I hope you don't mind.'

Dominic sighed. All at once his temper seemed to leave him. His shoulders relaxed and he was no longer scowling. 'No, of course I don't mind. You must feel at liberty to invite whomsoever you wish to the house.'

A conspiratorial look passed between them that Geraldine intercepted, and she didn't care for it one bit. 'You might,' she said with malicious intent, with the look of an animal about to strike, 'if you were to know Miss Lockwood's brother had only recently been released from the Fleet prison.'

The silence in the room could be cut with a knife. Even the indolent Thomas sat up in his chair. In all the years Geraldine had known Dominic Lansdowne, she had never seen him immobilised by any emotion. The worse the pressure, the greater the disaster, the more energised he became. Now, however, he was staring at Miss Lockwood as if unable to absorb what she, Geraldine, had just told him.

'Of course I do not wish to intrude into a situation that is none of my affair, Dominic,' Geraldine went on, 'but neither would I feel right were I to conceal information that you have a right to know.'

Juliet was badly shaken by Miss Howard's unexpected pronouncement. Her heart contracted in sudden fear. Lord Lansdowne was looking at her hard and she stared at him with blind confusion and loss and disbelief.

'Is this true?' he demanded, his voice like steel.

'Yes, but that doesn't make him a thief,' she retorted, coming hotly to her brother's defence. 'He was in prison for debt, not stealing.' She looked at Miss Howard, doing her best to hold in the resentment and anger she felt. 'How dare you imply Robby might have taken the miniatures?'

Geraldine shrugged. 'I dare do and say anything I like, Miss Lockwood. Your brother had every opportunity to take them. Why, when I arrived he was in here alone, as I recall.'

'But you didn't actually see him take them, did you, Miss Howard?'

'No, but you have to admit it's a coincidence.'

Juliet watched the smug smile grow on Miss Howard's lips. If anyone had happened to look deeply into her eyes they might have been alarmed. Juliet saw it, saw the malevolence, saw the streak of red high on her cheekbones and her body froze so that she could not move.

'I seem to recall you were also alone in here for a time, Miss Howard, when I left the room to accompany Robby to the door. I also recall that when I returned, you were standing right by the display cases.'

Geraldine's face tightened. 'Just what are you implying, Miss Lockwood—that I took them? If so, it is quite outrageous and not to be borne.'

'I am merely pointing out that you also had the opportunity to take them. The time I was gone would have given you ample time.'

Geraldine laughed to hide her sudden nervousness. 'Don't be ridiculous. Why on earth would I want to take the miniatures, for what reason? They were painted by the late Duchess, Dominic's mother, and are of no value to anyone other than the family—although I don't suppose anyone outside the family would know that and would assume them to be of considerable value.'

Juliet looked at her hard. 'No, I don't suppose they would.'

Geraldine Howard was almost vicious in her ambition to secure Sir Charles Sedgwick, and to gain that end she would slander, abuse or destroy any woman who got in her way. Juliet, though Miss Howard believed she came from common stock, was no exception, since she was attractive enough to have drawn the attention of Sir Charles. Juliet had no doubt the woman would paint a wildly distorted vision for her employer, even to destroying her beloved Robby to do it, to remove her from the picture completely.

Drawing herself up, Juliet turned and faced her employer. 'Please believe me when I say that Robby would not steal. He is not a thief. Yes, he spent some time in the Fleet prison, but that was because he got himself into debt—debts which he has now settled in full.' She felt she was engaged in a battle except no one had told her the rules. She was telling the truth. Robby was not a thief, but she could see no way of persuading Dominic Lansdowne to believe her.

'You cannot say he did not take the miniatures with certainty,' Geraldine burst out. 'If he is a thief, the law will deal with him as he deserves. If he is found guilty, the court will sentence him to hang.'

Juliet's entire body vibrating with panic, she faced Miss Howard, having felt each of her harsh words, as if it was a blow to the head. 'No, dear God, no—not for a crime he is not guilty of.'

Geraldine sneered. 'If he is guilty, it will take more than a prayer to save him.'

'While I freely acknowledge my brother's reputation is not perfect—and whilst I also accept that his behaviour in the past is hardly above reproach—it is not for you to judge him.'

'Geraldine!' her brother rebuked sharply before she could say more, aware of a growing, uneasy suspicion as he looked at her. 'Do you have to frighten poor Miss Lockwood half to death? I apologise for my sister's behaviour, Miss Lockwood. She's being unforgivably rude.'

Juliet managed to smile at him. 'There's no need for you to apologise, sir.'

'I'm afraid there is,' Thomas countered, ignoring the look of pure venom his sister shot at him. 'Her manners can be quite appalling at times. Come along, Geraldine. I am sure Dominic would appreciate some time to sort this out. No doubt the miniatures will come to light in due course.'

'Thank you, Thomas. I can only hope you are right.' Dominic threw him a look of gratitude. 'Now, if you don't mind, I would like to speak to Miss Lockwood alone.'

Geraldine inclined her head briefly in a farewell gesture, irritated that she had been told to go. She consoled herself with the thought that if Charles or Dominic had some interest in Miss Lockwood, it was a wasted effort. She looked at Miss Lockwood and saw hate in her eyes, not shame. As she turned her back she breathed a sigh of relief. Things would play out as planned. With any luck Dominic would see the error of employing a woman with a criminal for a brother and send her packing.

As Juliet was left alone with her employer, her heart began to beat in heavy, terrifying dread as she sensed her lover of last night had seemingly withdrawn from her, as if the closeness, the tenderness they had shared had never existed. They faced each other, an invisible wall between them, and she felt a terrible pain inside, felt tears she was too proud to shed. The face of a stranger, not a friend or a lover, was looking at her—angry, hard, judgemental.

She couldn't believe this was happening. She could not believe it was ending. She wanted to shout at him and make him see how unnecessary this was, but she didn't say anything. Her pride prevented it.

When Dominic finally spoke his voice was tight as he tried to hold his inner tension under control. 'You are certain the miniatures were there yesterday morning?'

'As certain as I can be.'

'But you have no evidence of that,' he uttered sharply. 'You cannot be blamed for your brother's behaviour, but why the hell did you not tell me yesterday that he had visited you here?'

'As I recall, your Grace, you had other things on your mind,' Juliet uttered pointedly.

He nodded, accepting the truth of her words. Yesterday he had been unable to think of anything other than seducing her into his bed. 'And where is you brother now?'

'I really don't think that is relevant.'

'In other words, you are not going to tell me.'

'No I am not. Robby is my brother and he deserves my loyalty. He came to Essex to see me. He came to Lansdowne House to say goodbye because he had decided to leave earlier than he intended, not to steal.'

'So that was your brother?' That explained the identity of the man he had seen her with in Brentwood that day, and he could not believe the relief he felt knowing this, and that she had not been meeting some man she might have a yearning for.

A puzzled look came into Juliet's eyes. 'Pardon? You—saw him?'

'As a matter of fact, I did. In town. You looked— pleased to see him.'

Comprehension dawned on Juliet. 'I see. I really do. You assumed Robby and I were...' Her smile was icy. 'Did that hurt you, the thought of me with another man?'

'What you do when you are not working for me is your affair. When you bring your private life into my home that is another matter.'

'Robby has just been released from prison. His debts are settled and he has secured a splendid teaching position in New York.' She paused, feeling helplessness and anger that everything was about to go terribly wrong overwhelming her. Tears stung the backs of her eyes. 'I will not do anything that might jeopardise his career. I told you he is not a thief. He feels things deeply. Insults go deep with him. When he hears what he has been accused of, he'll make you see the truth.'

'Juliet,' Dominic said, sensing her distress and reaching for her shoulders in a helpless attempt to soothe her.

'Don't touch me,' she cried, flinging his hands away.

'Please don't upset yourself. I understand and I am sorry if I sounded harsh and judgemental—'

'*You* understand?' she repeated with bitter scorn, lifting her wretched, accusing face to his. 'How can someone like *you* understand how I feel, how my brother will feel, to be despised for something he did not do? I ask you to trust me, to have faith in me and accept my word on this.'

One sleep black brow rode upwards. 'Without question?'

She nodded. 'Yes,' she whispered.

'I can't do that. Are you asking me to overlook the missing miniatures?'

'No, no of course not... Will you inform the Bow Street Runners?'

'Not yet. I do not want them involved. There is still the possibility that the miniatures will turn up.'

'Do you think my brother stole them?'

Dominic evaded the question. 'As I said, they may yet turn up.'

'That's not what I asked.'

Dominic met her gaze head on. 'I remain open minded about whether or not he took them. What Miss Howard told you is correct. Those miniatures were painted by my mother—just scenes she loved that can be located within the countryside around here, places

that were dear to her and to my father. I want them
found. I shall instruct Pearce to question all the servants. The miniatures were in the display cases yesterday morning, so anyone who entered this room after
that will be questioned, including your brother.'

'Robby's life is important to me. I am not prepared
to see him arrested for something he hasn't done.'

'What goes on in my house is my business. The facts
are real. Your brother came here yesterday, and when he
left two of the miniatures in that cabinet were missing.
I do not know your brother, only that he has recently
been released from prison, which gives me little reason
to trust him. You cannot explain what happened to the
paintings, and my doubts will not be satisfied until I
receive some answers. If my natural concern offends
you, then that is too bad. Would you not feel as I do
were the situation reversed?'

His eyes, as they met Juliet's, were as hard as granite and uncompromising. He was icily furious and he
was allowing her no quarter in their argument.

'Yes,' she replied, unable in all honesty to disagree
with him. He looked at her for a long, unyielding
moment. She looked away, unable to meet his flinty
gaze. 'Of course I would. Robby left for London when
he left here.'

'Then he will have left an address where he can be
contacted.'

'I would like to speak to him myself first.'

'That would not be appropriate. *If*—and I mean *if*, he
did take the miniatures, then he would get rid of them
pretty quickly. In which case it would be hard to prove

anything against him and something precious to me and my family would be lost for ever. Do you understand what I am saying?'

'Yes, I do. And Miss Howard? Is she to be questioned also? Has it not occurred to you that she could have taken them in order to get at me by blackening my brother's name?'

'That is ridiculous. Why would she want to do that?'

'Because she is resentful of the time Sir Charles spends at Lansdowne House—here in the library—with me.'

'That is preposterous. Resentful Geraldine might be, but she is not a thief.'

'Neither is my brother.'

'And I sincerely hope you are right. Now, are you going to give me the address where he can be contacted?'

Juliet drew herself up straight and met his gaze directly, defiance in every line of her body. 'No, I will not, and I will not be bullied or intimidated by you into doing so.' Her voice was shaking with anger. 'I will question him, I promise you, and I know he will want to speak to you, but I know he is innocent.'

Dominic moved to stand over her and smiled. It was an absolutely chilling smile, his silver-grey eyes gleaming with a deadly purpose. 'If I want to find him I will, I promise you that. There will be no hiding place. I am a very powerful man, and I have very powerful friends, and if I find out your brother has come into my home and stolen from me, I shall destroy him quite cheerfully.'

Something shifted inside Juliet. She lifted her chin in that way she had of showing her defiance, of giving quiet rein to her anger. 'There has been a terrible misunderstanding. I take strong exception to my brother being branded a thief without a shred of evidence. Miss Howard's accusations are unjust—and it is clear to me that you share her opinion, which leaves me with no alternative but to resign my position immediately.'

The muscles of Dominic's face clenched so tightly that a nerve in his cheek began to pulse. 'Leave?'

'To save you from embarrassment I shall leave right away. Mr Lewis knows where I am up to in my work and I am certain will be able to carry on until you find someone qualified to finish the task.'

'I'm sure I shall,' Dominic drawled. 'You are not indispensable.'

'No one is that. Not even you, your Grace,' she uttered with unconcealed meaningful sarcasm. 'When you came in here with your sordid proposition, I had already made up my mind to leave. Your insult to my brother to which I take great exception has quashed any doubts I might have had. It is obvious to me that you don't want me here.'

'I don't?' he repeated cynically, while his gaze wandered over her body with insulting thoroughness, before lifting to her face. 'Looking as you do there isn't any man of right mind who would not want you,' he replied with scathing, callous indifference.

Juliet moved closer to the handsome, forceful, dynamic man, her look contemptuous. 'How foolish I was to do what I did with you, to enjoy the simple and uncomplicated use of your body without remorse. I should have realised you were only amusing yourself with me, passing the time, which must hang heavily on gentlemen of your class in the tedium of the day. You are a libertine, your Grace—'

'My reputation has been grossly exaggerated,' he pointed out coldly. 'You should never believe everything you hear.'

'Oh, yes, and I'm a Chinaman,' Juliet said scornfully. 'A libertine is what you are, and I am saddened to think I spent useless hours in your arms. So return to your current mistress with my blessing. She is welcome to you. I have given you my notice and now I shall get on with my life, whatever it might be. And please don't try to prevent me from leaving. No good will come of it.'

She turned then and began to walk away, but swift as a leopard he followed and took her arm, spinning her round to face him. She put up her hands, palms facing him, as though to ward him off. Her face was pale and she trembled, but in her eyes was the brilliance of her anger.

'Don't touch me,' she hissed.

Deaf to her plea, Dominic seized her upper arms and yanked her to his chest. 'Just a token kiss before you go to remember me by.'

Her face became suffused with a deep blood red. She struggled against him wildly, trying to free herself from his grip, twisting every way she could against the steel of his arms. He held her tightly, restraining her, and then his mouth came down on to hers, becoming gentle as he captured her pliant lips, their bodies welded together, his arms encircling her with all the masculine possession of a man who knows a woman is his.

One hand moved to her nape and when Juliet felt the hot sweetness flow through her, she moaned deep in her throat, arching her back as if offering her body to him as she had done in the depths of the bed they had shared.

They might have gone on, lost in mindless pleasure, but suddenly Juliet recollected herself, her sanity returning, and in her fury she shoved him away, her lips swollen, her eyes blazing. She would have left immediately, but he blocked her exit.

'How dare you? How dare you play with me as if it's some despicable game?'

'I don't play games, Juliet.' He arched a brow, his eyes resting hungrily on her lips. 'Is there to be no farewell kiss?'

'You can go to hell, Dominic Lansdowne, and the sooner the better as far as I am concerned. I'd see myself dead before I let you touch me again. Get out of my way,' she demanded through gritted teeth, 'because you've had all you're going to get from me.'

His eyes were laughing now, maliciously so, and he had the greatest difficulty, she could distinctly see, in preventing himself from laughing out loud at her discomfiture. Her rage increased. If she had held a pistol in her hand she would have shot him, glad to see his flesh shatter, the blood flow. Her heartbeat quickened and deep within her, where no one could see, the core

of her female self began to throb, and she hated him
for it.

Teetering on the brink of despair, she gazed into her
tormentor's implacable, handsome face, fighting back
the tears and trying to hold on to her dignity. She raised
her head, and though her eyes were hot and angry with
her need to hide from him what was inside her, she
managed to keep her voice cold and contemptuous.

'Will you please step out of my way?'

To her surprise he stepped aside. She walked across
the room to the door, moving resolutely, her step light,
as though freed from a burden she had laboured under
for a long time. She turned and looked back at him
one last time, wanting to remember the scene, the
moment, so that she would never soften towards him.
She welcomed the coldness that was sweeping away
her wretchedness and demolishing all her tender feelings for him.

When she finally turned and walked out, her head
was held high and proud, and Dominic felt his heart
move painfully beneath his ribs, aching with some
strange emotion in which shame and sorrow were
mixed.

He watched her go, telling himself he was a fool
to let her walk out on him. Of all the women who had
passed through his life, not since Amelia had he wanted
any of them like he wanted Juliet Lockwood. What was
it about her? Her smile? Her touch, that set his heart
beating faster like a callow youth in love? Her innocence? Her sincerity?

He frowned and went and poured himself another

drink, throwing it back in one. Whatever it was it was not love. Love was not for him. He was immune to love. And yet Juliet Lockwood affected him deeply.

The thought of her walking out on him, on her work, became a growing torment. It flared into anger.

Chapter Seven

Juliet went straight to her room, her mind on one thing only: leaving Lansdowne House immediately. She was angry—angry, resentful and very afraid. Afraid for Robby, for even though she knew he was guilty of no crime, the mere breath of a scandal could ruin him.

Dominic Lansdowne, her lover of one glorious night, would not overlook the matter, and nor could she blame him, for the miniatures meant a great deal to him.

But she would never forgive herself for her abandon. How could she have let this happen? How could she have let things come to this? She had no work, for she could not possibly continue working for Dominic Lansdowne, and she had no prospects.

What she had done was shameful, sinful, but she was honest at least with herself and there was no one to blame, only herself. Not Dominic Lansdowne, not anybody, only Juliet Lockwood, who had wanted him to make love to her with a madness that was alien to her, and who even now, with her brother facing prison— or worse, God forbid—would not change a moment of what she had done.

Travelling to London, Juliet was overwhelmed by the significance of the moment. She felt she was standing at a crossroads, with paths stretching out in every direction leading to an uncertain future. Everything that had been before, everything that was yet to come, depended on what she decided to do now.

With her grandfather's letter burning a hole in her pocket, by the time she reached London she had decided. The die was cast. She had made her choice. What remained was determination to see things through whatever the consequences.

She tried not to think of the night past. She could not allow herself to weaken. If she did then, Dominic would have taken everything of worth from her. The time for regret and recrimination would come later. Now, how to prevent Robby being arrested mattered more than her breaking heart. But the images of her lover of last night sleeping, of his silver-grey eyes filled with passion, the curve of his lips as he kissed her, were memories so powerful they hurt and brought tears to her eyes.

Of course, deep down she had known nothing could come of it, and it was a relief now there was some distance between them, but it was no less painful for that. Her pride was battered and her heart was bruised.

* * *

Fifteen minutes after Juliet had left Lansdowne House, the entire household was lined up before Dominic in the hall, answering his questions. After intensive questioning, all he learned was that the previous day Miss Lockwood's brother had called and a short while later Geraldine Howard had arrived and both had been shown into the library, both having spent some time in there alone.

Later that same day a strained-looking Thomas came to see him, carrying a small package.

'Thomas?'

'I'd like a word with you, Dominic.'

'What about?'

'This.'

Thomas placed the package on the desk between them. Dominic raised questioning brows.

'Is that what I think it is?'

'The miniatures, yes. Knowing my sister, I suspected she was behind their disappearance. I tackled her about it when we got home and she admitted it.' He combed shaking fingers through his hair, clearly embarrassed and nervous about facing his friend concerning his sister's wrongdoing. 'Resentful of the attention Charles has been paying Miss Lockwood of late, she did it for no other reason than to frame Miss Lockwood's brother in the hope that she would leave.'

'My compliments to Geraldine on her duplicity, her vindictiveness and her dishonesty. She succeeded admirably,' Dominic snapped. 'Miss Lockwood no longer works for me.'

'Dominic—I'm sorry. I had no idea…'

Dominic shrugged. 'It doesn't matter. And if you've come here to ask me to keep this between ourselves, then you have my word on it. Not to protect your sister from scandal—feeling as I do right now, nothing would give me greater pleasure—but your parents. I value their friendship too much and would not wish a matter such as this to damage that.'

Thomas's expression was one of immense relief and gratitude. 'Thank you, Dominic. I can't tell you just how much that will mean to my family. I would like to keep this unfortunate incident to ourselves. I am deeply ashamed of Geraldine. If what the silly girl has done gets out, it will become a scandal that will explode all over the district.'

'I agree. Just one thing.'

'Yes?' Thomas saw his friend's jaw clench so tightly that a muscle began to throb in his cheek.

'If Geraldine is wise,' Dominic said in a soft, blood-chilling voice, eyeing his friend coldly, 'she will avoid me very carefully in the future.'

When Juliet reached London she took a hackney to the address in Cheapside Robby had given her. A small but fashionable, well-appointed house, it was the home of a friend of his who had accompanied him on his tour through Europe. Thankfully her brother was at home and received her with considerable surprise, but one look at her unhappy face and he knew all was far from well.

When Juliet was seated in a small sitting room and the door closed to the rest of the house, Robby sat down beside her. 'Juliet? Something is wrong, I can see that. Tell me.'

'You won't like it, Robby. It concerns you.'

Robby listened in silence as she told him what had brought her to London. In the immediate aftermath of such grim news and its dire ramifications for him, Robby sprang to his feet and immediately began disclaiming all knowledge of the theft. He was appalled that Miss Howard had implied that he was responsible, insulted, angry and upset that Juliet had been put in a position to have to defend him and resign her position, a very good position that she valued and enjoyed. Taking her hands in his, he raised her up to stand before him and looked deep into her eyes.

'You must believe me, Juliet, when I say I did not take those miniatures. I am many things, but I am not a thief.'

'I know that, Robby. You wouldn't do such a terrible thing.'

'And I think Miss Howard is mischievous and vindictive.'

'I think so too. Ever since I arrived she has resented the time Sir Charles Sedgwick spends at Lansdowne House, even though time and again I have tried sending him away. I think she saw me as some kind of threat, which is quite ridiculous.'

'Her trumped-up theft charges against me in revenge

could easily see me hanged for something I haven't done.'

Juliet blanched. 'It won't come to that.'

'I'll go and see Lansdowne, speak to him.'

Juliet's eyes filled with alarm. 'But you could be arrested.'

'If he believes I've stolen his property, then I shall be arrested anyway. And how can I prove that I have not? Better for me that I make the first move.'

'I believe the Duke is to travel to London himself tomorrow, Robby. He has a house somewhere in Mayfair. I don't know where, but with him being such a well-known, important personage, it shouldn't be very difficult to locate.'

'Then I'll call on him later tomorrow. But what of you, Juliet? What will you do now, with no work and no prospects of another position? And where will you live?'

'I shall have to find another position before my money runs out. I can't expect the Duke to give me a reference—and I wouldn't want him to now, so I'll write to Sir John. I know he'll be only too pleased. In the meantime, I've decided to go and see my grandfather. I don't know what will come of it, but it is something I have to do. I am not going to be reunited, never having met him, merely to listen to what he has to say. I also intend finding myself a position—somewhere away from London. I might even return to Bath, since I have friends there.'

Robby looked surprised and then he nodded. 'I'm glad you've decided to go and see the old man. That is good and it will be a relief to me. Despite his refusal to become reconciled with your mother, she would never allow any wrong to be said against her father. She always said he was a good man, reasonable and fair.'

'But not when she wanted to marry our father, a widower with a child—you, Robby—a man who was not very well off. He had nothing to offer her—certainly not for her to be kept in the lifestyle she had become accustomed to. But they loved each other. They wanted nothing more than that, and for the time they were together they were devoted to each other. One only had to look at them to see that.' She sighed, her wistful gaze staring into empty space. 'Not many married people can say that. For myself, I would settle for nothing less.'

Robby gave her a quizzical look. There was a sadness about her and a look of regret in her lovely dark eyes. And he was sure he could see the hint of tears. 'Hey,' he murmured gently, placing his finger beneath her chin and tipping her face up to his. 'What's brought this on? If you hadn't been in isolation in the country, I'd say someone had caught your fancy, Juliet, and stolen your heart.'

Juliet looked at down at her hands, and when she spoke her tone was guarded. 'Don't be silly, Robby. You know I'm not like that. I've no time to fill my head with foolish fancies.'

'What?' he lightly teased. 'Not even if the exceedingly handsome and charming Sir Charles Sedgwick pays you attention.'

Juliet flushed furiously. 'No, Robby, especially not

Sir Charles. I've told you he's to marry Miss Howard; and besides, the Duke disapproved of his visits, which he complained about distracting me from my work.'

She sensed Robby's sudden stiffening even before his eyes narrowed in a sharp glance.

'The Duke? Knowing his weakness for a pretty face, I have a distinct feeling that he was not averse to distracting you himself. Am I right, Juliet?'

Juliet checked abruptly, realising that, in her weary state, her expression had given away more than she intended.

'I am right, aren't I? There's something you're not telling me.' With a terrible suspicion growing inside him, gripping her upper arms, Robby thrust his face close to hers, his eyes hard and searching, the gentleness having vanished from his voice when he spoke. 'Did something happen between the two of you? What was it? A kiss?' When she looked away and bit on her trembling lip, he knew there was more. 'He gave you more than a kiss, didn't he? Did he compromise you? Did he dare to lay a finger on you?' He shook her harshly. 'God damn it, Juliet, tell me.'

His bright colouring told Juliet he was angry, and after the gruelling journey all her defences were down. The moment of reckoning had arrived. Robby waited, studying her every expression, and Juliet glanced over his shoulder while weariness crashed over her in waves.

'What did he do?' Robby persisted.

Forcing herself to look at her brother's tortured face, she swallowed, trying to drag her voice past the aching lump in her throat. 'Please don't make me tell you.

You'll hate me—although you can't hate me more than I hate myself just now.'

He stared at her in silence, and as his suspicion turned to reality, he was outraged over the enormity of it all. At length he said, 'He seduced you, didn't he? That—that bastard seduced you.'

Juliet shook her head, trying to control the poignant tug of her heart at the memory. White faced, she stared at him. Her disgrace was total. To have her brother question her virtue was damning. Her position was irredeemable. She felt the sharp sting of tears at the backs of her eyes. 'No, Robby,' she said, for to be fair to Dominic Lansdowne, she must shoulder some of the blame for what happened, 'he didn't seduce me.'

Appalled, he said, 'You mean you—you...'

'Yes,' she answered in an agonised whisper as she stared into her brother's beloved face. 'I did. What I mean is that I wanted him to. You said yourself that Dominic Lansdowne is irresistible to women. I can vouch for that. I know how disappointed and angry you must be, and I—I'm sorry, Robby.'

Robby's body stiffened as if he were trying to withstand a physical blow. 'Sorry? Is that all you can say when you have demeaned yourself? Dear Lord! You cheapened yourself by tumbling into bed with a renowned libertine, a man whose string of mistresses is so long he's lost count.'

Her brother looked taller than usual, older, angry. Juliet could not bear to look at him. 'He—only has the one, and it wasn't like that.'

'No? That's the way it looks to me. Lansdowne is a rake of the first order, for God's sake.'

'Robby, please stop it. Please don't be angry. I can't bear it.'

Robby couldn't believe it. He wanted to go and strike out at Dominic Lansdowne for taking advantage of his lovely, vulnerable sister, whom he had never stopped thanking God for the gift of her, for her beauty, her gaiety, her joy. And now Dominic Lansdowne had brought her to this.

'I am not a violent man by nature, Juliet, but when it comes to something as serious as this—when a damned rake has stolen my sister's virtue, then I can be as outraged as the next man. I could kill him. Do you love him?'

'In truth, I don't know,' she murmured, shaking her head miserably. 'What I do know is that it hurts.'

'You do realise that this cannot be overlooked, don't you? I shall confront him tomorrow.'

Her head shot up. 'No. I won't permit it, Robby, do you hear me? Go and see him over the matter of the stolen miniatures, but not this. I am a grown woman. I know my own mind and what I do is my affair.'

'He won't marry you, you know that, don't you?'

'Of course I know it, which is why he wanted me to be his mistress. He will marry someone like Geraldine Howard—a woman worthy of his own inflated opinion of himself. A woman to whom he will offer marriage, not some sordid liaison in exchange for her virtue.'

'Damn it, Juliet, you are still my sister—if I can't look out for you, then who can?'

'I don't need anyone to look out for me, Robby, do you hear me?' she said as he strode towards the door. 'I have had to look after myself for a long time.'

'And look where that has got you,' he threw back at her. 'You have fallen prey to the first dissolute character that comes along.'

'Where are you going?'

'To make arrangements for you to stay here tonight. It's too late for you to go to your grandfather now. You have to stay somewhere.'

She moved quickly across the room, halting him as he was about to leave. 'There is just one thing, Robby. Promise me you will not tell the Duke where I am. I don't want him to know. There is some money owing me for the work I have done. I would rather not have to ask,' she retorted bitterly, 'but I am going to need it.'

'You'll get what you're owed, Juliet. I'll see to that. And trust me. I will not tell him where you are.'

The day following Juliet's departure, Dominic's sleek, well-sprung travelling chaise left Lansdowne House for his house in London.

He was dictating a letter to Mr Lewis when Pearce tapped on the door of his study and entered.

'Yes, what is it?'

The butler cleared his throat. 'There is a gentleman to see you, your Grace.'

'Who is it?'

'A Mr Lockwood.'

To Dominic's annoyance his visitor pushed past Pearce, whose jaw dropped and his look became one of indignation. As he was about to voice his objections, Dominic said, 'Leave it, Pearce,' as with deadly calm he laid down his quill and stood up, shooting a look at his secretary that told him to leave.

Mr Lewis and Pearce left together, leaving Dominic and Robby glowering at each other.

'I would like a word, if you please, your Grace,' Robby retorted coldly.

'And if I don't please?'

'That's too bad, because you're going to listen to me. I will come to the point right away.'

Dominic hadn't known what to expect of Juliet's brother, but he had not expected him to be a man capable of delivering a scathingly descriptive, eloquently worded tirade that would put even him to shame.

'I am here to defend myself against some very serious charges laid against me, but I will begin by saying that since I am unskilled in both pistol and sword I cannot call you out as I would like, and if I were a violent man I would take a horse whip to you, damn you. You style yourself a man of honour, yet you readily dishonoured a gently bred, innocent girl to satisfy your lust. You seduced my sister while she was in your house, in your care, subjecting her to public censure and ridicule. Because of you, her reputation is ruined, compromised by a renowned reprobate. Deny it if you dare.'

It was madness, but at that moment Dominic admired everything about the man—a deeply concerned brother with principles above what was acceptable and what was not, a man of integrity and honesty. He intended to make Dominic feel ashamed.

He was succeeding.

'And then on some trumped-up charge against me, Juliet resigned her position and you damned well let her, a defenceless young woman, to face the world alone. Of all the cowardly, irresponsible bastards I have come across, you beat them all, *your Grace*,' he emphasised contemptuously.

A muscle moved spasmodically in Dominic's throat, but he made no effort to defend himself to Juliet's enraged brother. The accusations hurled at him combined with the torment of his own cruelty to Juliet before she had left. For a moment he stood locked in his memories of her, until the force of Robert Lockwood brought him back to the present.

'I apologise,' Dominic said, speaking for the first time since the tongue-lashing had begun. 'I confess that such behaviour was beneath me.'

Surprised by the quiet control of the other man, Robby stared. He didn't know what he'd expected, but it certainly wasn't an apology.

'And I will apologise to Juliet,' Dominic added.

'And the charge of theft?'

'Does not apply. When the miniatures went missing, only two people could have been responsible. You and one other.'

'Miss Howard?'

Dominic nodded.

'Did it not occur to you that my sister might have taken them?'

'No. Not for a second. And I did not accuse you. Even after Juliet left I remained open minded.'

'I take it the miniatures have been found?'

'Yes, and let that be an end to the matter.'

'I'm relieved to hear it. One spell in the Fleet is enough for any man.'

Dominic sensed a subtle reduction in the other man's hostility, but it wasn't evident in his next acid comment.

'If you'd exercised any decency and restraint in your lust when my sister was in your employ, she wouldn't now have the worry about whether or not she is with child.'

Torn between anger and embarrassment at having something pointed out that had already occurred to him, Dominic lifted his brows and looked at the angry young man. 'Which is a matter that has crossed my mind. If this turns out to be the case, I promise you I shall make provision for the child.'

'And Juliet?'

'Juliet also.'

'Pay her off, I think you mean,' Robby said scathingly.

Dominic's eyes narrowed ominously. 'I will not marry her.'

'That is the only decent thing you have said. Whomever Juliet marries, she deserves a man who will treat her with reverence and respect—as God intended men to treat their women. A man she can love. You, *your Grace*, are unworthy of her love.'

Robby's words hit their mark. Dominic blanched. 'Where is she?'

'That is none of your damned business. Any monies

owed my sister are to be sent to me.' He slapped a piece of paper on to the desk. 'That is the address where I am staying. I will see that she gets it. Good day.'

That said, Robby turned on his heel and left.

In the aftermath of Robert Lockwood's visit, his grace, Dominic Alexander Lansdowne, Duke of Hawksfield, descendent of three hundred years of nobility and possessor of wealth and estates beyond comprehension, was forced to admit that everything he had been accused of by Juliet's brother was true.

He had deliberately ruined a thoroughly decent, innocent girl and awarded her the final insult by suggesting she become his mistress.

Seeking some kind of succour, he called on Frances Parker, his current mistress, who welcomed him warmly by throwing her arms about his neck, with her low, throaty laugh telling him how much she'd missed him and that he really shouldn't spend so much of his time away from her in the country.

Until a few weeks ago Dominic had enjoyed her seductive voice and sensuous beauty. But now he found her lacking. Her eyes lacked a certain dark, warm lustre. She didn't look at him with that impudent, appraising sideways glance. Nor did she tremble in his arms with shy, slowly awakening emotions she couldn't understand. Frances was too practised, too eager to please, too available—but then he was paying her to be. She didn't stubbornly defy him. She wasn't intelligent or witty, nor did she call him your Grace.

She wasn't Juliet.

* * *

And so he left. Returning to his fine empty house, he poured himself a drink and then another, but finding he was unable to dull the ache that came with just the thought of Juliet.

He tortured himself by thinking of the way she had refused to become his mistress, and how he had cruelly mocked her. He dragged his thoughts from the torment of that time. He preferred the more refined torture of thinking about the joy of her, their light banter in the cornfield and on the day of the steeplechase, and he could visualise her exactly as she was in the garden at his sister's house, her lovely face aglow with innocent anticipation of what was to happen next. He thought of the way she had melted against him and kissed him with innocent passion, how warm she had felt in his arms, wonderful and loving.

Closing his eyes, he cursed himself for the fool he was for letting her go. He should have told her he did not believe her brother was guilty of stealing those wretched miniatures, and maybe if he had she would still be at Lansdowne House, but then, hadn't she told him she had made up her mind to leave anyway, when he had asked her to become his mistress?

Slamming his glass down, he left for his club, knowing there was nothing he could ever do to atone for the profane act he had committed against her, but when he found her he would apologise to her, as he had promised her brother he would.

That day following Dominic's confrontation with Juliet's irate brother, Cordelia arrived at his London house. Having heard of Juliet's sudden departure from her good friend Lady Howard, Geraldine's mother, she had come straight over to find out for herself what was going on. Looking both mystified and alarmed, she was admitted to the study, where Dominic was pouring over a column of figures.

'Dominic, I have heard Juliet has left,' she exclaimed, coming straight to the point.

'That is correct, Cordelia,' he replied, without looking up.

'Where has she gone, pray?' Cordelia asked, trying but without success to contain her impatience.

He shrugged. 'How should I know that? To her brother, I suppose.'

'I would like to know the reason why.'

Dominic threw down his quill and leaned back in his chair, knowing his sister would not be pacified until she knew the whole of it. Briefly he told her of the missing miniatures and that initially Juliet's brother had been suspected of taking them.

'Don't be ridiculous,' she snapped. 'Those miniatures are as precious to me as they are to you, and just because Juliet's brother has spent some time in the Fleet prison doesn't make him a thief. Some of the best people I know have spent time in prison for bad debts. Besides, he's hardly likely to risk his sister losing a respectable position by stealing from her employer.'

'The miniatures have been recovered, Cordelia. He didn't take them.'

'Well, that's a relief. Where did you find them?'

'All I will say is that they turned up. I would prefer to let the matter drop.'

'You must do what you think is best. But enough about the miniatures. It's Juliet I'm concerned about.'

'She left of her own accord, Cordelia.'

'That's a pity.' Cordelia was unable to conceal her mounting wrath by what she thought to be her brother's apparent lack of concern. 'That beautiful girl was enjoying her work at Lansdowne. Clearly she was put in such an impossible position by you that she must have felt compelled to give you her resignation.'

Dominic pushed back his chair and, standing up, stalked to the window, where he stood looking out, seeing nothing. 'Don't concern yourself. Miss Lockwood is clever. I am confident she will soon find a new position—or even someone to marry.'

It was clear to Cordelia that, while seeming calm on the outside, her brother was seething inside. 'That was *before* she encountered you.'

He spun round and looked at her. 'And what is that supposed to mean?'

'You tell me, Dominic,' his sister bit out, going to his side and glowering at his profile. 'My instinct tells me there is more to this than you want me to know about—and my instinct is never wrong. What did you do to her besides accusing her brother of being a thief? Seduce her? Running true to form, were you?'

'Damn it, Cordelia,' Dominic bit out, striding across the room and pouring himself a stiff drink. 'I don't have to listen to this.'

'No, you don't, but you're going to.' She went after him, determined to have her say. One look at his face told her she had hit upon the truth. Her expression was rigid. 'I am disappointed in you. You really are what everyone says you are, aren't you, Dominic? Your reputation for profligacy is well deserved. It was convenient for you having Miss Lockwood—young, attractive and desirable—living beneath your roof. And now if you have any decency, any honour, you will go after her and make amends, if you can and if she'll let you, because after this, she might very well tell you to go to the devil.'

'She already has—when I suggested that she become my mistress.' His tone was brutal and meant to shock. He succeeded.

Cordelia was so appalled her face turned chalk white. 'You really are quite heartless, Dominic. You took everything she had to offer and threw it in her face with an offer to prolong her humiliation by offering to make her your mistress. Did you have to insult the poor girl?'

'Why, what else could she expect? Marriage?' He stared at his sister, realising that this was precisely what she wanted. 'If I'd wanted to marry her, I'd have asked her,' he said acidly.

'So instead you insulted her by asking her to become your mistress in your usual autocratic way. Did you also tell her that you would set her up in a nice little house somewhere and shower her with jewels and fine clothes? Shame on you, Dominic,' she reproached harshly when his look told her he had done precisely that. 'And you being who you are cannot understand why she refused you.' Cordelia laughed bitterly. 'I was not wrong. I knew I liked Juliet Lockwood from the start—I also knew that you wanted her, but you wanted her on your terms. Nothing else would do.'

Dominic scowled darkly at her. 'I am gratified that you are enjoying this, Cordelia, but for once I wish you would see things my way.'

'On this occasion I am wholly behind Juliet. She is proud, a woman of principals, and she has the right to expect to be treated better than this. You want her, and you care for her, and you hate yourself for that weakness. If you wanted her to despise you, then you have gone the right way about it.'

Dominic's features tightened. 'You are intruding into a situation that is none of your affair, Cordelia.'

'I like Juliet, I care about her, so I am making it my affair. She is an extraordinary young woman, thoroughly delightful. Her manners are charming, she is easy and conversable and highly intelligent—and beautiful to boot—witty, too. You can't deny it. The girl's unique.'

'I don't deny it,' Dominic replied harshly, remembering Juliet's intriguing ability to look like a lady one minute, and a sweet, innocent child the next. 'But she's no longer here.'

'No. That's the pity of it. You humiliated her so thoroughly she probably won't forgive you for it. Now you can either enjoy your triumph or go after her.'

Dominic glanced at her sharply. 'And? What then?'

'Ask her to marry you,' Cordelia said outright, her words shocking Dominic to such an extent that as he was about to knock back his whisky his hand froze halfway to his mouth.

He stared at his sister as if she'd taken leave of her senses. 'What did you say?'

'I said marry her. I can't remember the last time a woman got you into such a lather. It's about time you stopped regarding women as mere bed warmers and entered into a more stable relationship. Amelia is dead. Yes, she humiliated you, damaged your male pride and made you a laughing stock among some of those you thought were your friends when she jilted you at the altar, but that was eight years ago and life goes on. You can't go on dwelling over former grievances. In my opinion, Juliet Lockwood is nothing like Amelia. She will make you an excellent wife.'

'God damn it, Cordelia,' he flared, his voice rising. 'I can't marry her.'

'Why not?'

'Because she's…she's…well…' For the first time Dominic was lost for words.

'What? Hasn't got the right pedigree?'

Suddenly Dominic's entire body tensed. His eyes jerked to Cordelia's and his face became a cynical mask. 'It isn't that she hasn't the right pedigree, she hasn't got any pedigree at all.'

'Does it really matter, Dominic? I have every confidence she will make you a good wife.'

'Society would never accept her,' he argued.

'I think that by now you are extremely secure enough in your position in society not to be bothered by such old-fashioned prejudices.'

'Cordelia, correct me if I'm wrong, but there was a time when you considered birth and breeding were the ultimate requirements in the woman I might one day marry.'

'I've changed my mind. And when did you care what society thinks of you? You've given society plenty to gossip about in your time—why should you worry about it now?'

'I am not thinking of myself, Cordelia.'

'Then that's a first.'

He shot her a look of annoyance and then sighed, his mood softening. 'I would not want her to be the victim of vicious tongues. Geraldine Howard has given her a taste of how it would be. Social prejudices will exclude her from respectable *ton* activities and I can imagine the society papers tearing her to shreds for being some kind of gold digger, an opportunist, attempting to ensnare a duke. I couldn't bear to put her through that.'

Cordelia's smile was one of immense satisfaction, and when she spoke she was almost purring. 'Well, well. Do I hear angels sing at last? It seems to me that you are quite besotted.'

'You can think what you like, Cordelia, but one way or another I will do right by her.' Putting down his glass, he played his hands deep into his pockets and with a brooding look stared past his sister, thinking of Juliet.

He saw her as she had stood against him, courageous and lovely, and he saw her as she had looked up at him after making love, her eyes filled with innocent passion. She was gentle and proud, brave and innocent, and with a surge of remorse he recalled how she had driven him mad with desire, and how she had filled his every waking moment since. His house should have been a place of safety, a place where she could live and work unmolested from the people within its walls, when the greatest danger to her had been the master himself. Self-disgust almost choked him.

'I know I treated her very badly and I will have to find a way to remedy that.'

'Marrying her would be a perfect way to redeem yourself. Will you marry her?'

'Damn it, Cordelia,' he uttered hoarsely, 'I can't.'

Despite his stubborn determination to stand firm, Cordelia smiled. Never had she seen her brother in such torment over a woman since Amelia. Nothing definite had been achieved, but she was satisfied that the outcome she was working towards would soon become a reality. 'But neither do you want to let her go. So, if she refuses to become your mistress, what else can you do?'

'What else indeed, Cordelia, but whatever I decide, I have to find her first.'

Dominic spent what was left of the day and all night fighting a mental battle against the insidious doubt and confusion that raged inside him, and it was all to do with one woman he could not rid his mind of no matter how hard he tried.

Most of the women he was acquainted with were available to him at the crook of his finger, some of the most beautiful women in London and beyond, but none of them especially stood out and appealed to him—

only one, who had particularly warm dark brown eyes
and a wealth of gleaming hair, someone with warmth
and goals and ideals, someone who would thaw the ice
inside him.

He sighed dejectedly. There wasn't enough fire in
the world to thaw him out and make him feel the way
he had for Amelia in those heady, golden days of his
youth when he had fallen in love, and even if there
were, he could not let it happen again. Behaving like a
lovesick calf was not his style.

But—and yet—Juliet, lying in his arms that night,
giving herself to him with unselfish ardour that had
driven him mad with desire, Juliet, with her glowing
eyes and musical laughter.

By the time the sun rose he'd lost his battle, and he
didn't regret it. After eating a hearty breakfast and calling on his sister to tell her that he fully intended asking
Juliet to marry him, he felt much better.

Three days after leaving Lansdowne House, Juliet
went to see her grandfather at his town house in Pic-
cadilly. Despite her cold detachment, she felt an odd
sense of unreality. She got out of the carriage and lifting her skirts slightly, climbed the steps to the house
with as much dignity as she could muster. The front
door was opened by an elderly, black-clad butler.

'Good afternoon. I am here to see the Earl of Fairfax.'

The loyal retainer's eyes rested on her face and Juliet
thought he looked on the verge of tears.

'Good afternoon,' he replied, his voice hoarse with

emotion. 'Would I be correct in thinking you are Miss Louisa's daughter?'

'Yes, you would,' she answered, smiling at the sublime pleasure that creased the butler's lined face. 'I am here to see my grandfather—if he is at home.'

'He is. I am his butler, known as Hewitt. I would like to welcome you to the Earl's London house, my lady.'

The smile vanished from Juliet's lips. 'I am Miss Lockwood,' she corrected him, seeing his eyes fill with disappointment. 'That is how I like to be addressed.' He recovered himself, however, and asked Juliet to step inside the wide, oak-panelled hall.

Footmen and housemaids seemed to be lurking about, several of them stealing curious looks at her. Her mind on the forthcoming meeting with her grandfather, Juliet was oblivious to the searching scrutiny, but she was faintly aware that a few of the servants looked at her with a profound sadness.

'I will just go and inform your grandfather you have arrived. Your coming here will mean a great deal to him.'

When Hewitt returned he showed her into a comfortable sitting room. She walked towards a chair where a man slowly rose with some authority. As he straightened he stood perfectly still, rigidly erect and aristocratic, but his eyes were warm as he faced her. Juliet felt an almost physical shock, for she realised that her own face bore a startling resemblance to the Earl's, whereas she'd scarcely resembled her own father. He was surprisingly tall and slender, with a good head of well-groomed white hair, and for a man in his early sixties, he was still very handsome.

Edward Fairfax was studying his granddaughter, too, his eyes clinging to the lovely young woman standing before him. He saw Louisa exactly as she had looked so long ago. How well and how lovingly he remembered his daughter. He smiled slowly, and an odd tenderness glowed in his eyes.

'You resemble your mother,' he said in a strong tone.

'Yes, I know.' Juliet firmly ignored the mistiness she saw in her grandfather's dark eyes, undimmed by age. 'You wrote to me. I have come to hear what you have to say.'

'Thank you. I appreciate that. Please,' he said, indicating a chair across from his own, 'will you be seated?'

Juliet did as he bade, sitting stiffly, perching straight backed on the edge of the chair, and waited until he'd settled himself.

'I have waited for this moment for a long time. Do not deprive me of an old man's pleasure of welcoming you home, for when all is said and done, this house and the estate in Scotland will be rightfully yours one day.'

'I have not come here to mend the breach. Only my mother could do that. And I have not come to claim anything. I am not interested in anything you might leave. I don't want your money or your property or a grand title. It's all meaningless to me, and in all truth I have never given it any thought. I have got on very well on my own for a long time.'

'You work for a living, I know that. I am grateful that you could take time off to come here—to see me.'

'I am between positions just now. I—intend finding a position away from London.'

'You worked for the Duke of Hawksfield, I believe.'

'For a short while—cataloguing his library.'

'He's an exacting man.'

'Yes, very. Are you acquainted with him?'

'No. I have seen him on occasion, but we've never been formally introduced. I know his sister—Lady Cordelia Pemberton—pleasant, likeable lady. Speaks her mind, which is what I like.'

'Yes. I like her too. I—do not know if my mother would mind me coming to see you. By your own actions I do not know you. You are a stranger to me.'

'I do not wish to remain a stranger to you, Juliet. Now, I am sure you would like some tea after your journey.'

Juliet looked towards the door when it opened. As if Hewitt were some kind of clairvoyant, he appeared bearing a tray of refreshment. He placed it on a small table between the Earl and his granddaughter.

'Thank you,' Juliet said with a self-conscious smile directed at Hewitt. With a slight inclination of his head he returned her smile and withdrew.

'Will you be so kind as to pour the tea?' Edward asked.

'Of course.'

There was silence as Juliet went through the familiar ritual of pouring the tea, all the while aware of her grandfather's eyes watching her every move, and she was unaware as she handed him a cup of the steaming beverage, how his heart swelled with pride at the lovely young woman who he sincerely hoped would carry on after him.

The news of Louisa's death had hit him hard and he would have made contact with his granddaughter then, had he not had to go through her father. Despite all the years, he had still found it impossible to face the man who had taken his daughter, and it wasn't until he, too, had died that he wrote to Juliet.

For many years his beloved Louisa had flung her defiance to comply to his wishes back in his face, and while that might have enraged another man, he had recognised in the gesture the same proud arrogance and indomitable will that had marked every member of the Fairfax family. At the moment, however, that indomitable will was on a collision course with his own, for he recognised that same strength of determination that marked Juliet as Louisa's daughter.

He was prepared to yield to almost anything to get what he wanted most in the world—his granddaughter; if he couldn't have her love and forgiveness, he would like her respect and her understanding. He also wanted and needed absolution, to be forgiven for making one of the biggest mistakes of his life, and for waiting too long to admit it, for his beloved Louisa had died. To that end he wanted Juliet to remain with him, to take her back to Scotland, to Fairfax Hall, to get to know her, cherish the time they would have together, and hoard the memories in his heart during the long, empty years ahead if she chose to leave him.

Suddenly he found himself saying, 'I missed your mother so much. When she left it broke my heart. I deeply regret what happened between us, but you must understand how difficult it was for me to accept that my only daughter—a young woman I loved and had such high hopes for—ran away and married a man without means and a son already.'

'His first wife had died. He did not abandon her.'

'No, I do know that.'

'It needn't have been like that. You could have accepted the situation, then she wouldn't have run away.'

He shook his head slowly. 'I couldn't do that.' Sipping his tea, after a moment's thought, he said, 'I have named you legally as my heir, Juliet. Despite your aversion to face the truth, you are endowed with all the wealth and estates that are your birthright.'

'There must be someone else you can leave it to.'

He nodded slowly, studying her, sensing a sadness in her. 'There are several cousins who would like to get their hands on it, but they are spineless ner' do wells and would bankrupt the estate within a year. When you marry—and I sincerely hope you do—should your husband have property of his own, Fairfax Hall could be kept in trust for any children you might have.'

Despite herself, Juliet smiled. 'I see you've thought of everything.'

He returned her smile. 'You are between positions, so will you not stay here for a while? I shall be returning to Scotland very soon and when I do, should you wish to, you could go with me—get to know the house where your mother grew up. Fairfax Hall is a lovely old house. It was a happy house once. It could be again.'

With a thousand emotions warring in her heart and mind, Juliet was sick in conscience. She'd spent a lifetime hating her grandfather for the manner in which he had treated her mother. But now she could see how he too had suffered the loss of his beloved daughter. But his love had remained constant. It had endured despite absence and silence. She could see how he grieved for her still. His face spoke of deep loss and regret.

Some stiffness went out of her shoulders and she began to relax. She poured them both another cup of tea and sat back in her chair to think over his proposal. She considered refusing, but there was something imploring and almost urgent in her grandfather's look when she hesitated, and she reluctantly nodded.

'Very well. I will stay here for the time being—but I am not sure I want to go to Scotland. I suspect there will be gossip. What will you say to everyone? How will you explain the woman living in your house?'

'By telling the truth if anyone asks. You are my granddaughter and I shall be proud to introduce you as such. And in the meantime I shall do my best to make your stay permanent—Lady Juliet.'

Beginning to warm to the idea of getting to know her grandfather better, Juliet found herself responding to his warm friendliness with an affection that all too soon was taking root in her heart. She had wanted to hold on to the resentment implanted after many years believing he was some kind of tyrant who had mistreated her mother, but this man was no tyrant, just a sad, lonely old man whose heart had been broken.

She smiled. 'You can try—although I must say that such a change in lifestyle would be hard to get used to. It will take some getting used to answering to Lady Juliet.' Her dark eyes twinkled with amusement. 'It doesn't sound like me at all.'

'Nevertheless that is what you are, and one day you will be a countess.'

Juliet's eyes widened. 'A countess?'

'Of course. As my only child, your mother would have taken the title. You are her eldest and only child, therefore the title—when I am gone, will be yours. Whatever you decide to do, a young lady needs much in the way of clothes and other fashionable things. I shall ask Hewitt to arrange for a dressmaker to call and fit you out with all the finery a young lady needs. While you are here I shall make you an allowance to spend as you wish.'

Juliet gasped. 'That is most generous of you, but I don't—'

He raised a hand, silencing her. 'Please hear me out. You have been raised feeling resentment towards me. I can understand that and I cannot blame you. I can only hope that once you have thought over the circumstances of your situation, your heart will soften towards me. Do not allow pride to prevent you from having the security my position can provide.'

Juliet drew a deep breath and nodded slowly, already feeling she could be persuaded to like this gentle man. 'We shall see.'

Chapter Eight

In London, Dominic went about his usual business, certain a reply from Miss Millington at the Academy Juliet had attended in Bath would arrive throwing some light on to Juliet's whereabouts. When it came, Miss Millington politely wrote that she was sorry, but she could not help him.

Both his confidence and his worry that Juliet had disappeared completely from his life were replaced by a deeper, darker feeling of uncertainty. It was a new emotion to him, and one of which he did not like. Behind closed doors he paced back and forth. One way or another he would find her. He would not give up.

When he did find her, what if she refused to speak to him? What if she was with child? How would she cope? She was proud and stubborn and, damn it, she had no right to conceal it. He could feel doubt eating away into his soul with every minute that passed without word from her. What if, when he asked her to marry him, she refused him outright? What if she refused to listen? He shook his head. No, he would not accept that. He had to press upon her how much he wanted her. How much he loved her.

He laughed at himself. No, not that. Love was for fools, and he was anything but a fool.

Word soon got about that Earl Fairfax's granddaughter had taken up residence at his London house, arousing much curiosity and speculation. Invitations for them to attend this and that began arriving by the dozen on a daily basis.

'I enjoy going out in society, and now you are here I shall enjoy showing you off,' the Earl said. 'To begin with I shall only accept those invitations I think suitable, nothing too extravagant, and I am sure you will enjoy Vauxhall. The gardens are quite spectacular and there's always a good turn out.'

The largest event they were invited to attend was Lord Fitzherbert's ball. He staged three balls and suppers yearly for the nobility, which the Earl decided would be the perfect occasion for her to make her entry into society. As he turned away he didn't notice how Juliet suddenly paled, and if he knew the true reason, that Dominic Lansdowne was to attend the same event and she never wanted to see him again, he might have declined the invitation. But Juliet knew her grandfather and Lord Fitzherbert were good friends and that he was looking forward to escorting her, so she kept her unease to herself.

Suddenly Juliet felt much more optimistic about her new life, and she wrote to Robby, telling him all about it. Her grandfather insisted on her having a complete new wardrobe and a lady's maid to assist her. At first she refused, but lost out in the end when the dressmaker arrived bringing with her a tempting array of sumptuous materials, the like of which she had only ever seen adorning the very rich.

Robby replied to her letter, telling her how happy he was to hear she was reconciled with her grandfather, and going on to tell her of his encounter with the Duke of Hawksfield. Juliet was relieved the matter of the miniatures had been settled. Robby didn't say how they had been recovered, but Juliet felt certain Geraldine Howard had been behind it. Certain that she had taken them as a means of getting Juliet to leave Lansdowne House, regardless of the dreadful consequences to Robby, it left her seething.

Only when she closed the bedroom door at night did her mind turn to the handsome Duke of Hawksfield. He haunted her dreams and with a tightening twinge of pain around her heart she realised how deeply she missed him. Remembering their one night of love, she would feel herself softening inside, along with a stirring of pleasure like a ray of sunshine peeping out from behind the dark clouds, and then she would abruptly pull herself together. Just when she had begun to feel alive again, she didn't want to risk her fragile, newfound tranquillity, and she had no intention of getting hurt again.

* * *

It was early afternoon. Arm in arm with her grand-father, Juliet strolled along the paths in Vauxhall Gardens, a slight breeze skimming her face.

The gardens, on the south bank of the river and frequently the venue for some landmark event, beckoned people from all walks of life. They came to enjoy themselves and to see the enticements—the beautiful pavilions and statues, temples and grottoes, to stroll up the famous Grand Walk bordered with elms, listen to the concerts that played throughout the summer and to dance and while away the time drinking tea in some pleasant corner.

While waiting for Cordelia to catch up after pausing to speak to an acquaintance, Dominic's attention was caught by a couple strolling arm in arm along one of the gravel walks. He recog-nised the gentleman as the Earl of Fairfax, but his eyes levelled on the lady—for that's what she looked like, a lady, fashionably and expensively attired in an emerald-green muslin gown. Her face was flushed and upturned to that of her companion. The two looked close and she was laughing delightedly at something he said.

Juliet! Dominic didn't stop to ask himself what she was doing at Vauxhall. It was enough for him that she was here that he had found her at last.

Juliet's grandfather paused to speak to a group of people, and, patting her hand, he broke away from her. She couldn't say what it was that made her turn at that moment—perhaps it was the prickling sensation she suddenly felt on the back of her neck—but turn she did, and with a shock that tightened itself about her heart, she looked into the face of Dominic Lansdowne. Happiness soared through her, and a joyous smile sprang to her lips.

He must have been watching her for some time, for he was not as stunned as she was. Juliet felt as though she had been struck, like Lot's wife to a pillar of salt, unable to move, unable to form any sort of coherent thought. She was like a senseless, inanimate object, mindless, and she thought she might have remained this way for ever, with the crowd milling around them. Although there was noise, laughter, the conversation of people who came to these pleasure gardens to absorb the atmosphere and socialise, there was stillness and silence about them.

Juliet felt herself relax, her limbs coming back to life, her eyes still fastened to his, drifting on the enchantment of being in the same place as him, breathing the same air. They stood quite still in those first few moments, savouring each other, their eyes seeking the truth, which was what they had felt for one another was still there. But too much had been said, too many insults that were still deeply painful for Juliet, too much humiliation remembered for her to succumb once more to this man, and had she not vowed that she would not be hurt by him again?

Having made up his mind to make her his wife, Dominic was even more eager to speak to Juliet, to feast his eyes on her again and hold her in his arms, to hear her soft, musical voice and to know the exquisite sensation of having her slender, voluptuous body curved against his.

He was about to move towards her, but at that moment her companion returned. Juliet turned away and, smiling up at the Earl, linked her arm through his and sauntered on without a backwards glance.

Dominic continued to watch her and in the space of a moment his mind registered disbelief, shocked by what he was seeing. It started to shout denials, while something inside him cracked and began to crumble. The Earl of Fairfax? Impossible! Surely not! She was prim and proper, a woman of principal. Damn it! She was his!

But there she was, and she no longer looked like Juliet—his neatly dressed prim-and-proper employee. He stared in awe at the beautiful creature—an elegant goddess. Her gleaming rich brown tresses were swept up in a sleek and sophisticated arrangement beneath a fetching little hat. Small diamond droplets dripped from her ears, and her dress, in his opinion, was cut too low for an afternoon.

One only had to look at the way she clung to the arm of the Earl of Fairfax to see they were lovers. A murderous, crimson hot rage such as he had never known boiled inside him like fiery acid at the sight of another man touching what he considered belonged to him—and sickening jealousy, destroying his tender feelings for her. To think that while he'd spent the last few weeks searching for her, going out of his mind with concern for her and wanting her like a besotted fool, she'd been giving her favours to another.

Damn her conniving little heart. She was nothing but a cheap, mercenary opportunist.

It was later, when Juliet and her grandfather were taking refreshments with a group of his friends in one of the tea gardens that Juliet again saw Dominic, strolling along one of the serpentine paths with Lady Pemberton, who was looking her way.

Excusing herself to her grandfather, she went to speak to them, recoiling when she looked at Dominic. His face was expressionless, remote, but his silver-grey eyes gleamed hard and cold.

Cordelia greeted her warmly, genuinely pleased to see her again. Dominic had told her that Juliet was at Vauxhall with the Earl of Fairfax, and what he suspected, but unlike her brother Cordelia could not and would not believe her young friend had taken a lover.

'Why, Juliet!' She drew her into a secluded arbour, away from prying eyes. 'This is a pleasant surprise. And how well you look.' She turned to her stony-faced brother, who had reluctantly followed them. 'Doesn't she look well, Dominic?'

'Never better,' he ground out.

Juliet actually flinched at the ruthless fury in his eyes as they raked over her, but she raised her chin and held her ground, clutching her parasol in front of her. 'I am perfectly well,' she replied. 'As you can see, I have survived our last encounter without scars. I hope you were successful in finding someone else to continue the work I started.'

'Not yet, but I will. Your brother came to see me.'

'Yes, I know. Thank you for the bank draft. It settles things between us.'

'Do you often come to Vauxhall, Juliet?' Cordelia asked, aware of the tension between these two, which could be cut with a knife.

'This is my first time. There is so much to see and do. The gardens are extremely pleasant.'

'Indeed they are,' Cordelia agreed, suddenly distracted when she heard someone calling her name and a lady appeared in the opening to the arbour. Excusing herself, Cordelia sped off to speak to her.

'You will find them so during the day,' Dominic retorted, scowling darkly at his sister's departing figure before bringing his gaze back to Juliet, 'but at night they are altogether different. In fact, you might find them more to your taste.'

Juliet stiffened when his ice-cold eyes came to rest on her. 'Please explain what you mean by that.'

'At night they are not so genteel. A stigma of disreputability clings to Vauxhall then; in fact, they really do become pleasure gardens in every sense—gardens of vice, when sexual intrigue stalks some of the garden's remote avenues, when ladies of the town frequent the dark walks.' He smiled contemptuously. 'I'm quite certain you would find it interesting,' he remarked with unconcealed sarcasm.

His censure filled Juliet with a surge of angry rebellion, but, confused by his remark, she managed to hold on to her temper as she asked, 'Excuse me, but—what are you talking about?'

'That it must be quite an intoxicating experience for

you to parade up Vauxhall's Grand Walk on the arm of one of the most eligible men of the aristocracy—even if it is only as his mistress. In fact, if you play your cards right, with your looks and figure you could become the greatest demi-rep in London. Why, the Regent himself might show an interest—if the Earl permits if, of course.'

His insults sliced through Juliet, and it suddenly dawned on her what he was thinking; though horrified and appalled that he could even think so badly of her, she had no intention of enlightening him. She lifted her eyebrows coolly.'

'I confess that the Earl and I have become close. Indeed, I am very fond of him.'

Jealousy ripped through Dominic on hearing those endearing words for another man on her lips. Brushing back the sides of his jacket, he put his hands on his hips and planted his booted legs apart in a decidedly aggressive manner. 'I am surprised you settled for an earl when you could have had a duke,' he drawled in an awful voice.

Despite the outrageous attack on her character, Juliet's soft lips broke into a smile. 'One title is as much like another to me and means very little. My new status is certainly an improvement on the last.'

Dominic's face tightened with distaste as he looked down at her breasts swelling above the bodice of her elegant and expensive gown. She displayed no more than any other woman in the gardens, but this was Miss Juliet Lockwood who, apart from the one night she had revealed the glories of her body to him, had never revealed more than her face and hands.

'Isn't your display of flesh a little vulgar for this time of day?' His manner was chilling.

Juliet's eyes opened wide, and suddenly she wanted to laugh out loud. 'You should know the meaning of that word very well, your Grace, since your own conduct about town could often be described as precisely that. As for what I am wearing, this gown is the very height of fashion and extremely pretty.'

'And easy for the Earl to remove later,' Dominic uttered scathingly. 'Why are you with him?'

Juliet listened to him with outrage burning inside her, wanting to throw her new-found status in his face, but for some perverse reason she wanted to keep her relationship with the Earl of Fairfax from him. With as much dignity as she could muster, she replied evasively, 'I am with him for the usual reasons.'

'Money, influence and a very comfortable position, I suppose,' Dominic summarised with scathing disgust. 'I offered you all three, and much more, as I recall.'

'When you thought Robby had stolen those miniatures, I asked you to trust me, to have faith in me and accept my word that he did not take them. You refused. Everything that happened that day made it impossible for me to remain at Lansdowne House—with you. I am content with the way things have turned out. I happen to like the Earl of Fairfax very much, and he likes me.'

'Of course he does.' Dominic's sardonic gaze swept over her lovely face with its clear skin, slightly tilted warm dark eyes, and full soft lips that positively invited a man to kiss it. Tendrils of her hair drifted like whispered secrets against the curve of her cheek, precisely where he should have liked to place his lips. His eyes dropped to her voluptuous breasts trembling invitingly above the neckline of her gown. Desire poured through him. She had a body that was created for a man's hands, a body that could drive a man to lust.

Recollecting himself, he forced his gaze away, his pulse hammering. He had given her a taste for the pleasure love making could give, and merely knowing she was sharing those pleasures with another man sent ripples of unrest into the hollow place that was his soul. He despised himself for his sudden weakness.

'You are beautiful—you are also amoral, and I congratulate you on your success in snaring an earl. I thought you were a woman with heart and spirit, not some mercenary little opportunist.'

This unprovoked attack was too much for Juliet. 'I am not stupid enough to stand here and feel obliged to listen to you accuse me of being mercenary, lacking in morals—and—and some kind of parasite. How dare you say those things to me?' she flared, angry and hurt by this unfair condemnation from him of all people.

'Why not?' he bit out, wanting to hurt her as much as she had hurt him. 'Evidently, you are all those things.'

'And you are an arrogant, overbearing, spoiled aristocrat who, from what I understand, seems to spend all your time in the pursuit of pleasure and diversion.'

'And I am somewhat surprised you have come to this,' he said, without bothering to deny her accusation, since there was a modicum of truth in it. 'I am willing to concede I treated you badly, but I did not expect you to do anything like this. After meeting your brother— a forthright man with strong principles, I am surprised he allows it.'

Juliet gave him a mocking twist of a smile. 'Robby fully approves of my relationship with the Earl; in fact, he's encouraged it.'

Dominic was taken aback and exasperated beyond measure. 'Then the man's a fool.'

Juliet stiffened with indignation and her eyes flashed like fireworks. 'Do not insult my brother. He is one of the finest men I know. You're not fit to wipe his boots.'

'In your eyes, perhaps not, but he is also thoughtless and irresponsible.'

'And your standards are so perfect you consider yourself an authority to judge him, I suppose,' she uttered sarcastically, her cheeks aflame, suppressing the desire to hit him over the head with her parasol. 'I wonder why, when you have a propensity to insult me at every turn, you deemed to speak to me at all.'

'And I wonder why, since you left my employ with such haste, you approached me in the first place.'

'I was merely being polite,' she shot back, her voice rising.

'And were you merely being polite when you invited me into your bed?'

Juliet recoiled as though she'd been stung. 'It wasn't like that and you know it. Little did I realise when I agreed to work for you that you are a predatory amorist, and that my virtue would be seen as some kind of challenge to you, regardless of my station. Although since I have been given a full account of your behaviour, I would expect no less of you.'

He stepped closer to her, his eyes penetrating, cold and ruthless, his jaw tightening ominously. When she had left him at Lansdowne House she had looked like a wounded child. Now he was confronted with a woman he didn't recognise—an enraged, beautiful virago. Instead of apologising, as he'd intended to do when he had made up his mind to make her his wife, he clamped his hand about her wrist and said,

'Something I have always done is to steer clear of demi-reps, for their philosophy of making profit from selling themselves has always revolted me. I have never been that desperate.'

'You, your Grace, are a hypocrite,' Juliet accused coldly. 'After all, you are not averse to keeping a mistress or two yourself, are you?'

'That is different. While she is with me she is mine exclusively. No other man enjoys her favours.'

'Really? Well, it seems exactly the same to me—and don't manhandle me,' she warned, pulling her arm free with a wrenching tug that nearly dislocated her shoulder, then stepped back, well out of his reach, her chest rising and falling in fury. 'You are an animal,' she hissed.

His lips twisted laconically. 'Tell me something I don't already know.'

Juliet lifted her head to a lofty angle. 'This conversation is going nowhere. I think enough has been said between us.'

Dominic glared at her. 'Too damn right it has', and

then without another word he turned on his heel and strode swiftly away.

Juliet watched him stalk past the staring crowd, and knew that in all probability he had just left her life for ever. Forcing back her dammed-up tears, she turned to see her grandfather walking towards her.

Smiling, when she spoke she tried to keep her voice from trembling, but the strain in her face remained for her grandfather to wonder at. 'I'm sorry to have been gone so long.'

'Not at all.' He studied her closely. 'Unless my eyes deceive me, that was the Duke of Hawksfield you were speaking to?'

'Yes, it was.'

'I well know that he has not always lived a life that is above reproach. He ran with a wild crowd in his early days—gaming and drinking, before distinguishing himself in the army.' He looked down at her, a worried frown creasing his brow. 'I hope his treatment of you when you resided under his roof was exemplary?'

Juliet averted her eyes. 'Yes, of course it was. He was my employer.'

'Did you like working for him? I never did ask.'

'I enjoyed my work. Lansdowne House has a fine library.'

'You prevaricate, my dear. That was not what I asked.'

She sighed. 'I know.'

'Why did you leave? Was your work finished?'

'No. Far from it. The Duke and I—we—we had a

difference of opinion—and I considered it in my own best interests to terminate my employment.'

Her grandfather noted the catch in her voice. 'He upset you?'

'The Duke is very good at upsetting people, especially women.'

Her grandfather's face tightened as a terrible suspicion began to take root. 'Why did you leave if your work was unfinished? What happened between you?'

Juliet looked away. She couldn't possibly tell him how she had willingly let him make love to her, how she was unable to blot out of her mind the exquisite sweetness of the night she had spent in the Duke of Hawksfield's arms. The memory of his passionate kisses, of his whispered words of praise and passion, kept coming back to torment her, and there was nothing she could do about it. Sometimes she didn't even want to.

And so she looked for another answer to her grandfather's question, and said, 'It was about Robby.' She gave him a brief account of the missing miniatures, and how, because Robby had spent some time in a debtor's prison, and because he had been alone in the library that day, he was suspected of stealing them. 'My position became untenable.'

'And did he take them?'

'No. He wouldn't. The miniatures turned up after I left.'

'That must have been a relief. Did the Duke not ask you to return to your position?'

'No. Besides, he didn't know where to contact me.'

'Would you have gone back?'

'No. My leaving Lansdowne House was—unpleasant. Too many things were said—by both of us.'

Digesting what she had told him, her grandfather studied her unhappy face for a moment. 'You are a grown woman, Juliet, who knows her own mind and is her own mistress, so I won't interfere in what is not my affair. But I sense there is something else—something you're not telling me. I felt when you first came to me that you were unhappy about something. I'm a good listener if you want to talk about it?'

She shook her head. 'It's nothing, truly. Please don't worry about me.'

'When I saw him just now, the Duke looked decidedly put out about something.'

'He was—very. In fact it was all so silly really.'

'He knows you are my granddaughter?'

'No, I didn't tell him—he didn't give me the chance.' A mischievous twinkle entered her eyes. 'He assumed that you and I—because he saw us together—that we are...'

Comprehension dawned and seeing the funny side of it, her grandfather threw back his head and laughed out loud. 'For a man who is way past his prime, his youth just a distant memory, that is the most flattering thing that has happened to me in a long time. If that is what he believes, then he's been well and truly duped.'

'I know, and I can imagine just how furious he will be when he finds out the truth.'

Her grandfather's face settled in more serious lines. 'You know that I would give you my full support it you wished to stand against friend or foe, don't you?' he said gently.

His quiet offering touched Juliet and nearly destroyed her fragile grip on her emotions. 'I do,' she said, taking his arm and walking along the path. 'But it won't come to that. My time spent at Lansdowne House employed by the Duke of Hawksfield is well and truly in the past.'

Making her way back to Dominic, Cordelia saw him striding quickly away from the arbour where she had left him with Juliet. One look at the murderous fury on his face told her the meeting had not gone well. Shaking her head with exasperation, she hurried to his side and accompanied him out of the gardens to where their carriage waited. After handing his sister up, Dominic flung himself in after her and snapped orders to the driver. He leaned back. Not until they were travelling did either of them speak.

'Dominic—Juliet—'

'Can go to hell with the Earl of Fairfax—a man way past his prime whom she evidently prefers to me,' he said dispassionately. The words were devoid of concern; not even his eyes showed interest. Ever since Juliet had walked out of Lansdowne House he had been making desperate enquiries into her whereabouts, but it was as if she'd disappeared into thin air. And now he knew why he hadn't been able to locate her. The existence of a lover was the only thing that made sense.

When he'd asked her to become his mistress she had rejected him and would have left him anyway—despite that unfortunate issue with the missing minia-

tures—because she hadn't wanted him, and had sought
the protection of another man. But Edward Fairfax?
Dear God! Handsome he might still be, but he was old
enough to be her father—or her grandfather.

'You are jumping to conclusions, Dominic,' Cordelia told him. 'Did Juliet actually tell you that the Earl
of Fairfax is her lover?'

'She didn't have to.'

'But there might be an excellent explanation for her
being with him.'

Dominic turned and fixed his ice-cold eyes on his
sister. His face was white with rage, his voice hiss-
ing through his teeth. 'What sort of excellent explanation could she possibly have? She was hanging on to
his arm, for God's sake—for all to see.' Furiously he
looked away. The bewitching, artless young woman he
had made love to, had turned out to be a cold, calculating, beautiful—bitch.

Cordelia mentally recoiled from the blinding vio-
lence flashing in his eyes. Sighing, she shook her head,
remembering his actions when Amelia had died. He
would never give Juliet another chance to hurt him.
If she had shamed him voluntarily and betrayed his
trust—and he clearly believed she had done both—
then unless Juliet could make him believe she wasn't
the Earl of Fairfax's mistress, she was as good as dead
to him.

When Juliet returned to the house, the serenity she
had acquired so painfully over the past weeks had gone,
leaving her in mourning, grieving for the man she had

lost—grieving for the man she loved, for love him she did. Of that there was no doubt.

But, she asked herself, how could she possibly love a man who would hurt, humiliate her and insult her as he had done? It would seem there was no protection against love once it had you in its power. From the instant their eyes had locked together in Vauxhall Gardens, she had admitted that she loved him, and now she felt her despair flooding over her like a great wave.

How fragile everything was, this new world she had acquired, which had seemed so secure with her grandfather, but just a moment spent with Dominic had shown her it was nothing but a fantasy, a bubble that had burst with just one look at his face.

Her mind since leaving Lansdowne House had been filled with angry recriminations, with contempt for Dominic Lansdowne for what he had done to her, and what could have happened to Robby had the theft of the miniatures been planted at his door. But her female body was not concerned with matters that went on in her mind. Her flesh had not stopped loving this man. Her physical mind had not stopped wanting him, no matter how strongly she tried to push him away.

Refusing to wallow in self-pity, Juliet immediately began planning what she would wear for Lord Fitzherbert's ball, but as she put her preparations underway, she was nagged by the unsettling thought that she would come close to encountering Dominic.

* * *

When the day of the ball finally arrived and trepidation set in, it occurred to her, not for the first time, that during the time she had known Dominic Lansdowne, he had knocked her emotions all over the place. In fact she felt like a ball being slammed and bounced off his racket, never knowing where she was going to land. She was heartily sick of it and in no mood to let him do it again tonight.

Casting a last critical eye at her reflection in the long mirror, she accepted the fan and reticule her maid gave her, and, picking up her skirts, went in search of her grandfather.

'We must go,' she said, entering the sitting room where he was patiently waiting for her. 'We don't want to be late.'

'There is no rush, my dear,' he said, turning her in a full circle the better to admire her, elegantly attired, her hair arranged in shining curls. 'You look positively breathtaking and very elegant. I want everyone to be there when you make your entrance.' He beamed down at her. 'I feel twenty years younger.'

The stunned admiration on his face bolstered Juliet's faltering confidence. 'And you look it,' Juliet said, smiling broadly as she appraised his black evening attire, the diamond stickpin in his cravat twinkling like his eyes, and his thick white hair brushed smoothly back. For all his advanced years, he really was still a very handsome man.

'This is a proud moment for me—escorting my

beautiful granddaughter to her first ball. You do dance, by the way? I never thought to ask.'

She laughed. 'Of course I can dance. It was one of the things I was taught at the Academy—*and* all I need to know to go about in society—so I won't shame you.'

When they arrived at Lord Fitzherbert's impressive, elegant house, the streets round about were filled with the rattle of carriages and the jingle of harness, accompanied by shouts of coachmen and lackeys.

Climbing the steps to the house beside her grandfather, Juliet knew she looked her best. Her dress of pale green tulle suited her to perfection, although she had acknowledged some doubts about the deep décolletage, cut to the very limits of decency, displaying to advantage the pale flesh and full, rich curves of her breasts and shoulders.

With a warm, searching smile, her grandfather offered her his arm. 'Are you ready?'

She nodded and laid her gloved fingers on his arm. As they entered the house she concentrated on keeping her mind perfectly blank. They climbed the curving staircase that led to where the ballroom was located. Footmen dressed in dark blue livery trimmed with gold braid stood to attention along the staircase and landing. They joined the receiving line and eventually found themselves standing at the top of a short flight of stairs into the glittering ballroom.

'*The Earl of Fairfax and his granddaughter, Lady Juliet Lockwood,*' the butler boomed.

Surrounded by a group of glittering people, Dominic

raised his head. His eyes darkened with surprise and puzzlement as his glance slid over the guests pouring down the staircase, then instantly came to a halt when it reached her and froze when he saw the breathtaking vision in pale green tulle, the square neckline offering a tantalising view of smooth, voluptuous flesh, her fitted bodice emphasising a tiny waist. Her glossy dark brown hair was swept back off her forehead and held in place by an emerald clip, then left to fall artlessly about her shoulders in a wealth of luxurious glossy curls.

Dominic saw only perfection in the delicately sculpted cheekbones and slender white throat. She was too exquisite to be flesh and blood, too regal and aloof to have ever let him touch her. Drawing a long strangled breath, he realised he hadn't been breathing as he watched her. Neither had the guests around him.

'Good Lord,' one portly gentleman breathed. 'Is she real?'

'My thoughts exactly,' said another, helping himself to a pinch of snuff. 'I'd no idea the Earl had a granddaughter.'

'If she's who I think she is,' said one of the ladies, 'her mama created quite a scandal when she ran off with a widower, without her father's permission. Gently bred girls do not marry against the families' wishes in this country.'

'Society eventually forgets these things,' another lady continued conversationally. 'In the meantime, it would seem this young lady is the fruit of that unfortunate union and is the Earl's natural and legitimate granddaughter for all that.'

'Well, well!' Cordelia breathed, coming to stand beside Dominic, her gaze not having left Juliet since she had entered the ballroom, unable to believe what she was seeing. 'What a turn out! Who would have thought it?'

'Who indeed?' Dominic replied, beginning to feel like a complete and utter idiot when he remembered how, in Vauxhall Gardens, he had been too ready to judge and condemn.

'She's quite magnificent.'

'Isn't she?' Dominic ground out, watching the object of his gaze walk gracefully down the stairs, her hand resting on the Earl's arm, keeping her head high. 'She'll regret this.'

'More like you will regret your accusation. You were too hasty to judge her, and if her grandfather is aware of it, he will be none too pleased. Think about it,' she said, speaking for his ears alone. 'You have compromised her. If she has made him aware of that, the Earl might have something to say about it.'

'When she worked for me they were estranged.'

'It will make little difference. He is still her grandfather and your conduct towards her was inexcusable. You, dear brother, are going to be down on your knees for a very long time, begging for her forgiveness.'

'You know I never go down on my knees.' He glanced at Charles, who was also gaping at Juliet as if he'd lost his senses. 'And you, Charles? How do you feel about this turn up? Surprised?'

'Surprised and just as besotted as every other male present.' Charles looked pointedly at his bland-faced friend. 'All apart from you, it would seem. You must be made of stone. Miss Lockwood is so beautiful she'd tempt the Pope. It must be galling to discover one of your employees is really a lady in her own right—a lady who will become a countess on the demise of her grandfather, since the huge estate in Scotland is not entailed and she stands to inherit the lot.'

'Then she can watch out for the fortune hunters,' Cordelia said, wondering what Dominic would do about this new state of affairs. 'She's about to become the most sought-after young lady in London.'

'Are we likely to see you as a contender, Charles?' Dominic asked, eyeing his friend closely.

'I'm afraid not. Miss Lockwood is safe from me— *your* Miss Lockwood, unless my intuition deceives me, and actually, it never does. Geraldine will have me hung, drawn and quartered if I'm seen anywhere near the delectable Lady Juliet.'

On the stairs the Earl bent his head to Juliet. 'Come, don't be nervous. Just be yourself.'

As they proceeded down the stairs, Juliet's nervousness was superseded by a blissful sense of unreality. She was met by a wave of light and heat and music. The buzz of conversation was punctuated by the fluttering of fans and the swishing of silk gowns.

She had never been to a ball before, never seen so many fashionable people gathered together all glittering with jewels. The great white-and-gold ballroom, adorned with huge banks of flowers sent that very morning from the hothouses of Lord Fitzherbert's country estate, glittered at its most brilliant in the light of the immense crystal chandeliers ablaze with innumerable candles. The musicians were in an alcove across the room. The dancing had begun, and the music was sublime to her ears as couples twirled around the floor in a waltz.

Her eyes flitted over the crowd, seeing a sea of strange faces, and then her eyes were drawn to a tall, urbane figure in plain but perfectly cut black coat. The Duke of Hawksfield's shoulders were squared with rigid hauteur, his hands clasped behind his back, the candlelight gleaming on his black hair. His face was expressionless and for a brief moment their eyes met. He lifted his arrogant eyebrows, his look both suspicious and intrigued, but then Juliet looked quickly away, tempted to pick up her skirts and flee.

From a distance Dominic watched the well-wishers with furious persistence toadying around this gorgeous creature who had suddenly appeared in their midst. They were effusive in their compliments and attentions, requesting introductions and dances with her, vying for her attention and asking permission to call on her. Juliet took none of it seriously, but she treated them all with impartial friendliness. Her grandfather, the proudest man in the room, carried it all off with aplomb.

For the entire evening Sir Charles had Geraldine hanging possessively on his arm, her eyes full of malice whenever they rested on Juliet, both on the dance floor and off it. The sight of the woman who had caused her so much trouble evoked a burning ire in Juliet. It was when one of her partners returned her to her grandfather, who was in conversation with an acquaintance, that she heard Geraldine comment to a woman with an ear for gossip that the Earl of Fairfax's granddaughter had, until recently, had to earn her own living, and that she had been employed by the Duke of Hawksfield.

Smarting from Geraldine's idle talk and the malice behind it, having promised herself to remain calm whenever she came into contact with Geraldine Howard, the impertinence of the woman stung her to instant anger. Determined to defend herself, she turned, unaware of Dominic hovering close by, his eyes narrowed on Geraldine.

Dominic did not have a good feeling about the evening. If Geraldine was running true to form, she would lose no time in besmirching Juliet's good name. If she divulged what she knew of Juliet's lowly past to the *ton*, then she would need a miracle if she was to come out of it unscathed.

Geraldine, wearing a haughty expression, was standing just a few feet away with Charles and Thomas at her elbow. It was clear to Juliet that Geraldine had intended her to hear the remark. Her fingers tightening on her fan, Juliet moved towards her.

'If there is anything you wish to say about me, Miss Howard, will you please have the courtesy to say it to my face.'

Geraldine snapped her fan open and began vigorously wafting her face. 'Why, I am all astonishment.

I certainly never expected to see you at an event like this.'

'I can well imagine your surprise,' Juliet managed to say in a controlled voice.

'I was just telling Charles how people will be quite scandalised when they discover you were employed by his Grace, the Duke of Hawksfield,' she retorted with silken malice, 'and no doubt when it gets about you will be shunned by polite society.'

'If anyone can be bothered to listen to your vituperative comments. No doubt you will fuel the gossip and enjoy doing so.' Geraldine's vindictiveness turned Juliet's dislike into genuine loathing. 'It was brought to my attention when I encountered the Duke of Hawksfield the other day that the miniatures that went missing at Lansdowne House have been recovered.' Her eyes slid meaningfully to Thomas, who was shifting uncomfortably from one foot to the other. 'I cannot tell you how relieved I was to hear that. It has proved that my brother was not implicated in their disappearance in any way—nor were any of the staff.'

Geraldine stiffened and a wary, uneasy look entered her eyes. She glanced sideways at Thomas and then to Charles, to see if he was paying attention. He was, and he was looking at her with suspicious bewilderment. 'Then, like you, I too am relieved they have turned up.'

'You must be, although since there were only two people who could have taken them and one of them, my brother, has been vindicated, then I am of the opinion that the other person cannot be. You, Miss Howard. You resented my presence in your midst so much that you maliciously tried to have me removed by taking those miniatures yourself and having the blame placed on my brother. Theft is a hanging offence, and he wouldn't have had a prayer of proving his innocence.'

Thomas stepped forward, glancing awkwardly at Charles, who knew nothing about the miniatures Geraldine had taken. 'Lady Juliet, perhaps I can explain—'

She looked at him with cold disdain. 'I am sure you know what happened, Sir Thomas. You know your sister and what she is capable of, but I think it is for her to explain, don't you?' Suddenly her face broke into a smile and she said sweetly, 'However, this is neither the time nor the place, and since everything has worked out for the best, I have no wish to discuss it further.' She cast her eye at Sir Charles. 'You look somewhat puzzled by our conversation, Sir Charles. Don't worry, I'm sure Sir Thomas will put you in the picture. Now if you'll forgive me I see my next dance partner beckoning. I hope you all enjoy your evening—if you can,' she said, her eyes flashing momentarily to Geraldine. 'Although I dare say it will be difficult. Every time Miss Howard opens her mouth to speak I always expect to hear a rattle.'

Geraldine, her chest heaving with anger, snapped her fan shut.

Charles looked at her coldly. 'I would appreciate it if you would do as she says and tell me what the hell she was talking about.'

Throwing his sister a scathing look, Thomas took his arm. 'Of course. It is only right that you should know to what depths my sister will sink when she takes a dislike to a person.'

Having observed the short but heated interchange between the two ladies, Dominic's method of dealing with this was to speak to Geraldine himself before she dripped her poison into someone else's ear. Unfortunately he suspected that the damage was already done.

Geraldine was watching Charles and Thomas nervously. She whirled round in surprise on hearing someone speak her name, sucking in her breath when she saw Dominic. They hadn't met since that unfortunate business over the miniatures, and on Thomas's advice she had avoided him. Now she felt a shiver of trepidation.

'Not only do I find your presence here offensive, Geraldine,' Dominic said with quiet menace, 'I dislike what you tried to do to Lady Juliet Lockwood and I dislike the fact that the consequences to her brother could have been dire. I also dislike you intensely.'

Geraldine's mouth dropped open, her face turning a deathly white.

Dominic leaned closer, his voice like steel. 'You are a vindictive, malicious troublemaker and your life will be more peaceful, believe me, if you keep your mouth shut. I am more that a match for your devious schemes.'

'Why, I—'

He silenced the gasping young woman with a blistering look. 'The miniatures, Geraldine, the ones you stole from me and tried to put the blame on Robert Lockwood. Your brother knows you well. Suspecting you were behind the theft, he retrieved them and returned them to me without informing your parents.' He smiled, his ice-cold grey eyes full of meaning. 'Although from the way Charles is looking at you right now, I would say he looks fit to commit murder.' He had the satisfaction of seeing the rest of the blood drain from Geraldine's face. Shaken, she drew herself up with nervous hauteur.

'If I were to guess, I would say Thomas has made him privy to what you have done. Perhaps what Lady Juliet said to you has something to do with that—I did observe her walk this way. Remember—I am sure your parents would be extremely interested to know what their precious daughter has been up to, so be warned. Have a care what you say.'

He walked away, leaving a thoroughly chastised Geraldine to scurry away to make her peace with Charles, only to find he was dancing with a red-haired rival, Lady Caroline Buckley, who was gazing up at him like the cat that had got the proverbial cream.

Chapter Nine

It was during the break for refreshments that Cordelia, resplendent in deep rose silk and as regal as ever, approached Juliet, greeting her warmly, obviously genuinely pleased to see her.

'I see your circumstances are much changed, Juliet. I had no idea the Earl of Fairfax was your grandfather. Why, you could have knocked me down with a feather. It's certainly been an eye opener for everyone else.'

'I saw no reason to tell anyone, Lady Pemberton. Until recently I was as much a stranger to him as he was to me, so you must forgive me if you think there was any kind of deception on my part. The reason for our estrangement is long and complicated and I am happy to say it is now resolved.'

'Then what can I say except that I am happy for you both. He is a fine man is Edward Fairfax—and still a handsome one,' she commented, her eyes twinkling with admiration for the Earl. 'Have you seen Dominic, by the way?'

Juliet paled. 'Briefly. We—have not spoken.'

'Have you not?' Cordelia studied her young friend's countenance carefully.

'No, and I have no wish to,' she replied stubbornly. 'I am determined to have nothing further to do with that arrogant Duke—begging your pardon, Lady Pemberton,' she said, recollecting herself. 'However, it cannot be easy having someone as arrogant and self-centred as he is for a brother.'

Cordelia bit her lip to hide an admiring smile at the young woman's spirit. Juliet Lockwood might have been little more than a servant in a duke's house, but she bowed to no one. On the other hand, her refusal to speak to Dominic and her spirit were causing a stand off that Cordelia sincerely hoped would be remedied.

'I have grown accustomed to my brother, Juliet, and I agree with you. He is all you accuse him of being— and more. However, he missed you when you left Lansdowne.'

Hope stirred in Juliet's breast, but her expression displayed little interest. 'He did?'

'Yes. More than he cared to admit. When you walked out on him, you did the unexpected. His pride and his heart both took a serious battering.'

Cordelia wondered how Juliet would react were she to tell her that when Dominic had failed to locate her, her absence from his life had affected him deeply. Sleep had eluded him. His face had looked as hard and cold as granite, his attitude had been distant and curt, and there were deep lines of fatigue etched around his eyes and mouth.

'Are you aware of the reason why I left?'

Cordelia looked at her directly. 'Something to do with some missing miniatures, I believe. Although—I do know there was more to it than that.'

Juliet's humiliation was complete. 'Please don't judge me, Lady Pemberton.'

'I would never do that. I know the irresistible power that Dominic has over women.'

'He is like an irresistible force, like a wind that comes at you from different directions, so many sides, never knowing which one he is going to show you next.'

Lady Pemberton smiled her understanding. 'He is certainly complex—and private. He does as he pleases, when he pleases, and he doesn't give a fig what anyone thinks of him. He doesn't care about being disliked and he doesn't care about being admired either. The only thing he cares about is Lansdowne and his work.'

'He works hard, I know that,' Juliet murmured, remembering the times she had seen him poring over ledgers and holding meetings with businessmen in his study—and then not so long ago when he joined his workers to harvest the corn.

'It's not just the estate. Dominic has a shrewd head for business. Ever since he left his military career behind to take up his dukedom, he's been multiplying his fortune, by investing heavily in shipping and import-and-export companies, as well as others. In short, he doesn't need people and doesn't like anyone to get too close. I am probably closer to him than almost anyone—although I would like to think that very soon someone will replace me.' She fixed Juliet with a level gaze. 'He thinks very highly of you, Juliet.'

Juliet grimaced. 'I hardly think so. He sees me as a woman of easy virtue, who has used her body to get what she wanted. But I'm not like that. He will never understand.'

'Don't underestimate him, Juliet. Beneath that cold, dispassionate façade Dominic shows to the world, there is a heart that beats and feels like everyone else's.'

Because of her own experiences with Dominic Lansdowne, Juliet wasn't convinced.

'He condemns all women on the basis of one woman who hurt him very badly,' Cordelia went on. 'It was over eight years ago, but he will not allow himself to forget.'

'He did tell me a little of what happened, that she was called Amelia and that she betrayed him.'

Cordelia drew a long breath. 'Yes, but there was more to it than that. However, if he had wanted you to know the whole of it, he would have told you, so I will not betray his trust by doing so now. What I will say is that he needs a woman to heal the wounds Amelia inflicted, to teach him how to love again and how to love in return.'

'You—know he asked me to be his mistress, don't you?'

'Yes, I do know, and I'm glad you didn't. He didn't tell me what had happened between the two of you. He didn't have to—although I have to say that, to my knowledge, it is the first time he has dallied with a virtuous innocent—and he has never approached a woman in his employ. He behaved totally out of character—although I can see why he's attracted to you. There is a gentle strength about you I saw when I first met you. I remember thinking, when I saw the two of you together at my soirée, that someone like you would make him a perfect wife. I still think that.'

'It is very kind of you to say that, and I hope he finds someone like that. What would you have done in my place—had he asked you to be his mistress?'

'Me?' Cordelia's eyes sparkled with humour. 'I'd have given him what he deserved. I'd have taken a very heavy, blunt object and hit him with it.'

'Unfortunately,' Juliet said with a laugh of admiration for Dominic's forthright sister, 'I didn't think of that.'

'Pity. The arrogance, the sheer gall of my handsome young brother never fails to astound me.'

'I do not understand men like him. Perhaps when I am in full possession of society's rules, I will understand more.'

Cordelia tapped her arm reassuringly with her fan. 'I think you are amazingly perceptive,' she said with feeling, 'and very warm hearted and brave to have stood up to Dominic as you did. Good for you, Juliet. That's what I say.'

Somewhat cheered by her conversation with Lady Pemberton, Juliet went in search of her grandfather, but as the ball progressed, she could not prevent her eyes seeking out the object of her unease.

He looked breathtakingly handsome in his jet-black

evening clothes that matched his hair and contrasted sharply with his snowy frilled shirt and flashing smile. Beside him, other men were pale and insignificant. Many of the ladies thought so too, Juliet realised as she observed him dancing with one after another, several of those ladies flirting quite outrageously.

Just as Dominic had feared, thanks to Geraldine setting the gossip rolling with a single remark in an over-attentive ear, everyone in the room was rapidly becoming aware of Juliet's background and the fact that until recently she had been in his employ. It was also being said that she had left Lansdowne House in haste, the reason a mystery that had everyone speculating; given his reputation as London's most popular rake, they reached the obvious conclusion.

He looked at Juliet who was on the dance floor, laughing into the face of her adoring partner, enjoying herself so much she was sublimely unaware of the gossip, as was her grandfather that who was so proud of his beautiful granddaughter, the gossip passed over his head. Dominic couldn't let it hurt her. He had to set matters right.

Everyone was waiting for the Duke to invite Lady Juliet Lockwood to dance, but to everyone's disappointment he did nothing of the sort. In fact, the two of them seemed to be consciously staying well away from each other. It wasn't until the ball was in its final hour, when she was sitting out a dance to rest her aching feet, that Dominic, his mind on Juliet, who after tonight would be at the mercy of the *ton*, pushed himself off the pillar on which he had been leaning for the best part of the night, dancing a few duty dances in between.

Oblivious to the people milling about her, with a growing sense of unreality Juliet watched him move towards her with that same natural grace that seemed so much a part of him. He grew larger as he neared, his broad shoulders blocking out her view of the room, his silver-grey eyes searching her face.

He said in an unenthusiastic voice, 'Lady Juliet? May I have the pleasure of this dance?'

She looked up at him. 'No, thank you,' she said coldly. 'I don't care to dance.' She stood up. 'Please leave me alone. Excuse me.' Turning on her heel, she left him standing. Wanting to put as much space between herself and that arrogant Duke, she went in search of her grandfather.

'Good Lord,' one young dandy dressed in yellow pantaloons said to another. 'Did you see that? The Duke of Hawksfield asked Lady Juliet Lockwood to dance, and she refused and walked off, leaving him standing.'

'Must be insane,' commented his friend.

'I didn't think so when she danced with me. She was all sweetness and the soul of civility.' Lowering his voice, he bent his head closer. 'There is a rumour a buzz that she worked for the Duke before she became reunited with the Earl of Fairfax, and they did not part on the best of terms.'

'Really? I am all astonishment and curiosity.' Taking his friend's arm, he drew him to a quiet corner. 'Do tell me more.'

Dominic turned about and walked in the opposite

direction to Juliet, furious with her for her outrageous display of temper.

Resuming his stance against the pillar on the edge of the room, he folded his arms across his chest, watching an entire wall of young gentlemen descend on her and close round her. Laughingly she backing away, saved by her grandfather when he took her arm and escorted her on to the dance floor.

As she whirled past in her grandfather's arms, Juliet glanced at Dominic, realising from his aloof expression that he wouldn't ask her to dance again if someone held a gun to his head. As she caught his eye, his brows arched in ironic amusement, and then he casually shrugged himself away from the pillar and disappeared into one of the elegantly appointed card rooms.

Juliet had firmly believed that would be the last she would see of him, but her hopes of ending the ball without conflict were destroyed when she was leaving the ladies' retiring room. A hand shot out from nowhere, gripped her arm and dragged her into a curtained alcove before she had time to protest. She jerked back, furious, but Dominic's hand tightened sharply, preventing her from pulling free, forcing her to stand and face him.

'I beg you to release me. We have nothing to say to one another.'

'You think not? It seems to me we have a great deal to say to one another. I hope you're enjoying the evening,' Dominic drawled, without releasing her arm.

'I was, until I was approached by you,' Juliet

retorted, struggling to free her arm. 'Why have you dragged me in here?'

Tightening his grip, he pulled her close, towering over her, his darkly furious face hovering just above her own. 'Listen to me very carefully, *Lady* Juliet Lockwood,' he continued, ignoring her furious struggles. 'Never give me the cut again. I am not one of your fancy fops you can wind round your finger.'

'No, you're my seducer,' she hissed, infuriated by his imperious tone. 'Please let go of my wrist.'

He did as she asked and she stood glaring at him. 'Well? What do you want?' she asked ungraciously.

'To talk to you.'

'Anything we have to say to one another has been said. Your attitude and all those dreadful things you accused me of at Vauxhall were unforgivable. Of all the conceited, rude men I have ever met, you beat them all.'

As he looked down at her, Dominic reminded himself that no matter what she did or said, he would be patient and understanding. But with her chin held defiantly high and her eyes hurling scornful daggers, it was all he could do to bridle his temper.

'Juliet,' he said, on a softer note. She met his eyes, waiting, uneasy. 'I could happily strangle you.'

She noted the contrast between his words and his tone, but she wasn't softened by it. 'I know.'

'During all the time we have known each other, did it not once cross your mind to tell me who you were? You made a complete idiot of me at Vauxhall with that silly charade.'

'It was no charade, and I think you made an idiot of yourself, your Grace, without any help from me.'

'My name is Dominic, and based on your behaviour with me at my home, you cannot blame me for thinking you had got caught up in some sleazy affair. And you played along with it—no doubt enjoying watching me make a total fool of myself. I congratulate you. You are a superb actress, whose talents would be best suited to the stage. You knew who your grandfather was all along. Didn't you?'

'Yes, although I did tell you we were estranged. I saw no reason why I should tell you who he was since it was none of your business, and if you hadn't jumped to the wrong conclusion when you saw us together at Vauxhall and waited a while longer, I would have introduced you. He was sorry you went off so suddenly.'

'With good reason. You told him?'

'What? That you thought I was his mistress. Of course.'

Dominic rolled his eyes in mock horror. 'Good Lord, woman, have you no mercy? Is my shame not bad enough? And no doubt he is itching to meet me at dawn in some secluded place.'

'The idea did have a certain appeal, but he saw the funny side and was rather flattered that for someone as old as he is, he is still handsome enough to have secured a young paramour.'

Dominic's eyes softened. 'I'm glad I was mistaken.'

'Why did you drag me in here?'

'To talk to you. Since you publicly humiliated me

by refusing to dance with me, I could think of no other way of getting to speak to you.'

'What about?'

'Geraldine.'

'Oh. What has she done now?'

'Her worst. There is a rumour spreading like wildfire that while in my employ I got you in my clutches. It has also been noted that we have been avoiding each other all night, giving credence to the rumour. By breakfast it will be widely known that you spent some considerable time alone with me at Lansdowne House and left under a cloud.'

Juliet was mortified. 'I had no idea.'

'Society is neither discerning or kind, Juliet. By the time people have finished speculating, you will be in danger of being totally ostracised, your reputation in shreds, and everyone will cut you dead.'

Juliet felt sick at the very real possibility that this might happen. 'My coming here tonight is turning into a nightmare. I had no idea. It appears that I'm in danger of becoming a social outcast before I've even entered society. And you have taken pity on my plight?'

'And my own. We will both be teetering on the edge of a scandal. Being who I am—a Duke, a wealthy Duke who is also a bachelor—makes me the object of intense scrutiny.'

'But I have my grandfather. He will protect me.'

'Not even your grandfather or my influential self will be able to halt the gossip.' What Dominic didn't tell her was that tonight, any unattached bachelor who was foolish enough to show an interest in her was going to be a laughing stock. In the eyes of the *ton*, Juliet Lockwood would be considered used goods, and any bachelor who went near her would be deemed a fool or a lech and suffer her fate.

'What do you suggest we do about it?'

'You could dance with me.'

'I don't think that would be wise.'

He raised his brows and smiled wryly. 'Nothing you and I have done has been wise, Juliet.'

'Since acquiring your attention is like a holy crusade for some women, how do you know society won't admire my good sense for steering clear of you?'

'Because they will believe the damage has already been done. We were alone together at my home in compromising circumstances. Your estrangement from your grandfather will make little difference. You were still a young woman of birth and breeding and should not have been working for me at all.'

'At the time I had no choice. Besides, I valued my independence.'

'Independence?' He smiled. 'There are many who would say that independence is vastly overrated and is an odd notion for a female.'

'I still value it. But I suppose if I am condemned by society then it is no less then I deserve. I knew what the rules were. I broke them when I behaved like a shameless wanton and—and let you—' She broke off, biting her quivering lip, too embarrassed to go on.

'And who is to know that but you and I?' he murmured, his voice surprisingly gentle. 'I don't want to run the risk of looking too far afield for explanations, but it is possible that what happened between us was because we were attracted to each other. I sure as hell wanted you, Juliet. And I know you wanted me.'

'I—I'd rather not discuss it.'

The sudden glamour of his lazy smile was almost as effective as his admission. 'I refuse to regret or apologise for what happened that night,' he said. 'We wanted each other. It was as simple as that. I admit that the blame is entirely mine. You were innocent and totally inexperienced. By my actions I have wreaked havoc in your life and wronged you. I fully admit that and hold myself accountable. But since those people out there would never believe nothing happened, at least we can show them we are in harmony with each other. Come. Let's dance.'

Dumbly she shook her head.

He held out his hand. 'I insist. Let everyone see us together, and you will see how easily most minds can be manipulated. It may give the gossip a turn of direction, one they have not expected.'

Reluctantly Juliet relented and automatically placed her hand in his, but the eyes she turned up to his as he drew her out of the alcove were wide with fright.

'Juliet,' Dominic said severely, but with a dazzling smile for the benefit of the watching audience. 'You are the self-same woman who stood up to me at Lansdowne. Do not dare turn cowardly on me now.'

As they walked into the ballroom, heads turned as one, every eye focused on them, some filled with curiosity, some with sympathy and puzzlement, and some with condemnation. An odd quietness was creeping over the room.

They stepped on to the dance floor, where Juliet walked into Dominic's arms and felt his right arm slide about her waist, bringing her close against the solid strength of his body. His left hand closed round her fingers and suddenly she was being whirled gently around in the arms of a man who danced the waltz as though he had danced it a million times before.

She should have felt threatened and overpowered, especially with almost every eye in the room focused on them, but instead, feeling his broad shoulders beneath her gloved hand, and the arm encircling her waist like a band of steel, she felt safe and protected instead.

Lowering his head to hers, Dominic murmured, 'Lift up your head, smile at me, look as though you've never enjoyed a dance more.' His eyes twinkled wickedly. 'Flirt with me if you like, but do not on any account look humble and meek, because these people will interpret it as guilt.'

Juliet drew a shaking breath and a smile curved her lips. 'Lift my head and smile I can do, but flirting is definitely out. Look where it got me before.'

'How can I possibly forget? The memory will be with me for ever.'

Juliet sighed, her mind attuned to his as she too remembered that exquisite night that would be branded on her memory for all time. 'You dance divinely,' she complimented softly.

Dominic relaxed and smiled down at her. 'I'm supposed to say that to you.'

'Really?' She frowned. 'It would seem I still have much to learn.'

'Society has rules to govern absolutely everything.'

'It seems to me that society requires a female to be utterly useless.'

Dominic laughed at her observation. 'And we know useless cannot be applied to you, Lady Juliet.'

'I sincerely hope not.'

'Try to relax.'

'I am relaxed.'

'Your body tells me something different.'

'My body is my own affair.' She was acutely aware of his hand against her waist and she had a sudden impulse to shy away.

'I well remember what your body looks like, Juliet.' His eyelids were lowered over his eyes as he looked down at her upturned face, gently flushed by his remark. 'I remember everything about it, every curve, every hollow and every inviting, secret place.' He grinned at the shock that registered in her eyes and spun her round more vigorously than the dance required. 'I am a duke after all.'

Juliet scowled up at him, seeing sparkling humour in his eyes. 'You're loving this, aren't you?'

'Every minute,' he admitted shamelessly. He looked at her mouth and his smile vanished. 'After all, you did walk out on me and make a fool of me by letting me believe your grandfather was your lover. I must take my revenge where I can.'

'I had good reason to leave your house, as you well

know,' she said in her defence. 'And you were so fired up at Vauxhall you gave me little chance to explain.'

'And I don't want another quarrel with you, Juliet, so I will not start one.'

'Thank you. Neither do I.'

'Although I do feel compelled to point out that a young lady should never, under any circumstances, contradict a duke, or ignore him as you did when you refused to dance with me,' he uttered with mock humour. 'We don't like that. Did they not teach you that at the Academy you attended?'

'I cannot remember being taught any such thing, but your character and my own sense of fair play make it hard for me not to contradict you, *your Grace.*'

As he swung her round, Juliet's heart began to beat in heavy thuds. She knew she should not let him hold her so close, but she did not try to pull back, for it was almost as if she were under some sort of spell. It was not until she felt his arms tighten slightly about her waist that she came to her senses. With a glance from side to side she realised that there was no escape until the dance ended.

'So,' he murmured, as if reading her thoughts, 'you would like to leave me again. Well, with everyone watching our every move, finish the dance now and walk away, if you can.'

Juliet looked up into his face, and in the silver-grey depths of his eyes she saw something relentless and challenging, but though she felt a quivering inside, it was not with fear.

'Do you want to?' he asked.

His voice was deceptively soft and Juliet felt she should take her own advice and end the dance prematurely, but the intensity of his gaze was enough to keep her trapped in his arms.

'No.'

His gaze lingered on her face. 'You know, Juliet, you could have such power if you knew how to wield it.'

'Power? I don't understand.'

'If a woman goes about it the right way, she can get anything she wants out of a man. Some women know this instinctively. You, Juliet, do not have the faintest idea.'

'Stop it,' she retorted, trying to sound calm and in control, while melting inside. 'You are playing a game with me and I'm in no mood for games.'

His lids were half-closed over his eyes. 'I admit it. I am playing a game with you, and I will not let you win. But I can teach you how to play.'

Something in those words made the melting stop. 'You forget that you already have, and look where that has got me.'

He laughed low in his throat. 'You, Juliet, are an interesting young woman—a challenge for any man. You want to be a proper young lady, while being captivating and alluring at the same time. Is that possible? An interesting question, don't you agree?'

'I see no reason why a woman can't be both.'

'As I have found out to my satisfaction.'

She looked at him, knowing he was referring to the night she had surrendered herself completely to him. 'You said you are playing a game with me and that you always win. What, then,' she asked, 'do you want from me?'

His gaze moved to her mouth, lingering there. He wasn't smiling any more, his face having taken on a serious expression, and in the moment that followed Juliet felt again that wild surge of excitement and anticipation, remembered the times she had been in his arms.

'I want you to marry me.'

Juliet's surroundings disappeared into a haze. Shock stunned her, but somehow her feet carried on dancing. After a moment, unable to work out where his proposal had come from, amazed that her voice sounded so calm and controlled, with a strong a hint of sarcasm, she said,

'What? Am I to understand that you are offering to raise my status from mistress to wife?'

'That is precisely what I mean.'

'And am I expected to feel flattered by this?'

'Not at all.'

Juliet stared at him dubiously. 'Just exactly what makes you suddenly so desperate for a wife that any woman will do?'

Instinct and experience told Dominic that a little tender persuasion could vastly further his cause, and he was prepared to resort to that, but only if logic and complete honesty weren't enough to persuade her. 'You are not just any woman, Juliet, and I have given marriage to you a great deal of thought. Had I made the offer before you left Lansdowne, what would your answer have been?'

'Despite having surrendered my virginity and my

honour to you the night before, my answer would have been a very firm no. I am ambitious, but not in that sense, nor am I interested in luxury. So you see, *your Grace*,' she said, addressing him with contempt, 'I am not interested in your offer. I am still trying to get over the last one.'

Dominic winced at the reminder. 'Will you at least listen to what I have to say?'

Juliet glared at him with feverish wrath. 'No. Not now. Not ever.'

The strains of the waltz died away and as they left the dance floor Dominic took her arm. Believing he was going to escort her back to her grandfather, she let him, but he led her to a secluded corner, away from prying eyes and sensitive ears.

'You will listen—if I have to tie you down you will hear me out.'

All Juliet's past experiences rose up to taunt her. Just the thought of those things was enough to hurt, but she did still want him. Heaven help her she did. She was a fool. Damn him for toying with her. Damn herself for letting him. But despite his supreme confidence that he could have it all his way, she would not let him.

'This is your game, not mine, Dominic. I don't like the kind of games you play.'

'But I do. We are involved in a power struggle, you and I. Do you not see the power you could have over me?'

'What? By becoming your wife?' she threw at him. When he opened his mouth to reply, she looked away. 'Leave it,' she hissed. 'The games you play are by your rules, not mine. I will not succumb to you twice, so in my book that makes me the winner. Understand that I don't want you. You've already used me. Have you any idea how ashamed I feel?' Her laugh was bitter. 'The lowly employee falls for his Grace the Duke! It's all so trite. So—disgusting.'

'It was never that.'

'It was sordid.'

'Juliet, I am offering you my name and all I possess.'

'Then give it to someone else,' she flared heatedly. 'I don't want it. You can have any woman you want. You only have to crook your finger and a hundred desirable women will come running.'

His eyes narrowed dangerously. 'Remember what I said. I always win.'

'Not this time, your Grace. Not this time. Now please go away and let me walk away from you with a shred of my pride intact. Goodbye, Dominic.' She turned and left him, and as she did so a part of her died inside.

When Juliet returned home, after bidding her grandfather goodnight, with a fixed smile on her face she headed directly to her room. Normally she would have undressed and got into bed, but after dismissing her maid she went to the window and stood staring blindly out. The energy she had forced into her parting from Dominic and the happy conversation about the ball with her grandfather in the carriage vanished. She felt as though she had fought a physical battle with a pride of lions and lost.

Shame and disappointment overwhelmed her. Covering her face with her hands, she bitterly faced the awful truth that physically she was no more immune to Dominic Lansdowne now than she had been when she had worked for him. She could withstand his insults, his anger, but not his smile, his touch, his kiss—the kiss that twisted her insides into knots, that made her burn, that wreaked havoc on her heart, her body and soul.

Yes, she was still as susceptible as she had ever been.

Feeling slightly better, the following morning she was alone in the garden when Hewitt came to tell her the Duke of Hawksfield was asking to see her. Reluctantly she agreed to see him.

Automatically she backed away. He was looking every inch the elegant, handsome duke today. Despite the civilised elegance of his superbly tailored dark blue coat and dove grey trousers and silver and gold striped waistcoat, he had never looked more dangerous, more overpowering than he did as he came toward her with that deceptively lazy, stalking stride.

Standing straight, she faced him, folding her hands calmly at her waist. 'Your Grace.'

'How many times do I have to tell you to call me Dominic?'

'This is not a good time to call.'

'No? I apologise.'

'My grandfather is not at home.'

'You know perfectly well it's not your grandfather I've come to see.'

'Nevertheless he will be sorry to have missed you.'

'There will be plenty of time for us to become acquainted later.'

'Why are you here? Anything I had to say to you I said last night.'

'You've had plenty of time to reconsider.'

A crushing weight settled in Juliet's chest. She should have known he would never give in. 'I have not changed my mind.'

'Then allow me to change it for you.'

There was no time to protest, for his arms reached out and he pulled her close.

'You won't find me a cruel husband, Juliet, if that's what you think.'

'That is not what I think.'

'You'll find me a very generous husband, that I promise you.'

She felt herself being drawn relentlessly closer to him. She shook her head slowly, feeling a knot of emotion in her chest. 'I won't marry you, Dominic.'

'Juliet,' he said softly, feeling her capitulation, 'you will. You know you want to, so don't fight it.' His voice turned husky and persuasive and her breast came into contact with his chest. 'I can give you everything a woman wants.'

Everything but love, Juliet thought miserably. And that was the only thing that she wanted, would ever want, the one thing he seemed unable to give.

'Everything a woman *really* wants,' he murmured, and before Juliet could understand that cynical remark his lips began a slow, deliberate descent towards hers. 'You'll have jewels and gowns and furs and more money than you have ever dreamed of.' His free hand cupped the back of her head and tilted her face up for his kiss. 'In return, all you'll have to give me is this.'

Before Juliet could react to his words her mind went blank as his sensual mouth seized possession of hers in an endless, stirring kiss that slowly built to one of demanding insistence. She moaned and his arm tightened possessively around her, as he began a slow and erotic seduction. By the time he stopped and lifted his head, Juliet felt dazed and inexplicably afraid, for she knew that for moments such as this, she was in danger of giving him what he wanted.

Anger stirred in her heart, anger that he thought he could simply offer her marriage and all the trappings that went with it and she would fall at his feet with gratitude. Pushing him away, she lifted her head haughtily.

'I gave you my answer last night. It is still the same. My decision is final. You really are as cold and heartless as your proposition makes you sound. I told you once before that money and possessions are meaningless to me, so do not feel you have to sell yourself.'

'I will not take no for an answer, Juliet. My proposal is sudden, I realise that. You must have time to get used to it.'

She gazed at the cool, dispassionate man standing before her. He looked so powerful, aloof and completely self-assured. It was impossible to believe that he wanted to marry her. Perhaps beneath his unemotional façade, Dominic felt as lonely and empty as she did. Perhaps he really did want her and no other would do. Then again, perhaps she was only trying to fool herself into believing it.

'I've had all the time I need. But why? Why?' she found herself asking. 'Why do you want to marry me? What's so special about me that, above all the women you could have, you choose to marry me?'

He expelled a harsh breath and the ducal dignity faltered. 'Dear God, after what happened between us, do I have to explain? I am attracted to you—surely you know that by now. And I know you are attracted to me. Otherwise you would not have let me make love to you.'

'True,' she agreed, 'and I was not so ignorant of these matters as to realise that marrying me then would have been a bit extreme. I believe the usual custom for that sort of thing is to pay the woman off, so I suppose I should have felt honoured that you offered to make me your mistress.'

'Since then I've had a great deal of time to consider what is between us more seriously. I deeply regret making you that offer and you were right to feel insulted and degraded by it. Now things have changed.'

'They most certainly have,' she retorted, her voice trembling with bitterness. 'Not so very long ago I was a nobody and hadn't a pittance to my name. I was only fit to be your mistress, to be cast off when you grew tired of me. Suddenly you find I am a lady, the granddaughter of a man who is a wealthy earl with an estate in Scotland to rival your own, and all of a sudden I have all the requisites for you to marry.' She thrust her face towards him, her colour rising with indignation. 'Just how low can you get, your Grace? How many more insults will you heap on me before you are done?'

He stiffened, with all the hauteur and dignity that befitted a duke, and when he spoke his voice was low and furious. 'My proposal of marriage was well meant. You insult my honour.'

'As you have insulted mine. Now we are even.'

'Quite, so now we can begin afresh.'

'You conceited beast! Why should I want to be your wife? I mean nothing more to you than the woman who would bear your children, a woman you would pack off to your country estate while you continue to enjoy your dissipations and corrosive pleasures in London.'

Dominic's eyes narrowed and were brittle with anger. 'You have a harsh opinion of me, Juliet.'

'That, your Grace, is putting it mildly. I would not be a complaisant wife. I would not turn a blind eye to your dalliances. You have a notorious reputation with women—a reputation which is undoubtedly earned.' She took a step closer, her cold eyes fixed on his. 'Know this, Dominic Lansdowne, and hear me well. The man who marries me will put me above all else. There will be openness and trust between us, and love.'

'Ah, love!' A glint of humour lit his eyes. 'Will you not settle for my everlasting adoration within the firm bonds of matrimony? I could add,' he gestured casually, 'the first night as already—'

'Be quiet and allow me to finish without resorting to crudeness. In short, there will be no mistresses. I will *never* be second best, and you, your Grace, are a rake, a libertine, call it what you like, and rakes never change. So as far as I am concerned, you can take your amorous self off to one of those beds where you can be assured of a warm welcome and forget all about me.'

'Ever since I made up my mind to marry you, Juliet Lockwood, not even in my weakest moment have I considered letting you go. And if I had,' he added, bluntly reminding her of her passionate response to him a moment ago, 'do you think I would consider it after that?' Dominic tipped her chin up, forcing her rebellious gaze to meet his implacable ones. 'I'm going to marry you, so get used to the inevitability of it. You have obviously convinced yourself that I will treat you harshly. I won't. In fact, I will grant you anything within my power.'

'Very well. I don't want to marry you. Will you accept that?'

'Anything but that. Why are you so angry with me, Juliet?'

That was the moment when she realised that it wasn't anger that was upsetting her, it was because she was hardening herself against him, but the sudden tenderness in his voice was unsettling. She looked up at him, looked away, and looked back at him again. 'I'm not angry. Not really.'

He slowly brushed his knuckles along her chin, up to her earlobe, sending shivers down her spine. 'Allow me to itemise my crimes, Juliet,' he said calmly. 'I may have appeared unfeeling and selfish, often dictatorial and self-seeking, and I do have a reputation I am not proud of.'

'And do you expect me to overlook that defect in your character and marry you in spite of it?'

'Where you are concerned I want to give you my name and my protection and to raise you to the unassailable peak of society. Do not condemn me for wanting to shower you with gifts. Yes, I want to shower you with the very best of luxuries it is within my power to grant you.' He looked at her closely. 'Is that just cause for your bitterness and animosity?'

Juliet's body seemed to droop. There was something in his eyes, something intense and passionate. She could feel herself trembling inside. She was afraid—afraid of being his passion today and cast off tomorrow. And she was afraid of how much it would hurt if she let herself believe him now. She swallowed and looked away. Suddenly she felt confused and utterly miserable.

'I don't know. What I do know is that it's not enough for me. Why will you not accept it?'

'Because I cannot stop thinking of you. Of the times when you would grace my library, of our conversations and the very first time I ever heard you laugh—in the harvest field that day, when your face was all pink from the sun and you had straw in your hair. You were enchanting. I cannot stop thinking of that night we made love,' he said, his voice low and husky, 'how you filled my senses until I could not think. I remember how you looked with the moonlight on your naked body, and I remember how you looked when you fell asleep in my arms.'

'Please stop it,' she demanded in a fierce whisper,

fury rising in her chest, for he evoked memories of her own she had tried so hard to forget. 'It is cruel of you to say such things to me when we both know it is only your determination to have your way that makes you say them.'

'We both lost control that night, Juliet. I should have known better, but I could not stop myself. You were so very lovely. You call me cruel? It is you who are cruel, for not allowing me to make up for the wrong I've done you. If I am determined, it is because I want you. You are unfair to deny me that.' He looked deep into her eyes. 'Tell me you don't want me, Juliet. Can you do that?'

She shook her head. 'No, in all truth I cannot. My feelings for you are—complicated; if you cannot commit yourself to me—if you cannot share yourself with me, and only me—I will not marry you.'

Seeing someone come out of the house on to the terrace, she suddenly smiled. 'My grandfather has returned. Come, I will introduce you, but then I want you to leave.'

They walked towards the man who was waiting for them. Dominic took the other's proffered hand and introduced himself, watching the Earl's face for a reaction. His eyes measured Dominic up in a slow, exacting way that gave him every assurance that he was successfully assessing him. Then the older man smiled and nodded slightly, seeming satisfied.

The meeting went well, the two having much in common. Juliet flinched when her grandfather insisted that the Duke take some refreshment, and as she sat through the long drawn-out ritual with angry impatience, sipping her tea while their conversation drifted across many topics, Juliet knew that Dominic was doing his utmost to add to her frustrations and that he was prolonging and was highly amused by the whole affair.

When he finally rose to leave and he had taken leave of her grandfather, she went with him into the hall.

'I was quite embarrassed by your blatant and transparent attempt to curry favour with my grandfather,' she hissed. 'Whatever you're up to it won't work.'

Arching his brows with mock innocence, he looked down at her. 'Why, I have no idea what you mean.'

Juliet lifted her head imperiously, throwing back her head, and Dominic felt his blood run warm in his veins and the heat of it move to his belly with wanting her. Her round chin squared up to him and her eyes gleamed, warning him that he had no authority over her.

'Yes, you do. You are many things, Dominic Lansdowne, but I didn't think you were devious and calculating. Now I think you had better leave. I am not going to marry you.'

Dominic looked at her for a long moment with those magnificent silver-grey eyes, and then he smiled. 'We'll see about that.'

'I've given you my answer. Sometimes even a duke must take no for an answer.'

Juliet watched him go, her emotions all over the

place. She had not chosen to love him, for what woman in her right mind would choose to love a man who employed her to work for him, and treated women as less than human? No, she had not wanted to love him, nor wanted his love, but from the moment he had put his hands on her, had wrapped his arms about her, arms that were strong and masculine, and placed his lips on hers, she had been lost in him. The very essence of Dominic Lansdowne was an irresistible magnet she couldn't deny.

Despite her decision not to marry him, she had not forgotten their night together nor anything else about him. Memories of him were etched into her brain like engravings on a stone, memories of how he had held her and kissed her and made love to her.

Sweet Lord in heaven, she knew she had committed a sin when she had let him make love to her, but she loved him—hopelessly, enduringly, and compulsively. But she could not go on like this. Somehow, some way, for the sake of her sanity and to find some peace, she had to get away. The way she saw it, she had only one direction open to her and that was to go to Scotland with her grandfather two days hence—how much further could she go?—but she would never forget Dominic.

How pleased her grandfather would be. At the thought of leaving London and Robby she felt a pang of loss, but it was offset by the knowledge that he was soon to go to New York and a new life, and she would find peace somewhere else. Scotland was far enough away for her to do that.

Chapter Ten

'I like the duke,' Juliet's grandfather said, studying her strained features carefully. 'You're drawn to him, I can see that.'

'Yes, I cannot deny it. He—he wants to marry me, Grandfather.'

His eyes opened wide and then he was quiet for a moment. 'He has asked you?'

'Yes.'

'And? What was your reply?'

'I refused him, of course.'

'Why "of course"?'

'I have no intention of becoming involved with him. I came to know him through working for him. He is an aristocrat. At the time I was his social inferior and had to work for a living—which put me quite beyond the pale. Marriage between us is quite out of the question.'

A smile lingered on her grandfather's lips. 'You've

made quite a life for yourself. The Oxford professor's daughter has come a long way. Everything is changed now, Juliet. Marriage between you and the Duke would be a good match.'

Afraid her grandfather was about to encourage her to accept, she went on, 'Please don't tell me I should consider his proposal.'

'No, my dear, and nor would I be so indelicate as to enquire as to your reasons for not marrying him. Having been absent from your life for so many years, I have no right to play the heavy-handed grandfather and insist that the Duke should have approached me first. You are you own mistress.'

'Do you think I am being foolish—refusing him?'

'My dear girl, I have come to have a great deal of affection for you. You have worked hard, and therefore you possess a good deal of sense because of it. You're an intelligent, grown woman and you know your own heart and mind. I am sure you've given the Duke's proposal a great deal of thought.'

'Yes, I have, but I would still be grateful if you were to offer me your counsel and advice. Lord knows I need it.'

'Being a duchess would be an enormous responsibility and I can understand your reluctance to take on such a role.'

'It's not the role I object to. It's the Duke. He would never have asked me to be his wife before he knew I was the granddaughter of an earl.'

'So it's your pride that rules your decision. I can appreciate that, for I possess a great deal of that myself.

You might call it a family trait. I would feel just as indignant as you at his sudden change of heart, but, despite his motives, do not let your pride get in the way of what you truly want. Whatever you decide, you will have my full support. You know that.' He sighed and took her hand, looking at her fondly. 'I am going to miss you when I leave for Scotland. You have been such excellent company and I've become used to having you near me. It's selfish of me, I know, but I am reluctant to let you go.'

'You won't have to. I've decided to go to Scotland with you.' She smiled and leaning over kissed his cheek. 'It's about time I saw my ancestral home.'

Her grandfather expressed his delight. There was nothing he wanted more, but he suspected her sudden desire to see the house that was part of her inheritance did not outweigh her need to put as much distance between herself and the Duke of Hawksfield as possible.

'If that is what you want,' he said, studying her thoughtfully, 'then maybe it's as well for you to get away from London at this present time.'

'Why do you say that?'

'If everyone thinks the Duke is interested in you, then every move you make will be observed and commented upon. You will be inundated with callers, watched and discussed at length in the society papers. Some of the gossip will not be favourable, for dukes are a rare commodity and ladies who are looking for a good catch for their daughters will be full of envy and more than a little avaricious.'

'That would be absolutely dreadful,' Juliet gasped with alarm. Such a thing had not entered her mind. 'All the more reason for us to go to Scotland as soon as possible. I'm not worried about gossip since there is nothing to gossip about. There is no romance and the sooner everyone understands that the better.'

Her alarm increased the following day when the largest bouquet of white roses was delivered. She stared at the card that told her they were from Dominic. Why had he done this? She didn't want it. She didn't want him sending her flowers. She didn't want him to be romantic and courtly—because if he did, she might start to believe he cared for her.

He did not love her, but she knew from the terrible pain in her heart that she wanted him to.

Three days later, after Dominic had called at the Earl of Fairfax's house and been told by the housekeeper that the Earl and Lady Juliet had gone to Scotland and did not intend returning for the foreseeable future, he had known a wrath that was beyond anything he had ever felt in his life. Obstinate, infuriating little fool!

Calling at his sister's town house, which was close to his own in Mayfair, with a face like thunder he restlessly paced up and down her drawing-room carpet.

'You seem in poor temper, Dominic—and be careful not to wear out my carpet. What is it?' Cordelia asked impatiently. 'Do be still.'

He came to an abrupt halt in front of where she was sitting. 'It's Juliet.'

'What about her?'

'She's left London for Scotland. How could she do that?'

'Oh, I see. Surely there's nothing unusual in that. It's only natural that she would want to see her ancestral home. Did she not tell you that she would?'

'She does not impart confidences to me,' Dominic ground out.

'Little wonder you are vexed because you've been dealt a cruel blow by fate.'

'Hardly by fate,' Dominic scoffed. 'More by a wily young woman who seems to delight in provoking me at every turn.'

'Dominic, did you propose to Juliet?'

'I did.'

A wide smile lit Cordelia's face as she sprang from her chair. 'How wonderful…'

'Not so wonderful, Cordelia. That infuriating woman turned me down flat.'

'Did she, indeed?' Her eyes narrowed. 'Did you ask her, Dominic, or tell her? Dear me! That is just like you. Juliet has every right to be courted without being rushed into things. Marrying her is simply the right and honourable thing to do, and you are going to have to figure out a way that would persuade her to accept your suit. So, what will you do now? Let her go?'

Paralysed with a mixture of urgency and fear, he shook his head. 'I can't. May God help me, Cordelia, I can't,' he uttered fiercely. 'I cannot bear this gaping emptiness in my life I feel without her. I have to go to her.'

'Then to bring about a reconciliation, you have to do something to bring it about. Go after her and show her how you feel. Tell her, Dominic.'

Cordelia watched him stride swiftly out. Her heart soared. It was evident to her that Dominic loved Juliet so much that he would have flown to Scotland if he'd had wings, to tell her of his love.

With a sense of urgency she went to her desk and began to write to Juliet. She would lose no time having it dispatched, since she wanted it to reach Scotland before her brother got there. While ever Juliet believed it was her new-found status and wealth that had drawn a proposal of marriage from Dominic, her pride would stand in the way of her acceptance, so perhaps a little push from Cordelia would not go amiss.

When Juliet had her first look at Fairfax Hall, a luxuriously appointed mansion in the heart of the breathtakingly beautiful Scottish borders, she was enthralled. Gazing at the sweeping expanse of undulating, neatly tended parkland and the sprawling mellow stone mansion—grand and impressive and very fine—brought tears to her eyes. It was to have been her mother's inheritance, an inheritance she had turned her back on to marry the man she loved.

The more Juliet saw and got to know of her own ancestry and the place she had come to, she found it difficult to understand how her mother could have left. The house embodied and expressed to all who saw it the continuity of a rich history as it had affected one Scottish family, her own. In not a few instances throughout the times of both peace and unrest, the members of this family had themselves helped to shape events of national importance.

Fairfax Hall was a significant bastion of her heritage and it was only by appreciating and understanding the vicissitudes under which her ancestors had lived that she could draw on the wealth of experience which had been passed down and, unbeknown to her, moulded into her own life.

Her days were filled with simple pleasures. Her grandfather escorted her on visits to their neighbours and to local events, and she walked for miles in the surrounding countryside. She soon became a popular figure and was much sought after. It wasn't long before she attracted the interest of the local swains, and they began calling at Fairfax Hall in ever-increasing numbers. But not one of them drew her interest. She missed the rich voice of Dominic, and his absence from her life made the days seem somehow lacking.

Two weeks after her arrival at Fairfax Hall, Lady Pemberton's letter was brought into the dining room where Juliet was lunching with her grandfather. Excusing herself, she went out onto the terrace. Holding the letter in her hands, she looked at it for a long moment before opening it, her fingers shaking, and began to read Lady Pemberton's sprawling writing.

It would seem that Dominic had told his sister of his proposal of marriage and she wanted to express how sorry and saddened she was to learn that Juliet had turned him down. Suspecting Dominic's clumsy proposal might have some bearing on her decision, she felt it only right to disclose what had been said in a conversation between herself and her brother when Juliet had left Lansdowne—before Dominic had any knowledge of her being the Earl of Fairfax's granddaughter and his heir.

As Juliet read on, she was unable to believe what Lady Pemberton was telling her. Pausing, she raised her head, her eyes shining with wonder and delight. Dominic had been so distraught when she had left Lansdowne that he had left for London to look for her, fully intending to ask her to marry him when he found her, and he would have asked her, were it not for that silly misunderstanding at Vauxhall.

Do not be fooled into thinking he only wants to make amends for the wrong he has done you. It's more than that. I know him better than anyone does and I have seen the way he looks at you. He's in love with you, Juliet, though I doubt he wants to be. Let him love you and love him in return. He has a great deal of love to give, but first you must let him see he can trust you. Then he will give you the world, a world that has nothing to do with material things.

Juliet clasped the letter to her chest. So he had wanted to marry her regardless of her lowly state. *Oh, Dominic, you fool. You should have told me.* At the time she would never have accepted, since dukes did not marry their lowly employees, but the main thing was that he had wanted to marry her without knowing anything of her new-found status and the wealth that came with it. The expression of disbelief on her face was real, and with it came the knowledge that no matter how much he fought it, he must care for her, or he would never have risked proposing a second time.

With a lighter heart she read on. The tone of the letter changed and a darkness seemed to enclose the terrace. Lady Pemberton went on to give her an account of what had happened between Dominic and Amelia. It was Lady Pemberton's considered opinion that to enable Juliet to understand why Dominic was frequently distant and unapproachable, Juliet should know what Amelia had done to him. They were in love—at least Dominic was in love, ecstatically so. The wedding was arranged. Guests were invited from far and wide. It was to have been a magnificent affair, London's wedding of the year with no expense spared.

Amelia did the unimaginable. She jilted him at the altar and ran off with a friend of his, taking a ship for America. Dominic's fury and humiliation were terrible to witness. I was the first to know the ship had gone down taking everyone on board with her. I was the one to tell Dominic. He didn't speak. He didn't even blink an eye.

Juliet bowed her head. At last she understood why he would not allow any woman to come close, why he would not allow his feelings and emotions to get the better of him. She could not blame him for not wanting to love any woman.

Her heart ached with remorse. For a man as proud as Dominic to have his proposal of marriage flung back in his face, which was what she had done, must have made him furious. Until now, she'd made trying to distance herself from him her goal, keeping every emotion carefully in check. But she wanted him, she realised with a despondent inner sigh. Despite everything he was accused of being—a libertine, a heartless, arrogant aristocrat—she wanted him, his love and his trust.

In the safe quietness of her heart, she was finally willing to admit that to herself, because now she realised he was much more than that. No matter how many women had known the wild, primitive wonder of his lovemaking, when he became her husband he would look no further than her bed. She would love him so much he would want no other. He would be hers alone.

'I'll make amends, my love,' she whispered into the air about her. 'I promise you I will love you for all eternity, and you shall never have cause to doubt it.'

Juliet was in the paddock with one of the grooms who was teaching her to ride when a tall, dark form appeared. It was Dominic. She'd been expecting him ever since she had received Lady Pemberton's letter telling her he would come. Handing the reins to the groom without taking her eyes off the man who was striding across the grass towards her, she went to meet him. Her heart began to hammer with a mixture of hope and dread as she recalled the last time she'd seen him. She had been less than kind.

Halfway across the paddock she stopped and waited for him to reach her. As he continued to walk towards her, she looked at his handsome face with its stern, sensual mouth and hard jaw, but what she saw was a man waiting at the altar for his bride, a man brought to his knees by humiliation, shattered pride and a fierce determination never to fall into the same trap twice.

A lump of poignant tenderness swelled in her throat and she unthinkingly walked towards him. She felt the heat of his eyes upon her, and they warmed her more than any verbal reassurance. The message in those compelling eyes was as clear as if he were whispering it. *You* will *marry me.*

'I'm so sorry,' she whispered achingly when she stood before him, wanting so much to reach out and touch him, but it was as if her arms had lead weights attached to them that kept them planted firmly by her sides. She gazed at the sensual mouth only inches from hers. It was an inviting mouth.

His eyebrows snapped together over cool silver-grey eyes. 'Sorry? Sorry for what? Sorry for running off and leaving me to kick my heels? Sorry that I've had to trail to Scotland to see you?'

Her lips curved in a wobbly smile and she had to clear the tears from the back of her throat before she could go on. 'Which tells me you are as determined to marry me as you were in London. What other reason would bring you all this way?'

'To thrash you to within an inch of your life for daring to provoke me.'

She laughed, a laugh that was sheer music to Dominic's ears. 'You may abuse me all you like if you think I deserve it, but all that would achieve would be a delay in the wedding, your Grace, for it would be unthinkable for a bride to walk down the aisle covered in bruises.'

His heated gaze seared her. 'Does that mean you agree to marry me?'

'I shall be proud to be your wife, Dominic.' Stepping closer, she slipped a hand behind his head and pulled his face close to hers and kissed his lips until his sanity began to slip away. She knew she had won when he took her in his arms and lifted her against him in a fierce, crushing embrace, her breasts flattened against his hard chest.

The desire Juliet had ignited in him had been eating into Dominic for weeks. He wanted her so badly he'd had to grit his teeth and fight against the urge to search her out and force himself upon her, and he felt like strangling her for refusing his suit.

Lifting his head, he looked at her. 'I imagined your life as being one long round of festivities since you arrived in Scotland. I thought that perhaps some handsome Scottish laird might have caught your eye.'

'My heart is committed, and fortune has decreed I shall have no other.'

As Dominic looked at her his eyes told her everything. He took her hand and it trembled as it hid itself in the encompassing warmth of his. 'Why did you not agree to marry me when I asked you?'

Pulling away from him, she pulled him down beside her on to a fallen log, where she sat facing him. 'Because I was afraid. I could not believe you were sincere. I apologise for the childish way I've behaved about this whole thing. I've been absurdly concerned about myself. I—loved you, you see, and I tried hard

not to. There were times when I told myself I didn't—
but I was deceiving myself.'

'My poor darling. I'm not worthy of such a love as
this.'

'Of course you are. I will always love you—and you
will love me. I will show you that I can be trusted with
your heart.'

For a moment he looked nonplussed. 'What are you
talking about?'

'Amelia. Lady Pemberton told me how deeply in
love you were, and that she—she…'

'Jilted me?' he uttered wretchedly.

'Yes,' Juliet whispered, knowing that what she said
now would determine their whole future.

His eyes blazed. 'Cordelia should not have told you.
She had no right.'

'She had every right. I can't begin to imagine how
you must have felt, but I can imagine how much what
she did must have hurt you. But she paid for it with her
life. Dominic, you should have told me yourself,' she
cried, unable to control the tears which began streaming from her eyes. 'The reason behind my refusal to
marry you was because you were only willing to make
me your mistress when I had nothing, yet as soon as you
found out about my grandfather, the haste with which
you proposed marriage seemed not only indecent, but
cruel.'

Through a blur of tears she saw him reach out and
she felt herself crushed against his hard chest. 'I don't
care what your reasons were any more,' she mumbled,
'that you loved Amelia so much—how she hurt you so

deeply that you couldn't bear to let any woman come close in case she hurt you again.'

'Hush. Don't cry, darling,' he whispered. 'Please don't. What I felt for Amelia is a pale imitation of what I feel for you. I asked you to marry me because I missed you so damned much. I wanted you, Juliet. I wanted you so much I almost went insane. I was so impatient to make you mine. And now, finally, I know that above all else I love you, I want you to be my wife.'

'I never knew. I never know what you're thinking— what's going on in your mind.'

'I don't have a mind. The truth is I lost it when I met you.'

She smiled and took his proffered handkerchief.

He cupped her cheek in his hand, loving her. 'How much time do you need to prepare for our wedding?'

'No time at all. When do you suggest?'

'Soon—dear God, soon. I will not wait. I'll make sure of you this time.'

Mesmerised by the seductive invitation in those silvery eyes and the velvet roughness of his voice, Juliet moved closer. His hands slid up and down her arms, velvet manacles pulling her closer to him, deeper into the sensual spell he was weaving about her. Without volition, her lips moved closer to his, and her heart began to race with excitement.

He laid his palm against her cheek, slowly running it back, curving it around her nape, urging her closer. 'Kiss me, Juliet.'

Her body went weak as his mouth opened on her soft, searching lips in a deep, hungry kiss. His fingers shoved into her hair, holding her mouth imprisoned, and she became lost in a wildly arousing kiss that sent heat racing round her body. After what seemed an eternity, Dominic raised his head and gazed down at her flushed face. He held her gaze for a moment, love glowing in the depths of his eyes.

'I missed you,' he murmured.

'I missed you, too.'

Pride surged through him. No man had touched her, he thought reverently, but him. This beautiful, unspoiled, brave girl would soon be his and his alone. 'Ours will be the shortest engagement in history.'

'I'd like that. After what happened with Amelia, I wouldn't want to put you through that again.'

He smoothed her hair back from her face. 'Bless you for that, but doesn't every woman aspire to a grand wedding and a honeymoon on the Continent?'

'I'm not any woman, Dominic.'

'I'm beginning to realise that.'

'And my grandfather knows the perfect place where we can spend our honeymoon.'

'You've spoken to him?'

'Of course. We've become close. He knows how I feel about you, Dominic.'

'And where is this perfect place?'

She smiled, her cheeks dimpling prettily and her eyes mischievous. 'Wait and see—but I'm convinced you'll approve of my choice.' She moved closer to him. 'It will not be easy for me returning to Lansdowne House as your wife, the Duchess of Hawksfield. As your employee I was readily accepted as such, but there will be a complete change in the household's attitude towards me. When I return I expect there will be a distinct reserve—there might even be resentment as well, now I am no longer one of them.'

'They will know by now who you are and by the time we get there you will be accepted as my Duchess. Dolly was close to you. I think it will be more difficult acquainting her with who you are than anyone else.'

'I've thought of that, and I think Dolly will make a perfect lady's maid with the right tuition. I shall see to that. I must also write to Robby. He will have left for New York by now.'

Dominic grimaced. 'Despite the severe dressing down your brother gave me when he came to call, I have to say that he impressed me greatly. It was obvious that he cares for you. I only hope he won't object to you becoming my wife.'

'Don't worry about Robby. When he knows how happy I am, how happy you have made me, he won't have any objections. But I don't know what the position of duchess entails,' she added, 'and I'm sure I'll be quite hopeless at it; still, I'm willing to learn.'

'If you find it too difficult, you could always retire to the library and finish sorting out my books,' he joked.

'At least I know how to do that. What other duties is a duchess responsible for?'

'She must run the duke's household, be diplomatic to the staff and sort out any grievances they might have. She must be charming at all times to his friends, entertain them and the dignitaries of the neighbourhood and the many charities he supports, be respectful and discreet—for the duke is a very private man.'

'I think I can do that, and if not I can learn. What else?'

'She must also keep herself available for the duke at all times. She has to learn how to please him—both in and out of bed, bear his children…' a tear found its way down her cheek and he tenderly wiped it away with his thumb '…and she must love him to the exclusion of all else.'

'The lady already does. And in return? What can she expect?'

Tilting her chin, he looked deep into her eyes. 'He will keep himself only unto her, and she can be assured of his undying love and devotion her whole life long.' He produced a ring from his waistcoat pocket—a simple diamond solitaire that glittered when it caught the light. 'I would like to give you this. It was my grandmother's and then my dear mother's. It's the truest expression of my love I can give you, but it's quite beautiful.' Taking her hand, he slid it on her wedding finger. 'Wear it for me, Juliet. I will get you a proper betrothal ring when I can.'

She looked at the ring—a perfect fit, and she smiled softly. 'I want no other. I shall be happy and proud to wear it.'

'Thank you.' Bending his head, he gave her a light, lingering kiss full of promise for the years ahead.

'Shall we go and tell my grandfather?'

'I've already spoken to him—on my arrival. He

knows why I'm here and has given us his blessing. He only wants your happiness—as I do.'

Just a small notice appeared in *The London Times* Society Page: *After a private wedding ceremony in the chapel at the Earl of Fairfax's ancestral house in the Scottish borders last week, the Duke and Duchess of Hawksfield are honeymooning in the Highlands of Scotland.*

The small hunting tower perched precariously on a high hill, commanded magnificent views of the Highlands of Scotland from every side. The only inhabitants were the bride and groom and a couple of servants to attend to their needs.

Lying in the large bed with her head resting on her husband's chest, sated and happy after their love making, wrapped in his arms beneath the blankets he'd drawn over them, Juliet smiled. The windows of the room opened to the east, so the lovers could see the first rosy glow of the dawn.

Time seemed to verge on eternity in this isolated place. Never had Juliet believed she could be so happy, and she owed it all to the man beside her. Their loving was magic, a stunning, beautiful, expanding rapture that she wanted to go on for ever. She felt a strange sense of rightness of being in his arms, as if here was where she was meant to be, like the air she breathed.

'What do you think?' she murmured, idly tracing her fingers over his hair roughened chest. 'Do you like my choice of honeymoon?'

'Mmm,' he murmured, brushing his fingertips across her jaw in a soft caress. 'I have always wanted to make love to a woman on top of a mountain.'

She smiled at that. 'And how long can we remain on the top of our mountain?' she asked, thinking whimsically of how cosy it would be to stay in the tower with him indefinitely.

'How does four weeks sound?'

'Perfect,' she murmured, lightly nibbling at the lobe of his ear with her small, perfect teeth, touching it with her tongue. 'But are you sure you won't be bored?'

To her surprise, her remark made him tighten his arms. 'Bored? I could never be bored with you, my love.'

Juliet raised her head, surprised by the unwarranted force of his declaration, and continued to tease. 'You're quite certain of that?' she murmured, trailing her fingers down the flat planes of his hard stomach, unaware that she could so easily stir his desire.

His breath caught in his throat, as again the hot coals of passion were fanned and flamed. Tipping his chin down and looking into her eyes, he did nothing to stay her wandering hand as it slid down the side of his thigh. 'Positive,' he said hoarsely. 'Juliet...' but it was already too late. Desire was pouring through him. With a smothering laugh at her startled expression, he rolled her on to her back and settled himself beside her. 'You, my love, are insatiable,' he teased huskily. 'Can you not control your lust?'

'No more than you, it would seem,' she breathed, nestling closer.

He lowered his head, his face brushing against her hair, stirring from it the sweet fragrance of jasmine, until his head reeled with the heavy scent of it. His finger touched and raised her chin until she looked full into those soft grey eyes. They were not smiling now—they were intense to such a degree that she shivered.

'I think we must re-think the time we intend to spend locked away in our tower, my love,' he murmured, his lips brushing hers. 'How does two months sound to you?'

'Perfect,' she murmured as he captured her lips, moving to welcome him, her woman's body reacting instinctively to the indescribably, splintering feeling that built with leaps and bounds within her whenever they made love. She was surprised by her abandon, for she came to him again, answering his every passion with her own.

* * * * *

A sneaky peek at next month...

HISTORICAL

IGNITE YOUR IMAGINATION, STEP INTO THE PAST...

My wish list for next month's titles...

In stores from 4th November 2011:

- ❏ The Lady Gambles – Carole Mortimer
- ❏ Lady Rosabella's Ruse – Ann Lethbridge
- ❏ The Viscount's Scandalous Return – Anne Ashley
- ❏ The Viking's Touch – Joanna Fulford
- ❏ Society's Most Disreputable Gentleman – Julia Justiss
- ❏ The Lawman's Redemption – Pam Crooks

Available at WHSmith, Tesco, Asda, Eason, Amazon and Apple

Just can't wait?

Visit us Online

You can buy our books online a month before they hit the shops! **www.millsandboon.co.uk**

1011/04

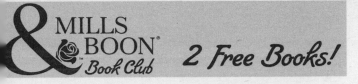